MW01060710

TRIUMPH

A NOVEL OF THE HUMAN SPIRIT

TRIUMPH

A NOVEL OF THE HUMAN SPIRIT

BY
JODI LEA STEWART

Progressive
RISING PHOENIX PRESS ®

No part of this publication may be reproduced, stored in a
retrieval system, or transmitted in any form or by any means,
electronic, mechanical, photocopying, recording, or otherwise,
without the written permission of the publisher.
Text Copyright © 2020 Jodi Lea Stewart

All rights reserved.
Published 2020 by Progressive Rising Phoenix Press, LLC
www.progressiverisingphoenix.com

ISBN: 978-1-950560-29-5

Printed in the U.S.A.
1st Printing

Edited by: Chris Eboch

Cover Illustration: Night Picture Of Milky Way And Rising
Moon Over The Lake, ShutterStock Photo ID: 461870854,
Copyright: Yuriy Mazur. Used With Permission.

Interior Illustration: Topographic Map Background Concept
With Space For Your Copy, BigStock Photo ID: 146501456,
Copyright: DamienGeso. Used With Permission.

Interior Illustration: Vector Antique Engraving Drawing
Illustration Of Black-Crowned Night Heron Isolated On White
Background, ShutterStock Photo ID: 1112195168,
Copyright: andrey oleynik. Used With Permission.

Book Cover and Interior Design by William Speir
Visit: http://www.williamspeir.com

Table Of Contents

Part I

Part II

As I traverse the hills and valleys of my life, I delight in the truth that relationships matter more than anything else. Love knows nothing if it knows not the heart.

In that spirit, I dedicate this special novel of my own heart to my family... husband Mark, Mother Vivian, Son Jason, Daughter Sunny, Daughter-in-law Cyndie, as well as to my brood of Grands: Page, Emily, Taylor, Bridgett, Scarlett, and River.

My own dreams, as well as my aspirations for all of you, are written in this book. Find them if you dare.

Part One

CHAPTER
One

Stolen

Near Old Ruddock, Louisiana
1903

Flo's piercing screech cuts the air like a sharp axe. "Simon-man, pull up on those mules for gawd's sake!" she cries.

"Whoa there, Gabriel. Easy now, Michael. Su-su-su, boys," utters the man called *Uncle Simon* by four of the six kids in the buckboard. He pulls the lead reins tight, resting them across his lap. He turns to gaze at Flo sitting in the seat beside him and swipes a hand with neatly trimmed fingernails over the beads of perspiration on his dark forehead.

"My soul, you scared me, woman. I thought Doctor John himself was come back to life." He chuckles in uneasy relief. "Or, for a minute, I was thinking, maybe, well... *you know who* had figured out some things, and—"

"Shush now. It's gettin' dark time, but I knows I seen a woman over to there by those trees."

Simon rises to his feet, his neck stuck out like a gander

eyeing a snake. His eyes canvas the trees slouched over the narrow trail before them. "Zeke, hand me that lantern up here, won't you, sir?"

Zeke, thirteen but growing fast out of his britches and shirts and appearing mostly to be grown, hands the lantern he fired up minutes before around the side of the buck seat to Simon. Simon's nerves are already taut from driving the buckboard wagon over the checkerboard ground greedily hoarding space between the swamps, marshes, and Lake Pontchartrain. Everybody knows that kind of ground isn't wholly stable, but Flo asked for a little drive-about for the kids before he left tomorrow morning on the train back to New Orleans.

Flo, with her exotic eyes and shapely form, gets about everything she asks for, and then some, and Simon finds that to be a pride unto himself.

Water mosquitoes ramp up their hungry search for blood as Simon strains to see through the humid tar of dusk slurping up the wagon and its occupants like a hungry towel. Five other kids besides Zeke jumble around in the back of the small buckboard to see what's causing the excitement. Curious eyes stare into the gloom spreading across the watery cypress as a pale moon rises over moss-swathed oaks on the shore. Hands slap at the carnivorous insects diving toward their skin for nourishment.

"There she is, Mama, by the black water!" Zeke shouts.

He and Flo jump from the wagon to the ground. Zeke takes the proffered lantern from Simon while Flo directs a silent finger at the small horde of squirming youngsters, warning them to stay put. As soon as her back is turned, they scale the wooden sides to the ground—delirious mice abandoning a ship long at sea.

Simon's gentle reprimands never make it past the toe board at his feet. He patiently climbs from the wagon and trudges toward the stranger standing in the lush St. Augustine grass spreading like a carpet from the banks of the water. An ancient crape myrtle burdened with fuchsia blossoms frames the unmoving figure standing before them. Zeke's high-held lantern casts a ghostly light over a brown-skinned woman of great beauty. She is swaddled in a pale-lilac shawl from her neck to below her knees. Her arms hold a rolled blanket about equal in size to a small log. Her hair is arranged high on her head and fastened in place with pins of creamy ivory. Red ribbons loop through her locks.

A surge of sickness invades Simon's belly as buried reminiscences dance on the edge of his mind. The woman mumbles incoherently in soothing tones to the blanket, sporadically covering it in tender kisses. Flo frowns at Simon, then looks back at the stranger. "Honey-girl, you be all right?" she asks softly.

The woman ignores her spectators, smiles at the blanket, crushes it flat to her breast. She commences a slow rotation, lifting her eyes to fall long seconds upon each person as she turns. She traps Simon in her gaze the longest, coagulating the air in his lungs. Long-forgotten memories creep from a deep pit in his subconscious. He swabs the rolling sweat from his face with a sleeve.

"Fl-Flo, we best be getting on-on back to R-Ruddock. It's g-g-getting late out here, and these young'uns n-n-need to be tucked in their beds." Simon coughs in his hand. "We're l-leaving now, ch-children." He turns toward the buckboard. The woman strikes up a humming rhythm replicating the cadence of a drum. Simon stops, turns back around.

Flo, confused about her Simon-man's stuttering, shoots

5

him a questioning look he doesn't see. She steps nearer the woman. "Come on, chile, let us bring you to town. Us womens'll help you with whatever's ailing yer purty self. We gots our medicines to heal yer heart and yer body, as well. Let's go now, honey. We understands how it feels to lose a little baby not barely in this world yet."

The woman seems not to hear Flo. Her feet move rhythmically, slowly—mesmerizing the onlookers. She gazes into the sky. Undulating. Singing.

Danse Calinda, boudoum, boudoum.
Danse Calinda, boudoum, boudoum.

Molten terror blossoms inside Simon, spreading hot into his arms and legs. The children sneak closer to gaze at the spectacle before them. Simon visualizes grabbing hold of his two children and the other four who call him Uncle Simon as an eagle hooks a fish to safely wing into the heavens, but he cannot move.

The woman sways side to side. She flicks her hand across her left shoulder. The swaddling shawl falls to the ground. She stands before them wearing a flimsy strip of material tied to her waist and dropping barely past her buttocks. Layers of gold chains hang from her neck and spread over her naked bosom. Her eyes gleam as she writhes and sings.

Eh! Eh! Bomba, ben! Ben!
Canga bafio, te,
Canga mou ne de le,
Canga do ki la,
Canga li!

Trapped by the gossamer web spun by the woman's beauty and peculiarities, the captive audience stares as she stops moving. For a few frozen moments, she deliberately gazes at each one. She tilts her face upward and shrieks, a strange animal sound. She tosses aside the empty blanket, bends to scoop up five-year-old Willy as though he is weightless, and dashes toward the brackish water of the estuary. She makes a sharp turn toward the swamp waters.

"My baby! Give me back my baby!" Flo shrieks, the heavy darkness quickly gobbling up her cries. Her screams shock the troupe from their trance-like stupor. One by one, they take to their legs.

"Mama! Mama! Mama!" Willy shouts.

The woman vanishes behind the curtains of Spanish moss draping the trees along the water bank. Her feet splash into the water. Willy screams.

Then, silence.

In moments, the agonizing quiet surrounding the band of confused people is filled with a cacophony of frog croaks and cricket chirps. A black-crowned night heron emits a barking-squawk complaint from a nearby tree.

Simon, running fast, reaches the water's edge and strains to see through the darkness. He cups his hands. "William! Willy-Boy! Where are you, son?"

An insect ensemble begins strumming nocturnal melodies across the calm waters before him, rendering his soul bloodied and bare. He sinks to his knees, lost in an agony for which there are no words. Flo witnesses his collapse. She falls beside him onto the damp earth.

The wails of her other five children rise like a pillar to the cold moon eyeing the scene below.

CHAPTER
Two

Invisible Eyebrows

St. Louis, Missouri
1958

Sooty St. Louis air hugs the concrete schoolyard making it hard for me to get good air. Course, my stupid asthma is the cause of my breathing problems. A wheeze comes out of me, and I look around scared someone else heard it too. No one's noticing me, so I go back to watching the kids squeezing every drop out of our first recess on our first day of school. I press my open hand into my chest to help me get a deeper breath.

The sound of the busy city pushes through the cyclone fence around the schoolyard like dirty putty—the globby, gray kind that sits for years on old wood around glass windows. Brake squeals and car honks outside the fence have put me in a kind of spell. I'm already bashful about my new school and all the kids I don't know. We moved here from Pevely only a few weeks ago, so I'm a stranger to every kid hollering and running around on the broken concrete.

I stare at one big crack with weeds growing out of it. My eyes kind of move up and there she is—a girl I first seen when we settled down in our new classroom this morning. The girl's green eyelet dress with a white underlining petticoat is flat out a sight to see against her pretty skin. I start getting ashamed since I know my own dress looks pitiful. The tiny patch on the hem feels like it's taking over the whole skirt part since I feel so shy about it. Momma said last year's Easter dress would do fine for the first day of fifth grade since we're so broke after our move to the city. I said, "But, Momma, it's got a patch, and it's faded from Aunt Vel washing it so much for Sunday School all last summer."

What did Momma say back to me? Nothing. She just smiled that tired-looking smile of hers and brushed my bangs off my forehead. Same thing she always does when there's not a thing in creation she can or will do about something. Truth is, I forgot how used-up my dress was till I seen that girl standing there looking fresh as a fistful of daisies.

For some reason, we get fixed in each other's stare. She's looking me over, and me? I'm doing the same. I suppose we're walking closer and closer 'cause, all of a sudden, we ain't far apart. I guess I never seen a prettier little girl in all my life.

She says, "I haven't seen anyone without eyebrows before. What happened to yours?"

Why, what a thing to say, and it ain't even true. I *do* have eyebrows, but first, I have a question of my own I want answered.

"Why's your hair in all those braids and barrettes?"

"Because that's how my mama fixes it."

"Oh. Anyways, I got eyebrows. Feel."

The girl's stretched-out finger slides across my brow.

"They're there, but they don't show up at all. I can't see

your eyelashes, either. You have any?"

"Course I do." I blink hard as she leans in close.

"I see them now. Can you turn around?"

"Turn around? Why?"

"So I can see the back of your hair."

I turn in a circle, my arms stiff as rails at my sides.

"Your hair's the same color of yellow as a baby chicken. It's pretty."

I touch my hair wondering if what she says is good or bad.

"What's your name?" I ask her.

"Mercy Washington. What's yours?"

"Shirley Ann Blackburn, but everyone calls me Annie."

Mercy nods and snaps the gum in her mouth a few times on one side of her mouth. I look around, biting my lower lip wondering what I should say next. I get an idea.

"Hey, Mercy, you like to play with dolls?"

"Not as much as I used to since I'm growing up. But if they have their legs and arms and pretty clothes, I do. If I see a naked, dirty doll, I throw up." She turns toward the swing set. "I don't even like anyone who doesn't dress their dollies nice."

"I got one with all its arms and legs. She ain't naked, neither."

"Don't say *ain't,* and you said everything else wrong, too. Say it like this, 'She isn't naked, either.'"

I stare. Nobody but one teacher in all my life ever said I wasn't talking right. I swallow hard. "Okay, I'll say it different next time. Anyways, my doll's wearing a pretty dress and bonnet. Her name's Molly-Mae."

"It's *anyway,* not *anyways.*"

My mouth drops open 'cause I'm so surprised at this.

"Where is Molly-Mae?"

I put my hand on my chest and breathe in some air. I let it out slow so no wheezes come with it. I don't know if I can say anything right in front of this girl, but I try anyways. "Um, she's in my school satchel in the cub-hole in our classroom. We can get her out at dinner time and play with her."

"Dinner?"

I nod.

"I think you mean lunch."

I don't answer 'cause I don't know if I mean that or what. What I do know is me and Mercy are going to be best friends. I know it plain as day.

"You want to share my gum, Annie?"

"I shore do! What kind is it?"

"Spearmint."

Mercy drops her gum into her palm and pulls it apart. She holds the halves up to examine them. The halves seem to please her, so she hands me one. I pop it in my mouth and grin at my new friend.

She smiles back.

It was a smile I'd count on for the rest of my life.

CHAPTER
Three

Ernest and Arlene

Denton, Texas
1903

All he knew was this baby girl was the gift he and Arlene had prayed for, yearned for day after day. When his friend Jack got word to him asking him if they still wanted a baby, he had answered promptly. Throwing a few vitals in the small trunk and loading it on the wagon, feeding the chickens, milk cow, and the horses early in the day, and getting his neighbor to come feed them until he returned was what he did. Then he hitched up his horse team and started the two-day wagon ride from Denton to Fort Worth to pick up the baby Jack had stumbled across with no explanation of how he had done so.

Arlene cried most of the way, and it wasn't sad crying, he didn't think, but tears of joy and relief. Once, she said, "I'll call her *Ruby*, after my mother," and that's the most of what she said on the journey.

By now, he was used to Arlene's weeping. She'd done it

continually ever since little Rosemary was laid in the ground that awful blustery day. Her little brother Thaddeus had preceded her in death by a week. Both youngsters gone, victims of the fever. Unable to have more children, Arlene had taken to her rocking chair holding the little clothes she had sewn for her babies and crying for the better part of a year.

He had watched helplessly with his own heart breaking but not willing to put any more burden on his grieving wife by showing his own sorrow. Quietly, he kept up their ranch without a word, tiptoeing around Arlene, sometimes carrying her to bed or to the table to pick at the food he clumsily prepared.

When Jack—who had ridden in the Texas Rangers with him in their wild youth—came through the Territory for a visit before his annual trip to New Orleans, he was shocked at the state of his friend and his wife.

"In all haste, you must do something!" he proclaimed in astonishment. "Both you and your missus are skeletons. For the love of God, take in an unfortunate child who has no home, Ernest."

"I would gladly take any child under our roof, Jack, if only the Good Lord would bring us one." Ernest buried his head in his hands and wept for the first time since the horrible tragedies.

Jack had witnessed this man chase outlaws through New Mexico and Texas into the burning sands of Old Mexico for days at a time with only his iron grit to sustain him. Ernest had tamed killer horses no one else dared approach, engaged with gusto in shoot-outs with banditos so cruel they were barely human, men who fought to the death rather than surrender. Now, here was his friend lost in an agony Jack sympathized with but did not understand.

Jack had been fending for himself since orphaned at the age of twelve, had never seen fit to marry, and had no children he knew of. The raw pain of his friend had touched him, nevertheless, and when he traveled to New Orleans for his yearly gambling venture with his previous, now pooch-bellied and cigar-smoking Texas Ranger compatriots, he stumbled upon a circumstance that would forever change his own life and the lives of his Texas friends.

CHAPTER
Four

Lateral Moves

St. Louis, Missouri
1958

I don't know Debra, but she smiled at me a lot when we lined up to go back in the classroom on this first day of school. Pretty soon, we're trading seats so I can sit in the back of the room by Mercy. Me and Debra settle in our new seats grinning big at each other until something happens—a stillness. It comes in the room and hangs there making me squirm and I don't even know what it is. I look around and notice a lot of the kids gawking at me and her. Others are looking at the front of the classroom, so I do too, and there's our teacher staring me square in the eyes. I smile at her. She doesn't smile back. She gets up from her desk looking all pucker-faced like a hunting dog with a stopped-up nose. She walks round her desk and leans herself against it with her arms crossed in front of her chest.

I find myself thinking how her ironed white blouse shore looks nice tucked into her skinny blue skirt. The blue color tumbles down Mrs. Patterson's legs starting from the thin, black leather belt around her waist and ends in the middle of her calves. Her ankles are crossed above her black high-heeled shoes that have little white bows on the top.

A few coughs around the room and a giggle or two, and now I'm feeling troubled like I done something wrong. I smile again as friendly as I know how, and that's real friendly since I'm from a little town and we smile all the time at each other there. My teacher stands up from leaning on the desk, drops her arms, and takes one of those big breaths that raise the shoulders up and puts them back down. I know about those kind 'cause sometimes they help me get more air in my chest.

"Annie, get up here to your assigned seat," she says, pointing to where Debra is sitting.

So that's what has her all riled, me switching seats? She probably thinks we got mixed up and don't remember where she put us this morning. "It's okay, Mrs. Patterson, me and Debra traded seats so I can be by my new friend Mercy." I smile again just knowing things will be fine now with my good explanation.

She chirps out a small chuckle that sounds kind of like a hiccup, moves her head back and forth for the longest time, still giving me the eye. She walks around her desk to the side facing the chalkboard where her rolling chair is. She opens a top drawer and pulls a book out.

Me and Mercy sneak a look at each other. She lifts her shoulders. I do too. Looks like we're both confounded. Debra turns around and frowns at me like it's my fault the teacher is acting like this.

Mrs. Patterson starts talking while her head's bent over that book she took out of the drawer. She flips the pages real fast and says, "Girls, I'm about to give you five seconds to get in your previously assigned seats, or… it looks like I'll have to introduce you personally to Mr. Reasonable. Is that what you want?"

Me and Debra skedaddle fast to our old seats. Mrs. Patterson's fifth-grade class was introduced to Mr. Reasonable like he was a real person right before first recess, only he ain't a person at all. He's a wooden paddle about a foot long. On his handle is a leather strap threaded through a hole. He hangs from a nail on the wall next to the chalkboard. I ain't looking to get that paddle across my behind since I never had a whoopin' at school and don't intend to ever get one.

Soon as I'm settled back in the other desk and my face is burning real good, Mrs. Patterson walks over to my desk and plops that book open in front of me.

"Here. Pages three to eleven. Copy all the spelling words on those pages five times each on lined paper. Turn them in tomorrow morning with the other homework assignments I shall give the class at the end of the day. Be sure your name is at the top on the right-hand side of each page, along with the date and our classroom number."

I know I'm getting a dadgummed punishment, and my face burns hotter than ever. I can see I have some explaining to do to our teacher, and I do it now in my nicest voice. "Mrs. Patterson, some of the other girls traded places, and you let them."

"They traded laterally, not vertically."

That don't make no sense. I think my teacher ain't hearing right, so I try again.

"But why can't I sit by my new friend?"

"Why…?" Her raised eyebrow feels like a snowball rolling down the back of my dress.

"I mean, can you tell me why I can't do it, ma'am?" My mouth's so dry now my words sound like a squeak mouse spitting sawdust.

Mrs. Patterson gets red across her cheeks, and I shrink down in my seat.

"I will tell you one thing, Miss Shirley Ann Blackburn..." she says, pointing a long finger at me... "I shall make it a top priority this school term to teach you some respect for rules."

CHAPTER
Five

We Bad

Near Old Ruddock, Louisiana
1903

Simon didn't want Flo to come with the other townsfolk who work in the Ruddock logging mills and in the homes of the mill owners, but she wouldn't be persuaded elsewise. That woman was near beside herself with grief, and who wouldn't be with her little boy snatched away in front of her very eyes only a few hours before? Well, to be exact... one hour and ten minutes before now, but that was beside the fact. Things like this didn't happen to decent folks, and yet, it did.

Leaving the water's edge earlier, Simon, being full of rage and grief, had, for one horrible moment, felt like taking his riding whip to his mules, something he had never done before. Instead, he wrapped his arms around Gabriel's neck and let the tears fall like raindrops on his coat. He nodded at Michael and rubbed his hand across his neck. The mules felt his pain and trotted doggedly all the way back to Ruddock with nary a flick of the whip in the air or a spoken command from Simon.

In town, Zeke and his younger brother, Eli, ran along the raised sidewalks to the Colored-people church and told the minister and his wife what happened. Then, they banged on the doors of the elevated shanties housing the mill workers to sound the alarm about Willy. In minutes, folks were hitching up wagons, saddling their mules or horses, some riding two and three on the backs of their animals. A fevered fear hung on their brows and swam in their eyes. Black magic was in the air, and it horrified young and old. Zeke and Eli repeated to any listening ear how they saw flames in the woman's eyes right before she stole their little brother.

Now assembled, Simon leads the searchers through the darkness to the unholy place of Willy's disappearance. He let Zeke and Eli join the search. The younger kids—all crying their eyes out about Willy—were directed to stay behind with Gertie, the preacher's wife.

As soon as the wagons and animals stop behind Simon's wagon, Flo leaps from the buck seat and runs to the edge of the water where Willy's last scream was heard. "Willy! Willy! Where are you, my *bébé?*" she yells across the dark and scornful swamp. She pulls her hair. "Willy, it's your own true Mammy. Come back to me, honey, come back to me!"

The night sounds seem to mock Flo's distraught mind with their blasphemous normality. "Willy, you my angel. Don't leave me. Please don't leave me! Mammy can't do without her sweet boy."

Silence.

Flo screams and crumples into the sweet grass along the waterway. Her fingers dig into the wet soil below the blades. Women folk and Simon rush to her and stare at the tormented woman moaning on the ground. Simon carries her to the back of the buckboard and places her tenderly on the boards.

The searchers vigorously renew their hunt. They look around every tree within reason, even climbing them, lanterns in hand. They look behind the sodden ghosts of moss wrapping the tree branches alongside the water and walk lengthwise every inch of the swamp and lake banks in the area. They beat the tall reeds with sticks and call Willy's name in every imaginable tone, loud to soft—pleading to commanding—begging him to answer. The women sing hymns and shout out prayers. A man cries out in a rich voice, "Merciful God, release that boy from the hand of the she-devil!"

Simon puts his cheek to Flo's hot forehead as she lies sobbing. When he rises to join the volunteers, she grabs his arm. "Simon-man, take my hand," she whispers.

"Flo, I am beholden to join the others and look for our boy."

"No, you listen now. We ain't gonna find him. He gone. He gone shore as we know the Good Lord make it rain on both the evil and the good folk in this world. We gots us a bad omen here, and it's truer than both of us. We done this. Oh, my Lordie-lord, we done it." She sobs into the back of her hand.

"Flo, baby, you're getting yourself in a dreadful state. Rest here while I go to look for our Willy. I won't be long."

"No, no, it ain't no use."

"Why are you saying that, honey? You never give up on anything. We'll find him. Don't speak such terrible things."

"We done it, Simon-man, we done it by our sin."

Simon's heart stops. The mortar between the bricks of his carefully constructed wall of self-lies sprouts a crack.

"We done broke them Ten Commandments, sweet man,

and you knowed it same as me."

He squinches his eyes, his stomach tightening with guilt. His coming to Ruddock every two weeks on the train from New Orleans was business, yes it truly was, but it was something else, too, only he never allowed himself to think of it that way. Here now was the truth laid bare before him. He had been with Flo as her husband and as a daddy to her other four offspring even though he had a wife and two daughters of his own in New Orleans.

He hadn't meant to have two families, but Flo was a woman a man didn't... couldn't... walk away from. Her smile, her walk, her warm affections, her kindnesses brought him back to her arms again and again for nearly eight years. Alice, a sweet girl of seven, and Willy, only five, are his very own children bore by this woman of his heart.

"I knows it, and you knows it, Simon-man. God's let this evil comes here on us this day. Oh, such a dark evil it is!"

Simon can't move, not so much as a muscle. If an angel of Heaven materialized to read a proclamation of his guilty deeds from a golden scroll, he couldn't raise one finger or utter a single word to defend himself.

"That devil woman... she come from Hell itself to get our Willy, and it mean we sinned, and we sinned like David do in the Bible when he lays with that woman from the roof and sends her man offen to die in the wars. God took away his little baby, too. We bad, Simon-man. We bad."

Flo rolls onto her side whimpering softly.

The years of practiced numbness of his wrongdoing becomes a weight Simon can no longer bear. If Flo is right, the boy who delights him—the only son of his loins—that innocent, sweet child, is gone forever. He steps away from the wagon to vomit.

CHAPTER
Six

Here's How We Do It

St. Louis, Missouri
1958

I'm leaning as far back in the public bus seat as I can, my face smushed against the window. I don't like it since it's grimy with handprints and kids' nose prints and who knows whatever else, but I do it anyways. Behind me, Mercy is leaning up as far as she can with her face close to my seat and the window. That's how we be together and talk when we take a bus somewhere around the city. It's best if there ain't many people on the bus so we can talk a little louder when that noisy bus stops and when it pulls away from the curbs. We're quiet when we have to be, and talk when it's loud.

We can't help it 'cause I found out we ain't mostly allowed to sit in the same seats beside each other. Bus drivers and nosy folks with mad faces tell us so all the time. Seems just because we're kids, they think they can mouth off like that. I never knowed about any such rules before me and

Mercy got to be friends 'cause I was never on a bus or streetcar except with my momma or my brothers, or by myself when Momma puts me on a bus to go to my widowed aunt's town of Belle about eighty miles away.

What I've learned since me and Mercy been doing this is everybody gets all riled up if we try to be together just about anywhere we go. We made up some tricks to keep them from going crazy. Take going into a grocery store or department store… see, Mercy, she being as smart as all get out, just like my momma says about me, too, steps in close behind a nice Colored lady like she belongs to her. I follow a little bit behind like I'm part of someone else's bunch. Mercy goes in the store ahead of me pretending she's the woman's kid. Once we're inside, it don't seem to matter so much.

Sometimes, a bus driver or a shop keeper wants to know why I'm going around town with a Colored girl, that's what they say, and we got that worked out, too. I tell them, "She's my housekeeper's girl or our cook's kid, and we're doing an errand for my momma downtown."

I feel plain stupid saying those things 'cause we never had no housekeeper or a cook, unless you count my brother Donnie cooking us a cheese sandwich or making us a bowl of soup. The way I see it, we won't never have people working for us, but Mercy makes all this stuff up in her head, and I do whatever she says. She says her mama has a cook named Ettie and a woman who comes by three times a week who cleans their whole house and that's why it sounds dumb to me that I have to say her mama works for us.

Anyways, if we say all those things and people still act grouchy, I tell them my daddy said for us to be together when we're in public so's it's safer. Even if they don't rightly know if we're telling them the truth and give us one of those scrunchyeyed looks, by and by, they go on and mind their own business like they should have done in the first place. Sometimes, I tell them my daddy's a policeman, and that seems to soothe them a whole bunch.

It ain't really lying since me and Mercy just want to be left alone to be best friends, and we can't help it if folks act how they do. Anyways, maybe my daddy *is* a policeman. We don't know 'cause we ain't seen him ever since I was a baby. All I know is his name, and it's D.J. Blackburn.

So, that's how we do it, me and Mercy, going around the city using coins and tokens her folks give her to go back and forth to school and to the big public library. Course, we're going a lot more places than that, and, so far, no one's picking up on it 'cause they don't know about it. I think I never did have so much fun in my whole life as riding around the city with Mercy.

Today, we're headed to the Peach Garden to eat Chinese chow mein and eggrolls and drink tea in little, bitty cups with no handles. First, though, we got on this bus on our way to the Peacock Alley Jazz Club place where Mercy's Aunt Viola sings. I've got to say something here since it seems so important to everyone. Me and my youngest brothers, the twins who are two years older than me, are blond-haired and light skinned. We get terrible burns from the sun every summer, and it's no fun, neither. Donnie, my oldest brother, has lots darker skin than us, gray eyes, and brownish-black, wavy hair. My blond hair's wavy, too, but the twins' hair is like straw, not a bit of curl anywhere.

Now, Mercy's Aunt Viola is lighter skinned than my brother Donnie, but Mercy says she's still her blood aunt and her mama's half-sister, and she, Aunt Viola that is, don't want nobody judging her color in any way so to keep quiet that

Mercy's her blood niece. All this talk everywhere of skin color confounds me something terrible, but a whole lot of folks yap about it all the time.

Why we have to go see Mercy's Aunt Viola is 'cause Chinaman Bill gave us a sealed note to give her last time we sneaked off to the Peach Garden, which was about four days ago. He's the owner and the main cooker there, and he's sweet something awful on Aunt Viola. Anybody would be, you see, 'cause she's mighty beautiful like Mercy but older and wears glittery gowns and has her shiny hair all fancy in curls with diamonds in it and stuff.

Chinaman Bill goes to see her ever night after he closes the restaurant at ten o'clock, but he can't get too close to her. She's always wrapped around one of those microphones on a stage or lying across a piano or something Mercy says, so she can't be visiting with any visitors or men who love her.

"Is she sweet on him?" I asked Mercy one time.

"She sure smiles when we give her his letters. He slips her money in those things, too. Lots of men fall in love with my Aunt Viola."

"I guess so. Think she'll marry Chinaman Bill? Fact is, he ain't bad looking."

"Don't say *ain't*, Annie. Yes, he's handsome, isn't he? But, can you picture my Aunt Viola cooking Chinese food and doing the washing and all that?"

"No, I can't say as I can."

Now, here we are getting off the bus near Lawton Boulevard and walking to a certain third door on the right side of the building alongside the alley and giving it a few knocks. A large man with fluffy dark eyebrows wearing a hat and a tie opens the door a crack. The next part is important, and Mercy's training me how to do it right. I don't have it memorized yet, but I'm trying to.

"Um, I have a special delivery for Viola de la Maison LaRoche, and this is my cook's girl who's here with me."

The man leans down and stares me in the eye. "Who sent you?"

"My momma," I say, shivering a little inside because of my big windy-lie, and because the man shore looks like a mean one.

"Who's that?"

"Who's what?"

"Your momma."

"Oh, she's the one who does Miss Viola's marklet… uh, marble, uh…"

"Marketing," Mercy hisses from behind me.

"Marketing!" I shout with a grin. I have a hard time remembering that word for some reason.

"Lou, who is it?" half-whispers a soft voice behind the man.

"Two little girls who ought to be running on home and minding their own business."

"Well, for heaven's sake, let them in, Lou."

The man steps out of the doorway. We go into a room wrapped with purple and blue velvet curtains. On a gold bar the length of a whole wall hangs the most beautiful, sparkly gowns an eye could ever see in its whole life. Aunt Viola's primping dresser has a three-sided mirror attached to the back of it, and it's covered in bottles of perfume and powder-puffy things and a hairbrush and comb on a flat mirror. What always happens is I can't never stop staring at Mercy's aunt since she's so pretty. I almost think she's not real. She bends down and hugs us both at the same time with her good-smelling perfumed arms.

"My goodness, how sweet to bring me a message from my, uh, marketing manager today, ladies." She turns to the man and says, "I'll take it from here, Lou," and she waits for him to go through a door going into the building and not outside it.

When the door clicks, she says, "Mercy! You are a sight for sore eyes, honey. I love your sweet dress with those black patent shoes. Of course, you know to wear your darker shoes after Labor Day, don't you? My special fashion girl, you are."

Mercy just eats up that kind of talk from her pretty aunt, and I don't blame her. Aunt Viola sits down on a stool thing with buttons all over the top. It's dark red and velvet with curvy silver-white legs with a gold streak going up one side and down the other side.

"Annie, dear, it's good to see you, too. My, just look at your hair... so silky. Does the curl stay in all the time?"

"I think so," I answer, feeling my face heat up.

She smiles at me, and I think I'm maybe dead seeing such a pretty woman as her dressed in her long green relaxing dress with gold slippers and smelling better than cotton candy and baby powder all mixed into one good smell. Her eyes are beautiful green, and I wish I had a crayon that color. Her dark lashes sweep her cheeks like a broom when she blinks.

"What do you have for little Auntie Viola today, girls?"

She pats the side of the red cushion, and Mercy sits beside her and reaches into her black patent purse to bring out the note from Chinaman Bill. Aunt Viola's eyes get big. She looks at us a few seconds, then steps over to open a drawer on her primping dresser. She pulls out a paring knife and opens the envelope with a clean cut across the top. She reaches into it and pulls out a piece of paper. Several bills of money flutter out of the envelope. Why, it's more money than I ever did see before.

"That foolish man," she says, almost too soft for us to hear.

While she reads the letter, Mercy asks, "Are you going to marry him, Aunt Viola?"

I expect her to laugh her cute laugh at such a crazy question, but she looks down at the floor like she's seeing something there. Just like that, she stands up.

"Girls, it's time for you to go. My rehearsal for the early show starts in an hour. Lord knows I need to rest a little first. Now, be sure you're home before dark, and thank you for bringing my letter."

Before we know it, we're back outside in the sunshine holding an autographed picture of the beautiful Viola de La Maison LaRoche with red lipstick kiss marks on each of our hands. There's nothing left for us to do but catch the streetcar to Grand and Olive and go eat some Chinese food.

CHAPTER
Seven

Bone Tired

St. Louis, Missouri
1958

eenie is bone tired—the kind of tired that starts in the feet and runs up the leg muscles, spreads thick to the chest and arms, finally taking root in the head and splitting it open. Had she really almost hit that woman in the head with a bottle of seltzer last night? If Gerald hadn't caught her arm, who knows what she would have done. Well, the crazy old thing threw a full cup of coffee at her face for no reason in the world and barely missed her. What was she supposed to do?

The back-to-back shifts and working until morning day after day and—worse—night after night have worn her down this year. She's tired of slaving away in restaurants and drugstore food counters for measly salaries that barely cover rent and buy cheap food and clothes for her kids. Tired of seeing her kids do without. Tired of never having enough money to climb above her circumstances. Tired of being tired.

Lately, her weariness has turned into a rabid discontent mixed with a big dose of fear. St. Louis is becoming overrun with mobsters and crazies, not to mention the civil discord always running like a current between the races.

Her four kids are growing up without her in their lives, and it wounds her to the core. She wants to make them meat loaf and mashed potatoes, or fry up a skillet of pork chops and gravy every evening, not have someone else do it for hire, or tell her oldest son, Donnie, to fix dinners like grilled cheese sandwiches with a side of Campbell's tomato soup. Or canned mushroom soup and crackers. What kind of a mother lets her kids live on food like that and the occasional soda pop and bag of potato chips?

She needs out, and the only tiny patch of light to an escape tunnel seems too odd, perhaps grotesque, but it's something. She keeps the idea tucked into the back of her mind, afraid to take it out and look at it, and afraid not to. She sits up on the edge of the bed massaging her neck. Annie opens the door a fraction and peeks inside.

"Momma, oh, goodie. You ain't asleep yet. Can you tie my dress for me in the back? None of the boys do it right."

"Of course, I can, punkin. Come over here and turn around. Did you eat something?"

"Corn flakes."

"Oh, that's not much of a breakfast. You want to stay home with me this morning and let me fix us some eggs and biscuits? I'll put some sausage in the gravy, and—"

"Momma, today's the spelling bee. I told you about it the other day. You know I never miss one. Besides, Mercy's bringing me a piece of birthday cake from her house today."

"Her birthday?"

"Nuh-uh. Her brother's. She said it's going to be

chocolate with white icing. Her birthday is in the springtime, like mine."

"That's nice, but are you sure you can't—"

"Momma…" Annie's face is in a full frown.

"I'm just teasing you, punkin. Run along to school. See you later, alligator."

"After-while, crocodile." Annie smiles at their special goodbye as she closes the bedroom door behind her.

Zeenie knows she has no right to feel let down, but she does. Annie would never miss school. She loves it, but couldn't she sometimes love *her* more? Of course, it's a learned behavior, this desertion and loneliness, and it's patterned after her always leaving them to go to work. For nine years. Ever since she and the kids' dad split up when Annie was a year old.

How she hated that man.

How she loved him.

She pads barefoot across the room and opens the bedroom door to the empty apartment. The silence overwhelms her. She doesn't make it to the bathroom before the sobs come.

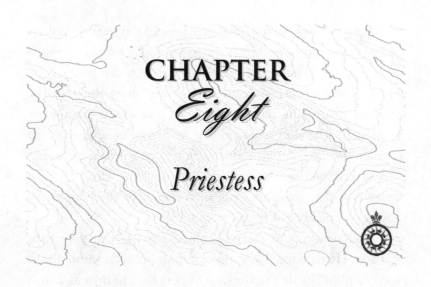

CHAPTER
Eight

Priestess

Lake Pontchartrain & Lake Maurepas Swamps
1903

Willy stares at the underside of a grey, frizzly beard above him. As his mind clears, he finds he's lying across a man's lap with the man's arm over his stomach. He's sick-sleepy, like he never felt before. He hears strange music—nothing like the music they sing and play at Mama's church. Drums beat rhythmically, but not fast. A chorus of strange humming and singing comes from somewhere, but he doesn't know where. Maybe it's the trees, but that doesn't make sense.

He struggles to sit up. The man puts a finger to his lips, staring down at him with aged, yellow eyes. Willy's captor is bare from the waist up. Sparse grey hairs curl across his dark chest. Thin leather straps dangling from his neck hold pieces of misshapen metal, a cross, and bone fragments. He's wearing loose, white trousers. Willy bends a little to the left and sees worn sandals on the old man's gnarly feet.

Water shines from somewhere behind the trees. People—young ones, old ones, but none so young as he—are dressed in purple and white. They stand or squat in the dusky light. Most of the women's clothes are loose, short dresses. The men are wearing purple shirts or have bare chests, with white trousers or loin clothes covering their privates like diapers. Lit candles and fires define a circle of gathering. Small, makeshift shacks propped off the ground surround the circle. A man walks into the circle, and a hush comes over the people. He kneels on one knee as if he's praying.

Willy squirms to escape the man's grip. "Dat dere Papa Rooster. He da King. He workin' up tuh bring da spirits for us and Mambo. She da Priestess," whispers the old man in Willy's ear. "Watch now, ya youngun'. Watch close."

Papa Rooster stands up, then falls forward utterly stiff, catching himself with his flattened hands on the ground. He coils to the left and strikes the ground three times with a clenched fist, shouting in Creole French. He springs quickly to his feet, grabs a jug and pours some kind of liquid on the ground. The drum beats are louder and faster. The man turns in a circle, slowly at first, then gaining speed. The crowd turns with him. He chants in a loud voice, so loud Willy covers his ears. Some people dance, others twirl, many holding torches and lit candles that never seem to tilt. The dancing becomes rapid. A woman screams. Some of the dancers lean backward, almost into the flames of the small fires along the ground. They come back up shaking violently.

A tall woman appears from behind the tree line. She is dressed in a long white robe with a blue cord tied around her middle. Papa Rooster yells something Willy doesn't understand, and people part like a river to make room for her. A table is brought from somewhere and placed in the middle of the circle. Four men lift the woman onto it as she stands rigid and looking forward.

Willy recognizes her as the woman who stole him from his Mama. He surges forward and twists off the old man's lap. He is instantly plucked up by a hefty woman who crushes his back into her ample bosom, binding his arms in front of his chest. No matter how hard he wiggles, he cannot break free.

The man they call Papa Rooster squiggles onto the table like loose liquid and stands beside the tall woman, who remains still with her arms at her sides. Someone hands him a can. He drinks from it with dark liquid spilling down his chin. He flings the empty can to the ground, flails his arms wildly over his head, and yells toward the sky.

Eh! Eh! Bomba ben ben!

Now, he is silent with closed eyes. He begins quivering. His movements make no sense to young Willy. The man's head doesn't seem to belong to his long-limbed body. He shouts in a language such as the boy has never heard before.

"He be full wit dem spirits," the woman holding Willy says to him. He looks up at her and sees a face brimming with joy. She kisses Willy's forehead. He shuts his eyes. The crowd gasps. Willy opens his eyes and jumps. The woman is naked and holding a long snake above her head. He gags as the woman guides the snake to her neck, chanting toward the sky as the snake slowly encircles her.

L'Appé vini, le Grand Zombi
L'Appé vini, pou fe gris-gris!

Drum beats escalate. Fiddles play. The woman's body quakes to the rhythm. Dancers stare wide-eyed without blinking; their feet move rapidly. Others stand with eyes closed, their heads and necks snapping in and out like Mama's old mean goose when he's trying to bite Willy's skinny leg.

Screams. Shouts. Laughter.

Willy's teeth chatter. His eyes seem to be glued open and staring. He shudders as darkness encloses him. His terrified expression dissolves into the peaceful countenance of an innocent child.

CHAPTER
Nine

Broken Home

St. Louis, Missouri
1958

Mercy's family is pretty rich and has some kind of *famous and worthy Negro folks,* as Mercy calls them, who they're awful proud of in their family line. I haven't heard much about them yet, but she says her mama and her grandpa will tell me soon enough if I keep coming around. What I found out the first time I went to her house is she gets money, an allowance, she calls it, every week for keeping her very own room neat and for making good grades. She keeps her money in a jar in her clothes closet. I've never heard of any such thing as allowances before.

Can you imagine a room all to yourself and getting money for just making good grades? My momma looks tuckered out and tells me *that's nice, punkin* when I bring home my straight A's all lined up on my report card and S-pluses for good behavior.

My momma works two back-to-back jobs and don't get

home until early in the morning right before we get up to get ready for school. Every dime has to be squeezed until it hollers, or that's what my Uncle Dew says. Me and Momma sleep on two little beds pushed against one wall in the small bedroom in our apartment with an old dresser-drawer bureau leaning kind of lopsided on the other wall. My three older brothers sleep in the living room—the twins on a couch that has to be pulled down every night and lifted up each day. My oldest brother Donnie, who's fourteen, sleeps inside a folded-over sheet with a blanket on top on our second couch. We call him Hot-Dog on account of how he sleeps in those sheets, and it's fun since he don't like it.

That droopy couch Donnie sleeps on hides an ugly hole in the plaster wall Momma was upset about the day we moved in this little apartment on Lee Street on the east side of St. Louis. That wall hole, and the roaches having a party all over the kitchen, about brought on one of her bad hissy fits, but she calmed down after the janitor brought up some borax powder and soothed her about how it would kill those nasty things as soon as they dared cross the white lines.

She pushed that worn-out old couch Hot-Dog sleeps on against the wall to hide the hole right after the janitor left, and then she got into one of her spruce-up moods and hung a picture of the President of the United States on the wall above our little television. Then the picture of Jesus with a light shining on his face my Aunt Josa gave us went up on the wall right beside it.

Over where our eating table and chairs are, she hung her matched picture set of Chinese ladies with big hairdo's and fancy pins sticking out of them. The women have on long robes of tangerine orange with black trim made of shiny foil. Momma won them in a poetry contest back before she got married to my daddy. I don't know anything about him except he drank a lot of liquor and rode horses all the time so she said we couldn't stay married to him.

When Mama don't have no one to watch us and has to work a triple waitress shift or some such thing, there's our Uncle Dew showing up in his white coveralls spattered with paint and smelling like everything you use to fix or build a house. He's Momma's younger brother out of seven brothers altogether, and he always settles down close to where we live to watch out for us. We shore do like him, not having our own dad around and all. When he ain't smelling like paint thinner or some such, he smells like cigarette smoke and Brylcreem, and he treats us kids like we're not from *a broken home* like the teachers and busybodies always say we are.

Donnie don't like it that Uncle Dew is supposed to keep an eye on him like he does us younger ones, but that's the way the mouse whistles, Uncle Dew tells him. He's fun saying silly things like that and with his shiny, combed hair and good-natured ways, Donnie don't get mad at him hardly at all about nothing.

He's the one who caught Donnie swiping a few dollars out of Momma's special keepsake box last year. Nobody knows about it but the three of us—that's me, Uncle Dew, and Donnie—cause I happened to overhear them talking about it when I was hiding under the raised porch of our house in Pevely.

I always went there to get alone by myself and all of a sudden, there was Uncle Dew and Donnie sitting on the front-porch steps. Uncle Dew was giving Donnie a big-man talk about stealing and how it would hurt Momma's heart to the point of breaking if she found out her oldest son, the one she counted on to be the Man of the Family, had broken her sacred trust in him.

My goodness, I was crying my eyes out listening, and so was Donnie. It was the only time I ever heard him cry, and it shore was sad. They don't know I heard them talking, and they never will.

Anyways, Mercy's mother didn't seem bothered about me being from a broken home or any such thing when I met her. She didn't mention it anyways. I rode the streetcar with Mercy to somewhere in town named the *Ville*, and my eyes about popped out seeing Mercy's house. Lord to goodness, it's nice. It's two-story with red bricks on the outside and a step-up front porch with painted white pillars and a roof over the porch that keeps you nice and shaded in the summertime. Inside, I about died it was so full of fancy furniture and carpets on the wood floors and a big huge circle of a stained-glass window in the bathroom upstairs that you can see when you walk up to the house. It even has two bathrooms.

Everywhere I looked was a fancy doily or a little glass animal or fish made from glass, and there was fresh flowers in vases in the big eating area Mercy called the dining room, and more in the hallway when you come in the front door.

I saw Mr. and Mrs. Washington first off since they came right to the door when me and Mercy came inside and told me who they were and shook my hand. No one ever shook my hand before, and I don't rightly understand why they did it since I'm just ten years old and not a grownup. Mr. Washington was dressed in a business man's suit of clothes, and Mrs. Washington had on a pretty flowerdy dress with a white collar and white cuffs partway up her arm and pretty shoes with not a scuff on them.

She said, "Children, Miss Ettie has a plate of fresh cookies just out of the oven on the kitchen table. Please help yourselves. Not so many to ruin your dinner, Mercy. We're having roast leg of lamb." Then she and Mr. Washington smiled so big at me before they went on their way somewhere in that big house that I know I turned three shades of red.

"Thank you, Mama," Mercy said, and led us through that wide hall just inside the front door and a little further to a kitchen bigger than both our living room, bedroom, and kitchen put together in our little apartment.

"Mercy, why do you go to our school so far away when you could go to a school here that's probably nicer and closer to where you live?"

"My mama and daddy want me to learn about the world by not being spoiled. My grandpa was one of the men helping make up the Elleardsville Financial Corporation in 1926 here in the *Ville,* so I can't be taking life too easy. He's got a history to be proud of, and I want to live up to it."

"What in the world are you talking about?"

Mercy sighed. "Oh, I'll explain it to you later. Sure, I could go to John Marshall School here on Aldine Avenue, but our school we go to, you and I, is one of the schools that's really letting Colored kids go to school the same as White kids. They ride the school buses together and sit together."

"Except in our classroom."

"Mrs. Patterson is thinking the old way. What's happening at that school and a few others is part of history, and now I'm part of it, too. My family says it helps me understand where we came from and where we're going to."

"But you're from here, ain't you?"

"Annie, don't say *ain't.*"

"All right, I just forget sometimes. But you're from St. Louis, so why do you have to understand where you're from?"

"It means we need to remember where our people, the Negro race, has come from. My grandpa says it's important to keep an eye on the past and the future and not just live in the present."

I am so confused when Mercy talks like that. No one in my family says anything of the kind. I have so much to learn from my new best friend, but one thing I know—her family don't treat me like I come from *a broken home,* and they shore are the fanciest folks I ever met.

CHAPTER
Ten

The Intruder

New Orleans
1903

*I*t happened so oddly, and seemingly by chance. Yet, upon reflection, Jack knew it was the work of something more that had caused the woman to select his room and no other on that crucial night. She could have selected any room, or shall we say—person— in the hotel that evening, and in great desperation it was, and yet, it was *his* room. Later, he would attribute this turn of events to Providence and perhaps the help of a kindly porter, or maid, or, perchance, several of them, who knew her and cared for their own.

Coming in quite late his first night in New Orleans from a full supper, brandy, and talk of the old days, he had been surprised to find his door unlocked. He retrieved the small derringer from the top of his boot and cautiously entered, but the woman inside was making no pretense of hiding. Not at all. She sat across the room in one of the two overstuffed, upholstered chairs provided in all the lush rooms of the St. Charles Hotel.

The bathroom light was on, its door ajar, and there she was, wearing a large shawl over her hair, shoulders, and part of her face. In her arms, a slumbering baby in a blanket. Next to her, an unsmiling lad of, Jack guessed, maybe four years old— a big-eyed, somber boy who stared a hole in him.

When he recovered from the shock of her presence, Jack, being mostly a scrupulous man, especially publicly, opened the door wide and, politely, of course, told her to take her leave. She placed the baby tenderly on the bed, closed the open door, then dropped to the floor on her knees. Head bowed, in a soft and pitiable voice, the woman implored him to listen to her dilemma.

"My dear woman, I am sure you have carried a burden unbearably heavy upon your small shoulders, but I cannot, in good conscience, entangle myself in your circumstance. I am, you see, an unmarried man, and you are a family woman alone in my hotel room. Look here, if you are hungry, I shall gladly see that you are provided meals tonight and that you and your offspring will have plenty of coin for a week of meals. Or, if you need a room—"

"Oh, no, please, please do not bid me leave you, *mon bon monsieur*," the woman tearfully mumbled in what Jack recognized as not the French, Haitian, or Spanish Creole dialects of the region, but rather in unadulterated French. It was obvious she had been educated and tended to in style. At last, she recovered enough to speak coherently, her head downturned. *"Monsieur,* truly if you turn me away, *moi et mes petit enfants* shall perish, *oui,* this very night."

"But what the devil am I to do? Are you wanted by the police?"

"No sir, no! I swear to you I have committed no crime that warrants taking me to prison. My crime is only that I trusted and delayed too long, and for that I am guilty, guilty, guilty!"

Jack sat down in one of the chairs and waited for the woman to regain her composure. While she sobbed into her hands, her serious-faced boy stood next to her staring at him as if all the sins of the world now and since the dawn of mankind were Jack's own fault and perhaps doubly so. *Disconcerting* was the word that skipped across his mind. Here was a nasty mess the likes of which he had never encountered before, and he wasn't sure how he was going to put the proper end to it. He had to admit the woman's obvious despair was compelling, the gloomy boy's eyes unnerving.

He sighed. "Just how can I help you, madam?"

In a few moments, she said, "Would you be so kind as to aid me in getting out of this city unnoticed, *monsieur*, and quickly? I have heard from many sources that you are a good man, and goodness and mercy are what I need more than my next breath. You see, the one who is even now turning over every stone in this city looking for *moi et mes bébés* is a very powerful man. Very rich with many connections all over New Orleans. Perhaps even at this hotel. Oh, yes, surely even here!"

"And your need is…

"I need only that you help this unworthy woman and her children escape terrible death and slavery."

Oh, is that all? Jack thought wryly. After a brief contemplation, he said, "Very well, then. Let me see how I can get you out of the city. I do have a few connections. First, madam, I think it befits you to gather yourself from the floor."

He bent and offered the woman his arm. She roused from her tearful agony to pat her face with a handkerchief, a very nice one, Jack noted. This accomplished, the woman took Jack's arm. At that moment, her shawl fell from her face and neck, and even though her flawless skin was covered in mean bruises, and a bloody gash smeared her generous but swollen lips, here before Jack was the most gorgeous female he had ever beheld—a woman the likes of which painters fought over, sobbed openly in front of, left their wives and lovers for, and begged on bloody knees to own... to keep... to paint.

A woman for which a man would fight a duel—perhaps a hundred duels—would travel around the world ten times to conquer and love, fighting to the death to rename any ship in which he found himself after this angelic creation's name, and Jack... Jack was smitten for the first time in his life.

In that one instant, staring at the graceful arch of her neck, the melting brown eyes, the radiant tint of her skin, he knew that whatever she wanted or needed, he was henceforth her willing servant.

CHAPTER
Eleven

What Momma Don't Know

St. Louis, Missouri
1958

I wonder what Mercy's family would do if they found out how we're running around St. Louis like we're all growed up and like we don't have no one we have to ask about nothing. I get worried sometimes my brothers will find out since they're so nosy. Truth is, they run all over the city, too, buying comic books and going to their friends' houses and slipping into the movie shows on Saturday afternoons. They don't tell no one neither. Donnie is supposed to be watching us most the time, and he does when he's home. Momma ain't never home anyways except to grab some shut-eye, so it don't make much difference is the way I see it.

Still, none of us know what she'd do if she knew everything, so we don't tell her. She thinks I'm with Mercy at school and that sometimes her parents come get me to take me to their house or else I'm home coloring or pretending or some such. That's not completely true, now is it, but how can I stop doing something I would never get to do except with my friend Mercy? Thing is, I've been home alone so much in my life, I can't stand it no more. Coloring pictures or drawing or pretending with my doll Molly-Mae by myself just ain't fun now.

The tricky part of me and Mercy's sneaking around is being careful when we go to the Peach Garden at Olive and Grand 'cause it's across the street from Walgreen's where Momma works her day shift at the lunch counter. When she gets through there, she walks across the street to The Royal Restaurant and works a whole bunch more.

She's dead tired and usually sleeping like a log when we get up in the mornings for school, so we don't see her hardly at all. Once in a while, she stays up and sees us off to school, but she's yawning the whole time and her eyes are red as a blood hound's. On her day off, she's doing the washing and ironing and buying some groceries or has Donnie go buy some at the corner grocery store, and she's yawning about all day long. She just gets one day a week off, so I don't spend much time with her and neither do my brothers.

"Hurry up, Annie," Mercy says since I'm being real slow about getting off the streetcar. The reason is 'cause I'm holding onto the metal bars by the steps and staring over at the Walgreens place.

"But I—"

"If you dawdle, she's bound to see you. Besides, my nice dress is getting rain spatters."

I reckon *dawdle* means being a slowpoke, so I jump past the last two steps you use to get in and out of the streetcar, and we hightail it fast to the Peach Garden's back door. Before we go in, I have to bend down to put my hands on my legs and push my chest up so's I can breathe better. The rain and running makes it hard for me to breathe with my stupid old asthma.

We go in the unlocked door in the back and walk around boxes and carts and the biggest cans of food you ever seen in your life to finally get to the kitchen. Chinaman Bill has us a little table with a white tablecloth against the wall in the kitchen, and we know it's 'cause he loves Aunt Viola so much that he does it. He lets us eat whatever we want till our stomachs almost bust, and we get to drink hot tea and soda pop with our food all at the same time.

We tell him hi, and I go sit down at our special table. Mercy digs in her purse and hands him a letter from Aunt Viola. I wish you could have seen his face when Mercy handed it to him. If he had a tail, he shore would have been wagging it. He hugs that letter to his chest and starts talking that Chinaman talk that sounds a little like buzzing in the back of the mouth. Then he trots off like he's got a whole stack of Christmas presents to open.

"When did you get that letter from your aunt?" I ask Mercy soon as she sits down.

"Last night. She came over for dinner and gave it to me secretly."

"What do you think it's about?

"I don't know, but something sure is going on."

"Are we going to stop by and see her after we eat?"

"Nuh-uh. Let's take the bus to that Jefferson Memorial Building and see the statue carved all from one piece of Italian marble. I've been wanting to go. My brother Jerome says it's almost twenty feet tall."

I don't say a word because the only marble I ever heard of are the marbles my brothers play with—cat's eyes, clearies, shooters, that kind of thing. The boys get on the ground and shoot those things in and out of a circle and act like it's as important as eating taters and gravy, which it ain't. Anways, I keep my mouth quiet so's Mercy don't think I'm ignorant when she says she wants to see a twenty-foot-high marble. Heck, I want to see that myself.

CHAPTER
Twelve

The Slap Heard Around the City

St. Louis, Missouri
1958

H er late-night streetcar trips home after work with a switchblade knife folded in her hand indicates where life seems to be going for Zeenie. Yes, she likes working at her new job at the Missouri Athletic Club better than the grueling two jobs she left at the Walgreens counter and The Royal Restaurant. Twelve hours on her feet are better than fifteen hours any day. The dollar an hour at the club instead of seventy-five cents an hour makes her take-home pay about the same as before, even with the reduced hours.

Truth be told, that new job most likely saved her life.

It was the kindness of one of the mob guy's girlfriend who came almost nightly into the Royal that changed Zeenie's place of work. However, what really turned everything upside down was what happened earlier. Zeenie had been so busy she'd barely looked up from taking orders, delivering food and drinks seamlessly to the tables of mafia men, their girlfriends, and countless other tables for hours on end and generally working her feet and mind into a numb frenzy.

Her shift at the Royal started at midnight and went until six in the morning, and that was after her three in the afternoon to eleven-thirty p.m. shift at the Walgreens cooking short orders and waiting on the counter and tables.

Altogether, she worked a solid fifteen hours a day with a half-hour lunch break at Walgreens and a half hour to walk across the street and get re-dressed for her other job. Sure, she took a couple cigarette breaks here and there, but only five minutes each. The pace was wearing her down, changing her into a web of nerves and exhaustion.

Her last night at the Royal had its usual crew of crazies show up. Queen Boggle, as the other waitresses called her, had been in talking to invisible people at her table and smiling into her napkin. She came in several times a week to order a slice of pie and numerous cups of black coffee. She got up twice to use the pay phone. As always, she didn't put any money in the slot before discussing huge real estate deals with important people, naming the mayor and other city officials in the conversation.

Every time Zeenie passed the big front window that night, she saw Augusto pacing the sidewalk outside the restaurant. He did that whenever his gang met inside for cocktails, wine, and planning sessions, which was every night except Sunday and Monday. He never failed to make eye contact with Zeenie, and it made her shudder to think a mafia strongarm was watching her so intently. No, it wasn't just that. He had a gleam in his eye that was unmistakable.

At two in the morning, Maggie came in to order her usual two meals to go. Zeenie felt sorry for Maggie, a prostitute just

Jodi Lea Stewart

twenty years old who came from a little town west of
St. Louis. Zeenie tried to talk to her once about leaving that
life and becoming a waitress or anything else besides her
present occupation, but Maggie told her, "Don't worry about
me, pretty lady. I'll take this life over putting up with a
drunken daddy any day." Even when she came in with a black
eye or covered in bruises, she still ordered those two meals for
herself and her pimp.

At two-thirty, Augusto sauntered inside and sat at the
Bonzarelli table in the semi-private cut-out in the back of the
restaurant. Zeenie came to take his order, and when she
turned to go, he ran his hand down her back, letting it rest on
the curve of her rear.

"My big broad from Broadway," he'd declared loudly
with an air of ownership that shook Zeenie to her toes. Her
exhaustion and nerves collided in an explosion of anger. She
wheeled around and slapped him across the face before she
even realized she had done it. The silence in the entire
restaurant was something she would never forget. No one
stood up to the mob, let alone hit one of them. Especially a
woman.

An eternity of silence was followed by Augusto's shocked
response, "Well, I'll be damned," he said.

She fled to the little locker room where the wait staff
went to sit, smoke a cigarette, and blow off steam about
difficult customers. What had she done? What was she
thinking? The night manager, Mr. Walker, came into the room
and closed the door behind him, his head shaking side to side.

"Zeenie, Zeenie, Zeenie. What got into you, gal?"

"I... I don't know, Mr. Walker. I didn't even think about
it, and-and... I've got to get out of here. He'll kill me sure as
the world."

53

A slip of a young woman wearing a full-length sable mink over her glittery cocktail dress came quietly into the room. Her blond hair in a French chignon was held in place with a diamond clasp. Red lips, tired eyes, pale skin. Mr. Walker and Zeenie watched her enter the room, their faces frozen. The young woman smiled at them.

"Miss Zeenie, I really like you. You're always so nice, and you work harder than any three people ought to. I-I want to tell you something now, and I hope you won't take it the wrong way. My sister, Annabelle? She works at the Missouri Athletic Club on Washington Avenue, and I think she can get you a job there if you want it. See, she says it's a grand place to work and our, uh, *boys* don't go in there like they do here. This place… this place and these late nights ain't, uh, I mean, aren't good for a fine woman with four children to work at."

Zeenie had the distinct impression the woman was taking a big risk coming in the locker room, especially from how often she looked over her shoulder at the door.

"Will you give her a call? I already wrote her number down for you." She handed a piece of paper to Zeenie. "You have a back way out of here, honey?"

Zeenie nodded.

"I think everything's okay, but, you know, just to be shore… uh, I mean just to be sure, maybe you should…"

Mr. Walker had already opened Zeenie's locker and was holding her purse out to her. She took it, looked back and forth at him and the young woman.

"I'll have Ed bring your paycheck to you tomorrow, Zeen. Don't worry about that. I'll put a little extra on it to tide you over till you get that new job." Mr. Walker stepped forward and gave her a fatherly hug.

Zeenie tried to smile, but tears were a blink away. She was

sure her smile looked as cheerful as chopped onions. "Thanks, Mr. Walker. I appreciate it." She turned toward the young woman. "I won't forget this…"

The woman pulled her coat tighter around her slim frame. "Don't mention it, honey. You're a real decent woman. Anyone can see that. I want you should, I mean… I think you should have a better job with better hours. You deserve it." She smiled and left the room as quietly as she had entered it.

Zeenie walked out of the service exit of The Royal Restaurant and never returned.

CHAPTER
Thirteen

Farewell, Old Buddies

New Orleans
1903

*I*n the safe privacy of the hotel room, the woman poured out her entire story and, afterward, pled with Jack to swear to keep her and her children a secret.

After hearing her strange story, Jack was in agreement that all care must be taken to depart the city in clandestine haste.

Tomorrow evening, as the men of the former Texas Rangers gather in the *Salon de Bourgogne* at the St. Charles Hotel for brandy, whiskey, cigars, tale-telling, and cards, he knows they will speculate and discuss at length as to where he might be. An annual ritual for years, bachelor Jack has never missed being among them every night for a week to reminisce—cuss and discuss, they affectionately call it—the Old West days when men were men and outlaws' antics were cut short by the bravado, guts, and glory of the vigilant few who dared to pursue them.

Yet, he knows had any of his fellow Rangers heard this poor woman's sad tale, they would have gladly taken to their pistols once again to right the injustice of the indignities she had suffered. Of that, he is certain. Revenge had crossed his mind several times as she told him about Samuel Allen Livingston, her somewhat elderly, yet rich and willing, former guardian and *paramour*, and how he had unexpectedly keeled over dead but a week before. The man's son, Bradford Allen Livingston, had shown up at her door this very night ready to destroy all that ever was of their "unholy liaison."

Bradford, a victim of a split family and having never lived with or cared for his father, growing up instead with a wealthy mother and her family back east, and he, being educated and in-process of becoming an esquire, told her he could not and would not abide the loathsome and vulgar habits of his now deceased father, especially considering his own future political aspirations, and that she, being a *quadroon*, was unrighteous already for that fact alone.

In an outrageous tirade inside the woman's well-tended cottage given to her by the late Mr. Livingston and situated just off Canal Street, he became so incensed looking at the beautiful woman who had so enraptured his father—a man who had taken up with her only after living alone for a decade after his divorce—that he, Bradford Livingston, took a brutal hand and strap to her to show the seriousness of his intent to scourge his family name of *such a vile, whoring woman and her unconsecrated progeny*.

He mockingly shared his ugly plot to sell the baby girl to a ship merchant who was on his way to Europe, one who would pay a handsome price for her. The baby would, thereafter, be sold to the highest bidder. In fact, he was planning to take her to the unscrupulous merchant that very night. The money from the sale would, in part, finance the young boy's voyage to a family upriver, a family growing cabbages and working in the lumber mills of Ruddock. The boy would henceforth be known by this foster family's surname, and not by the lie of the one he now claimed.

The younger Livingston's intention was to take the baby girl with him immediately. He said he would send his aide to pick up the young lad within the hour. She herself was to pack her things and leave New Orleans that very night, never to return. If she did not obey his orders, he promised she would face instant and horrible retribution by his own hand.

It was only by sheer craftiness of the woman's survival instincts and her quick mind that she had tricked the ruffian by telling him his father had left him a fortune in rare coins, along with an important letter, inside a box in the study. She produced a small key from a chain around her neck and surrendered it to him. While he occupied himself opening the ornate box that actually held nothing of significance to him, the woman seized her children and ran from the cottage screaming, "Bradford Allen Livingston is a murderer!" again and again as a ruse to humiliate and distract her tormentor.

People indeed stopped on the *banquettes* to stare, and the younger Livingston watched from the open door of the cottage, hatred literally darkening his countenance into a most hideous mask. The young mother's last glance over her shoulder at the man's face had terrorized her beyond reason.

As anyone of character would be, Jack was incensed upon hearing this grievous account. The woman swore on her own life she would get her daughter as far away from that man as was humanly possible, that her nightmare forevermore would be of Bradford finding the girl and selling her into slavery. Should that happen, she would surely die of heartache, herself having known, not firsthand, but of dearly loved ones, the bitterness of slavery on the one side of her family, as well as the bittersweet irony of being related to wealthy White people on the other side.

"But, my dear woman, don't you realize that I… Jack… a former lawman of the highest order, am fully capable of protecting all three of you to the death?" he had queried.

Her new deluge of tears and pleas had rattled him, and he gave in, swearing that he would never tell anyone the story of where the girl of six months of age hailed from or her dire circumstances. Further, he promised to find a way to hide her.

The St. Charles Hotel mezzanine is cheerfully lit with strings of colored lights. Jack walks from his room, down the hallway, across the mezzanine, and to the staircase straight-backed and dignified beside a woman who is heavily shawled about her face and shoulders. He holds the hand of a young lad in one hand. His other arm loops through the arm of the woman carrying a blanketed baby. They descend the wide, brass-railed and carpeted staircase into the lobby. The boy tugs at Jack's hand to explore the real-live trees growing inside boxed-in squares in the exquisite hotel lobby. The firmness of Jack's grasp tells the boy not one unnecessary move will be tolerated.

Out the doors and into the hubbub of St. Charles Street, Jack turns and tips the porter carrying his bags. After an exchange of words, the porter tilts his head slightly, then steps to the street to whistle for a horse-drawn carriage to take the entourage to the rail station. Thus, does Jack, without ado and with no explanation, exit New Orleans with a family he has never lain eyes on until a mere hour before—a family that is now his as sure as anything ever was.

Some secrets in life must be sealed as sacred documents dripped with hot wax, and this was truly one. That's how Jack sees it this night, and he, a man of his own mind and ways, is also a man of his solid word. Yet, a different man, he is, who now, at the ripe age of near forty, has lost his heart and head in one fell swoop to a goddess beleaguered by trouble and tragedy. She is his Helen of Troy, his Cleopatra, his beauty above all beauties.

Oh, sweet agony are the words playing inside his mind to the rhythm of the horses' feet on the paving-stone streets of New Orleans as they make their way to the rail station. That tempo gives way to an infatuated delight of future possibilities with Selene. He is, quite frankly and without a doubt, the man for her in every way from this day forward.

In the midst of fervent awakenings of long-buried, perhaps never-awakened, emotions, Jack's besotted mind roams to the tragic plight of Ernest and Arlene Adele, a couple who wants nothing more than a child to love.

CHAPTER
Fourteen

New Awlins Candle and Magic Shop

St. Louis, Missouri
1959

The New Awlins Candle and Magic Shop on Grand and Laclede sounded like a scary place to me, but Mercy said her cousin Christopher goes in there all the time and finds interesting things. She said her Grandpa Grafton and her parents would forbid her to visit a shop like that, so she certainly was bound to do so at least once or twice in her lifetime.

I don't know—Mercy's awful happy and proud of her family, so I was surprised she wanted to do something they wouldn't like. Anyways, Januarys are pretty snowy in the city, so me and Mercy can't go to the park or do something else outside. Saturday afternoons are too long to just sit around and do nothing, that's for shore. I guess visiting a different kind of shop like a magic shop was all Mercy could think of for us to do.

My Aunt Vel said magic stuff is a sin if it ain't just parlor tricks like hiding a card up your sleeve, so I guess I'm a little partial to not going there either. I said so to Mercy, and she said, "All right, what else can we do, Annie?"

We're at my apartment drawing and coloring ladies and queens and princesses and their clothes and making paper dolls out of them. I was coloring the rest of the red jewels on my paper doll princess crown when Mercy thought up the idea of us going to that shop. We already ate all the mushroom soup Donnie fixed us for lunch, and he'd taken off some place or other, probably to see a movie show with his buddies. We were sick of the twins arguing and watching their noisy cowboys and Indians shows on the television, the sound turned up way too loud, and even louder when I told them to turn it down.

I have no answer for what else to do to fill up the afternoon before Mercy has to go home in time for supper, so we dress in our big coats and boots and head for the bus stop. The bus is empty except for one old lady with a white paper sack with twine handles and a loaf of French bread sticking out of the top. She's sitting in the first seat behind the bus driver, so me and Mercy decide to sit beside each other, and you know what? The driver doesn't even seem to notice. That makes us giggle and talk up a storm.

When we see the New Awlins Candle and Magic Shop quite a ways down the street from the bus stop, I sort of don't want to go in. Mercy in her bright red coat takes off down the aisle of the bus and jumps off before I can tell her I might have changed my mind.

What I see first off inside the front door of the magic shop is a rack of cards explaining about oils, waters, powders, and stuff and what you use them for. Mercy walks right on by the rack, but I have to stop and read some of them since I read ever thing I ever see. I never heard of so many powders! There's Love Powder, Peace Powder, Anger Powder, and Drawing Powder. I guess that powder makes you draw pictures better? I shore don't know.

There are cards telling how to use things with names that make me shiver. Black Devil's Water, Hell's Devil Water, Mad Oil, Bad Luck Water, Sacred Sand, Follow Me Drops, and lots more. I feel kind of scared reading those names, so I hurry over by Mercy. She's looking over a whole shelf of colored candles.

"Look here, Annie. This pink candle is what you burn an hour a day for nine days to get your true love to love you forever. Maybe Chinaman Bill should try that," she says, then laughs. "The brown one is for when you have an enemy, and—"

"Can we go eat Chinese food now?"

She gives me a funny look. "We just ate two bowls a piece of soup at your place. I'm not a bit hungry. Don't be scared. Nothing in here can hurt us. Hey, look at that plant over there. It's really strange."

A man dressed in black droopy clothes steps out from the counter and smiles a crooked grin. "That's five-finger grass, ladies. You hang that up in your house or over the bed and it'll bring you good sleep and keep evil from your door. Kind of like Brimstone keeps away evil spirits when you burn it."

"We don't have any evil spirits to get rid of, mister," Mercy says.

"Sure, sure, course you don't, but see the five divides on that there leaf? This one here stands for luck. The other one for money. Then, you got the wisdom, power, and love fingers. Now, everybody wants those things, right? Don't have to have spirits for five-finger grass to do you good."

Mercy stares at him for a long moment. It's her stare that says *I think you're stupid,* and it's pretty powerful. She gives it out plenty when folks try to keep us from playing or going around together.

"My cousin bought a Dragon Blood Stick, and he said he found a twenty-dollar bill about an hour later. You got any of those?" she asks.

"Indeed, I do." The man rubs his hands together. "Aren't you the clever one to know about such things?" He steps to a shelf and pulls two sticks from a jar. "This here Dragon Blood Stick fits in your pocket or purse. It brings you money or luck or what have you."

"I'll take it."

"They come in sets of two. Fifty cents."

Mercy pulls a dollar from her purse and hands it to the man. He goes to the cash register and returns with Mercy's change and a small paper sack.

"I put a little *gris-gris* bag in your sack, honey. You'll need it if you're gonna study the ancient arts."

"I'm not studying any ancient arts," Mercy says.

He chuckles. "Uh-huh, sure, sure. Well, you come back and see me and let me know how those Dragon Blood sticks work for you. Say, ever wish you could find some treasure, girls?"

I look at Mercy, and she rolls her eyes, but the man doesn't see her do it. He walks back behind the counter and leans forward on his elbows.

"Everybody loves treasure, now don't they?"

He looks almost like he's wearing a scary rubber mask since his face gets all screwy-happy with a half-sided grin and yellow teeth.

"Mercy, let's go now."

"You're in luck, little ladies. I just got a shipment of Wonder-of-the-World Root in today. See, it's still in the packing box over there, and I, always thinking ahead of things, made up some Shem-Shem-Touras, the Tenth Seal of Mercury, last night."

He reaches under the counter and brings out a small piece of chamois like my Uncle Dew uses to wipe the water off his pickup truck when he hoses it down. Only, this chamois is cut real small and has funny drawings on it in red ink.

"You want to find the world's treasures and be rich? You have to know the secrets, don't you know? First, you decide where you think some treasure is. There's bundles of it in Luzianne, what with all the pirates, Spaniards, and those Aztec explorers who used to go there. Fact is, I lived in N'Awlins a spell, and that's how I learned all about this ancient knowledge. Finding treasure in St. Louis, well, you'll have to do some searching. Read you some old books in the library and some such, but it's here, oh, yes, it is.

"Anyways, when you think you know where some real loot is buried, dig a hole and bury the Tenth Seal of Mercury 'bout four feet in the ground. Then you gots to do some planting. Plant you some of the Wonder-of-the-World Roots, one to the west, one to the east, and one in the other two directions. I swear, the pores of the earth will open up for you!"

The man claps his hands together loud, and I jump.

"It's shore your lucky day, too, 'cause I have some Knaves Oil and Two Jacks Extract to wash your hands in after you bury those roots. Dang a'mighty, can you believe it's on sale? See, none of your work on that treasure matters if you don't use the oil and extract. Gots to have them to finish the deal."

"I never heard of any of those things," Mercy says.

"You ever talk to a treasure hunter, specially one from the City that Care Forgot, old New Awlins itself? If you do, you'll see. He'll know 'bout the proper roots and oils that reveal the earth's secrets. Girls, since you want to know, here's how it works."

I glance at Mercy, and I'm wondering why he thinks we want to know anything about anything he's blabbing his mouth about, but he goes right on talking. He reminds me of a tipped-over bottle without a stopper.

"After you do the burying and the washing up, you take a mirror and hold it over the buried Seal of Mercury. You'll see at least twenty feet under the ground!" He cackles and slaps his thigh, then leans down toward us. "Now take yourself a willow stick and fasten a gold coin on the end and pass it over the ground. This draws the treasure up to about four feet, and you can—"

It's a good thing Mercy takes hold of my arm and pulls me out of the store 'cause I was about to think maybe me and Mercy could find us some treasure for ourselves and get rich. My eyeballs had got glued to the man telling us that stuff in almost a whisper with his face going in all directions, his bloodshot eyes bigger than half dollars, and his long-fingered hands cupped together like they had an invisible globe in them.

Once we're outside, Mercy takes the Dragon Blood Sticks out of her sack and sticks them in the dirty snow mounded on the side of the street by the snow scrapers. She buries them so deep, you can't even see them in the snow.

"Why'd you do that for?"

"Because I didn't like that man, and I sure don't like how he rattles his mouth. Did you ever hear such stupid talking in all your life? Besides, he doesn't even pronounce New Orleans the way the people who live there do."

"How do they pronounce it?"

"Like *New OR-lins,* not *New Awlins or N'awlins.*"

"Oh. Well, you think maybe he was crazy?"

"Uh-huh. Didn't you see his eyes going everywhere when he talked?"

"Yep, I shore did. Hey, what was that other thing he put in your sack?"

"I don't know. *Agree-agree* or something like that. I've never heard of it. Let's get a look at it on the bus if we get to sit together. We'll check that big dictionary on the stand next time we go to the library. We might find it in there if we can figure out how to spell it right."

"Why didn't you throw it away, too?"

"Why?"

"I don't know. It might be something bad."

"Now you sound like Grandpa Grafton, Annie. He's so old-fashioned religious. I think superstitions might have a little truth in them but not like what we just heard. If that man could find real treasure with a stupid Seal and some roots, why isn't he rich himself?"

"How do you know he ain't, I mean *isn't?*"

"You can just tell. His clothes were sloppy. Not even ironed."

We head for the bus stop, and I shore am glad Mercy is my best friend. She's smarter than any ten kids all tied together.

CHAPTER
Fifteen

Awakening

Lake Pontchartrain & Lake Maurepas Swamps
1903

The flickering shadows through the palmettos outside the window brush across Willy's face, stirring him awake. He yawns, rubs his eyes, opens them. He sees a jumble of roots, glass, and small hunks of metal hanging by leather strings above his head. He sits up. His eyes dart around the room. His breathing quickens as he recognizes nothing at all. He kneels forward on the mattress to peer through a thick net nailed to a window over the bed.

Outside the netted window, he sees little houses made of swamp reeds, sticks, and old greying boards. An old woman sits on a metal chair in the clearing, hunched over, working on a partially finished reed basket. Willy watches adults walk here and there. A few kids chase a chicken from the clearing and disappear around the side of a shack. The old man who held him last night is shirtless and napping on the porch of one of the houses with a straw brim hat tilted over his eyes. His legs, clad in soiled white britches, are stretched out straight in front of him. A scroungy brown dog sleeps beside him.

"Mama," Willy whispers. "Mama! Mama!" he yells.

Willy bolts off the bed toward a line of amber beads hanging in front of the shack's only door. He falls to the floor, pain shooting up his leg. He looks down at the iron shackle circling his slim ankle. He pounds his fists on the dirt floor, crying bitterly. A few minutes later, he crawls back to the only security he feels in the room—the bed and mattress scooted against the wall. He presses his face against the window netting and calls his mother until he is hoarse.

The whole village, those who are not off working in towns, fields, or mills today, gathers outside the window opening. Some have tight, black curls on their heads like Willy, others have straight or wavy hair. He sees every color of skin… dark, light, golden, olive, white, and every shade of hair and eyes.

The crowd parts, and the woman who stole Willy, the one the old man called Mambo, walks toward the shack, Willy screams and wrestles against the iron chain. The door opens. The beaded curtain parts. Willy pushes violently with his head on the window netting to escape, but it stays firm.

"Hush fore ya go crezzie, *ti cheri a!*" the woman says. "Ya mine now for ta my udder boy swallowed by dem swamp gaters. Papa Legba make Loa gods gives ya ta me."

Willy draws into a ball, trembling. The woman talks strange, nothing like his mama or his sisters. He bites the back of his hand until it bleeds. The woman hums, then sings like she did on the road when his mama asked if she was all right. She moves closer to Willy. He pushes his small back hard into the wall at one end of the bed and stares at her with wet, horrified eyes.

She reaches her hands toward him. Shaking, he closes his eyes. Nothing happens. When he opens his eyes, he sees the woman has smoothed the covers around him. She takes a broom and sweeps the dirt floor, aiming toward the beaded doorway. She moves the beads aside and sweeps the circles of dust outside. She smiles tenderly at Willy. From the folds of her dress, she brings out a blue, crystal-clear candy stick and places it on the small table beside the bed.

"Ah, now, a sweet ting fer *ti cheri a.*"

When she leaves, Willy falls backward on the mattress sobbing. In the middle of picturing his mama's beloved face and of needing her arms around him, and of remembering her soothing voice, he thinks about that candy stick the color of the sky. It's so very close to him. On the table. He rolls onto his side and stares at it. It's pretty. He snuffles, his chest convulsing from his weeping. He takes the candy and holds it toward the light of the window. He licks it once and studies it again. It's sweet and what else?

One time, Willy chewed part of a tree leaf. It was bitter. The blue candy is sweet and tastes like a leaf, too. He puts the end in his mouth and sucks on it. In a few minutes, he is yawning. He lies back onto the bed. He takes the candy from his mouth. It remains standing up in his hand as he slips into a deep sleep.

CHAPTER
Sixteen

Does She Have Any Other Friends?

St. Louis, Missouri
1959

*I*f anybody had a druther, they wouldn't let their momma find out things like I had to. Momma was so mean when she found out, I almost don't love her no more. I didn't know she was one of them other kinds of folks. I know one thing—I shore am sorry I was ever borned in this family. Maybe that's bad to say, but it's the truth.

If it wasn't for those stupid twin brothers of mine being spiteful, Momma would never have found out. What happened is I left the same as usual for school this morning walking with Joey and Jackie. They always get sidetracked on the way to school and do some kind of mischief, and I go on to school by myself. Today was no different. They decided to cut Mrs. Arbol's flowers growing alongside the front of her house and try to sell them to any lady they came across so's they could buy more baseball trading cards. They always look so kind—and they're twins with all that blond hair—and I swear, I think people would buy a torn paper sack from them. I don't tell on them, but I should. They're twelve and old enough to know better.

Before they went to stealing flowers, I told them to tell Donnie I was going over to Mercy's house after school in case I was a little late getting home, but did they do it? No sir! They messed me up real good, and I won't be forgetting about it. I shore won't.

Me and Mercy's big plan this morning was for me to wait at the corner before I crossed the street to the school. At eight-thirty, here she comes right on time riding in the front seat with her grandpa. I've met him a time or two, and I shore do like him. He tells us about life and people and makes the most interesting faces at the same time. He lowers his voice, raises it, lets it get deep and all that. I never heard anyone tell things so excited like that before. Uncle Dew, kind of, but not as good as Mercy's grandpa.

This morning, he was all dressed up in a suit and bowtie and hat, and my gracious, if he didn't have a nice car! Shiny black with no roof and white on the tires. Lots of silver chrome, and the top of it was down. Soon's they pull up, Mercy gets out of the front seat all dressed in the prettiest two-tone blue dress with blue ribbons in her hair, white anklets, and black patent-leather shoes.

I had on a regular school dress that tied in the back—a washed-out pink with little faded flowers—pink socks that used to be red, and oxfords like Momma always makes me wear to school. I got frozen up with shame for how I looked, and down went my head on my chest.

Mercy said, "How do you like Grandpa Grafton's car, Annie? It's called a Ford Fairlane Sunline, and he bought it from a friend last fall before Thanksgiving. It's a little more than two years old, but it sure doesn't look it."

"I ain't never seen a car so pretty before," I mumble, head still down.

"Don't say… um, never mind."

Mercy's corrections of my talk always start with *Don't say*, so then I felt worse.

"Grandpa's the speaker today, so we better be leaving."

"I, uh…"

Something funny about me and Mercy is she knows what I'm thinking if I say it out loud or keep it to myself. She says, "Guess what? I have something for you since your birthday is next week. We'll take it inside to the lady's lounge when we get to the Center. We'll have time for that, won't we, Grandpa?"

Her grandpa turned to look at us. He smiled the biggest smile at me with more white teeth than I ever seen on anyone.

"Of course, we will. And how are you doing this fine spring morn, Miss Annie?

"I-I'm fine, sir."

"Good to hear, really good. We're blessed for sure."

He turned back around not looking at us, and Mercy opened the front door and leaned the car seat up. She pulled out the biggest birthday present I ever seen in my life from the backseat. It was wrapped in white tissue paper with a huge shiny yellow bow all across the top part. It was almost too big for Mercy to lift.

"What in the world…?"

Mercy laughed. "You can open it when we get to the ceremony." She handed me the present and climbed in the back seat. Me? I just stood there holding that big ol' present with my mouth hanging open. "Come on, slowpoke, get in the car. Here, I'll hold your birthday present until you get in."

I got in the backseat of that car with the red and white leather seats and sat beside my best friend in the whole world holding the biggest, prettiest birthday present anyone ever had. For the first time in my life, I felt kind of like a rich person. Only a little bit did I worry Momma might find out what Mercy and me done, but I didn't let it bother me much.

"After we visit the lady's lounge, we'll go hear Grandpa's speech. Afterward, we'll go have lunch in our favorite restaurant in the *Ville* for your birthday. Mama and Daddy are coming, too. Then, Grandpa and I will drive you almost home."

She winked, and that's because the rest of the plan was for me to get home right about the regular time from school and no one would suspicion me cutting school for a day. I'd never done such a thing before, but I wanted to go with Mercy this one time since she invited me.

Driving through town, I asked Mercy, "What's your grandpa talking about at this ceremony?"

"Equality."

"What's that?"

"It means every person should have the same rules and rights no matter what they look like, or where they're from, or where they're going to. Is that about right, Grandpa?"

"Honey, you got it just right," he said.

"That seems right to me, too," I said.

So, off to the ceremony we went to hear Mercy's Grandpa Grafton speak about something important, but first, I opened that big present in the bathroom and almost died. Inside it was three of the nicest dresses I ever imagined. One was red and white with see-through red stuff on top of the skirt part. Mercy said the see-through stuff was organdy.

The other one was checked on the top with white and

green and a velvet-feeling green skirt on the bottom. A dark green bow tied under the collar, and the tails of it went all the way to the hem. The third one was a banana-yellow eyelet dress with a yellow underlining. Also, in my box, was three pairs of white anklet socks and the most beautiful two pairs of patent-leather shoes with straps—one black pair and one white pair—in the whole world. It almost made me cry getting those pretty things.

"Why did your family give me all this, Mercy?"

"Because you're my best friend. They like you a lot, Annie, and that's just how they are."

"But—"

"Which dress do you want to wear right now?"

"I think the green one. What shoes should I wear?"

"It's not Easter yet, so wear the black ones. After Easter, you can wear white until Labor Day."

Mercy was the smartest girl I ever knowed.

What went wrong with our plan was so many people had to talk to her grandpa after he got done talking that we got late getting to the restaurant for my birthday dinner and getting me back to that corner near the school. None of Mercy's family knew I didn't have my momma's permission to spend the day away from school, and we didn't tell them. But, we couldn't hurry them up, neither.

When Donnie seen I wasn't at the apartment later on, he asked the twins if they'd seen me or knew where I was. Those brats said no. I swear I'll get them back for this. I have so much on them, it's pitiful.

Anyways, Donnie thought I was lost or something bad happened to me, so he went right away to see Mrs. Patterson at the school. She showed him the note Momma was supposed to have sent the day before asking for me to be excused today for a family reason. Only, Donnie knew right away it wasn't Momma's writing. It was Mercy's, and it was pretty since she's knowed how to write like a grownup for more than two years. Mrs. Patterson told him Mercy was also absent and showed him the letter her mama really wrote for her.

Mrs. Patterson got all aflutter, and that happens right regular with her. She told him she knew something like this was bound to happen eventually. Her and Donnie marched down to the principal's office to tell him, and the principal called Momma at work and told her I was missing and asked her if I had any other friends besides my little *Negra* friend, Mercy. He blabbed about all the kids calling us Salt and Pepper at school, and how we got to be best friends the very first day of school even when our teacher didn't like it.

All that talk from our principal sounded stupid when Donnie told me about it, but Momma didn't see it my way at all. She knew all along my best friend was Mercy, but she never asked me if she was different from me or anything. We ain't different just 'cause I'm lighter and she's darker anyways. My brothers don't let that bother them 'cause they never said a word either way.

So here was Momma hearing from the school and getting her feathers all fluffed up like a sitting hen guarding her eggs. She came right home from work, something she ain't never done before. I had come up the outside steel steps of our apartment building, hung my new pretty dresses on hangers in my part of our itty-bitty closet, and changed into my play clothes when she came flying through the door with a mad face.

"I thought you were lost!" she screeched. It seemed like she was mad 'cause I wasn't lost, the way she acted. She went on hollering at me for lying and not going to school and giving them a note she didn't write. I deserved being in trouble for all that part, but when she said I couldn't be friends with Mercy no more, I started screaming like a two-year old. I threw myself on the floor and had a bigger hissy fit than Momma ever had in her whole life. The boys all gathered around gawking at me with open mouths since I never throwed any fits like that before.

"I'll run away and I'll never come see you again as long as I live!" I yelled at her. "I won't ever love you no more, neither! You won't be my Momma!"

She grabbed the strap and gave me a dance step or two with it. It hurt, but I didn't cry. I just stared at her like I didn't know her no more. She got the strangest look on her face, put the strap down, and walked outside lighting a cigarette as she went. I ran to the bedroom to cry by myself. What hurts most is I never knowed my own momma was like those nosy strangers who think me and Mercy shouldn't be friends. Finding that out is the worst thing that ever happened in my life.

It was afternoon, not night, when I got my whooping, but I went to bed and wouldn't get up for supper or nothing else even when the twins came to ask me to. I sneaked out of bed all quiet while I heard them eating supper and hid all my pretty dresses, the socks, and the shoes in a flat box and put them under my bed. I ain't sharing my special things with nobody in this household I now hate.

I'm laying here right now, and here's what I know—there ain't no one ever going to tell me who I can like or be friends with. I'm thinking hard about what Mercy's grandpa said to that bunch of people today—that God hisself created all people in the world in His image and that we're all the same inside no matter where we come from, if we have money or not, or what we look like on the outside.

Soon as I get to see my Aunt Vel again, I'm telling on my Momma to her. Aunt Vel is the one who taught me the song about Jesus loving all the children of the world, so she won't like the bad way her little sister is acting about this.

CHAPTER
Seventeen

Dear Lonely Heart

St. Louis, Missouri
1959

Zeenie flicks the white linen tablecloth in the air and arranges artful ruffles on the top tier of the hors d'oeuvres table. She positions fake green and purple grapes around the sparkling-clean glass of the imported wine bottles. She takes another white tablecloth from her cart and spreads it smoothly on the bottom tier of the table. She can't put the silver receiving dishes on until she knows what appetizer and canape fare is being prepared for today's luncheon.

She puts the crystal relish plate she assembled earlier in the center of the bottom tier. Inside are glistening preserved watermelon rind cubes, cheese-stuffed Spanish olives, pitted black olives, crisp cucumber pickle chips, tiny carrot sticks, and Southern style spicy-sweet chow-chow. She can't seem to stop the thoughts inside her head, thoughts bordering on bitterness.

Imagine my kids getting to snack on foods like this instead of a measly bag of potato chips once in a while. What are they eating today? Baloney and Miracle Whip on white bread with a little tomato if Donnie slices it up for them.

She shakes her head, sighs, and pushes the cart through the brushed silver swinging doors into the kitchen. "What hors d'oeuvres are you making today, Danny?"

One of the white-garbed chefs in the massive stainless-steel kitchen stops chopping and gazes at Zeenie. "Maybe you're on the menu, sweets," he says.

Zeenie laughs, and so does Danny, but he isn't really kidding. Zeenie Blackburn is a good-looking woman, but she makes herself too scarce for him to even ask to dinner on her night off. He almost did several times, but she always averted anything close to an advance. She buzzes around the floor doing her duties from the moment she arrives and puts her personal belongings in the women's section of the staff lounge—ten a.m. on the dot every morning—and she never stops until the lunch crowd clears completely out by two.

After clean up, around three in the afternoon, Zeenie's in the women's lounge with several of the other waitresses having her hour lunch and smokes break before the afternoon shift begins. He can't go in there, and he's tried to get one of the gals on his side, but it's no use. She informed him Zeenie had enough worries without him adding to it. They seem fiercely protective of her—kind of a female society, he thinks, and so he carries an unrequited torch for Zeenie. Since he is actively looking for a wife, he doesn't let that torch burn too hot.

"So, what are we serving today, Danny?" she asks again.

He expels a long, resigned sigh. "Mushroom-liver pate with crackers, herring in sour cream topped with chives, warm stuffed deviled eggs, creamed lobster with toasted baguette rounds, and a lemon gelatin mold with crushed pineapple, shredded carrots and chopped pistachios. Oh, yeah, Sidney here…" he nods toward a young man… "is making one of those pineapple cheese things. He's studying to be one of the fancy chefs at the Tropicana in Vegas, you know. That is, when he gets the lead out of his pants."

Sidney looks up in surprise, then grins. Zeenie feels her patience ebbing, but makes an effort to join in the small talk. "What's a *pineapple cheese thing?*" she asks, trying to work up a genuine smile and commanding herself to stop drumming her fingers on the stainless-steel counter.

"Aw, Zeenie, it's easy to make," Sid says. "You cut the stem off a pineapple, rinse it clean, and set it aside. Give the pineapple meat to the cooks to dice and use for whatever they want. Mix together different soft cheeses with German mustard and a few spices and shape it like a pineapple. Don't worry. It's not hard. You score it all around in both directions diagonally, then you slice pimento-stuffed olives and put a slice inside each diamond shape. Put the green pineapple stem back on the top, place it on a fancy plate with some imported crackers all around, and voila! A Cheese Pineapple fit to serve to the president of the United States!"

"My goodness," Zeenie says.

"Show off," Danny grins, hitting the young man lightly on the arm.

Their friendly camaraderie leaves Zeenie tired inside. Lately, all she does is mechanically perform her life duties. Her emotions in totality are either weeping or hardness of heart, no in between. Her boys are growing out of their clothes and shoes monthly, it seems. The twins are a mess, and now Annie skipping school? Think of that! She never imagined such a thing possible for her little girl. Of course, it only happened because of the influence of that new friend of hers. Still, it's a shock.

How is it she never asked anything about Annie's new best friend of the last several months? Why didn't she try to meet the family that invites her daughter regularly to their house or to events? What kind of a mother has she turned into?

Waves of guilt leave her feeling light-headed and defeated. At least she put a stop to the situation between the girls. Yet, Annie's hardline stance on the matter had been unnerving, to say the least. Their blowout was three days ago, and Annie still isn't looking at her. She merely answers her questions with a word or two and avoids her as if she—her own mother—has a contagious disease.

The worst part was what Annie said when Zeenie went to bed the night Annie had cut school. She knew her daughter was still awake by her restless flopping, so, from her twin bed a few feet away, she said, "Annie, I know you don't understand this now, but I'm doing this for your own good. One day, you'll see I'm right. You and Mercy are both good little girls, but it's society that doesn't understand how you could be best friends."

Annie had answered right away, almost as if she had been expecting her to say something.

"Nuh-uh. You're the problem, Mother, and so is ever body who acts like you. You only look at a person's skin color and not their insides."

Zeenie felt the sting of Annie's comments like a backhanded slap. She hadn't said another word. Couldn't. What do you say when your soul is exposed? And Annie, for the first time in her life, had called her *Mother* instead of

Momma.

It sounded so distant.

So cold.

Just like Zeenie's own heart.

The next morning, Zeenie steps into the public telephone booth outside the Athletic Club fifteen minutes before her shift begins.

"Dew, hi, I was sure hoping you were home. You're taking an early lunch break? What? You guys were up painting that city bridge at what time? Three o'clock! Sheesh, I'll bet you are. Yeah, the kids are fine. Mostly, anyway. Um, I-I've been thinking. What? Oh, smart-aleck! Yes, I do use my brain for more than a hat rack. You're terrible. Listen, um, okay… I'll do it. What? You know what. Why do you want me to say it? Oh, you're still such a brat. Okay, I'll take a look at those Lonely-Hearts ads. I d-don't think it'll lead to anything, but… anyway, can you pick me up during my lunch hour here? You can? Remember, I take it at three this afternoon. You might as well bring all those ads you've been saving. Yep. Out front. Bye now."

Her hand trembles as she hangs up the phone. That crazy idea of Dew's just jumped out of the shadows and into reality.

CHAPTER
Eighteen

Dem Gators

Lake Pontchartrain & Lake Maurepas Swamps
1905

Willy twists the perforated lid on his jar of water and tadpoles. He has a few more days to catch frogs and tadpoles before the village inhabitants close up the summer swamp shacks and fade back into their city jobs for the cold months. The villagers, except those who are too old, go back to work in private homes, sawmills, restaurants, and other businesses.

Mambo… Mam, makes a good living in New Orleans in a story-and-a-half cottage off South Rampart Street selling potions and *gris-gris*, leading seances, and advising abundant clientele of every societal strata and color how to entice a lover, remove a sickness curse, get rich, or make an enemy sick.

In Isabelle's opinion, everything those customers want magic to do, they should be asking for on their knees. Instead, they come in veiled secrecy to ask Mam to use her magic for them.

Isabelle, the oldest of Mam's five daughters, is assigned to guard Willy this afternoon from every unforeseen thing that might happen to him, especially alligators. She is, too, but not in such an overbearing way as Mam bosses her to do, so much so the poor boy can't do anything but sit and be still with his little mind and body yearning to do childish things like running and playing.

It's not his fault Isabelle's only other brother Tohn was eaten by the alligators. Tohn wandered off alone that fateful day, and Mam got it in her head the *Loa* gods owed her another boy. She stole Willy to replace Tohn, and Isabelle watched as Mam gave him the sleeping candy for six months so he'd stop grieving and remembering his *before life*. Sometimes, she thinks, but only for mere moments, it would be better for Willy if he were taken by the alligators rather than live the life destined for him with Mam and the others.

Isabelle used to secretly ask him the names of his family, and he'd tell her right off, especially about his mama Flo, his daddy Simon, and his biggest brother Zeke. Soon, he was forgetting their names. In a few more months, he had no memory of his other life at all, mostly because of the powders Mam gave him. Earlier, he told Isabelle his name was Willy St. Clair, and she wrote it down and all that he told her and kept it at the Franklins' home in the city.

Now the poor boy believes he is Judeson Lavolier, Lavolier being Mam's last name, at least, the best she can recall. Isabelle remembers how the light disappeared from the child's eyes as each day passed and never came back.

A secret outsider, Isabelle is nothing like her mother, her grandmother, or any of the females in this sect of mixed Creoles who follow the god Vodou and other unseen Haitian gods, the *Loa*. Most of the villagers are descendants of slaves stolen from Haiti many decades before. Isabelle knew no differences of her life from anyone else's until she was seven years old, the age the young girls from her village are sent each winter to work and learn from prosperous families in New Orleans. They start as helpers to the other household servants and later train to be maids, cooks, or seamstresses. The family that hired Isabelle was different from most.

Right away, the lady of the house, Mrs. Franklin, who has no children of her own, began teaching Isabelle to read and write using biblical primers and church hymn books. She took Isabelle on numerous missions with her and her doctor husband to help the less fortunate gain health and stability. Isabelle attended twice-weekly religious meetings with the couple. The process changed her, and she, in time, accepted the faith of the family she worked for.

Her personal principles make her summers away from the Franklins gut-wrenchingly grim. So far, she has avoided participating in the ceremonies by using a myriad of clever illness excuses… mainly, a made-up disease that causes her to "pass out cold" when she is too excited or worried, even having fake seizures as required for proof.

All that changed only a few days ago when the sect elders criticized Mambo for allowing Isabelle to reach age fifteen without consecration to Zombi, the snake-god Mam conjures in her rituals. Especially disgraceful was the fact that one of Isabelle's younger sisters was dedicated last year. Many younger girls of the faction already had one or two children. The public shame from the elders hardened Mam's heart. When Isabelle begged her to have one more year before consecration, Mam became angry and drove her from her shack with a belt.

Today, Isabelle watches Willy giggling as two frogs hop along a tiny rock-lined path he made for them. How can she view such innocence and know, at the same time, what lies ahead for her if she does not flee? Consecration is, in Isabelle's mind, debauchery of the vilest order. She cannot and will not be dedicated to Zombi. The ceremony is hellish. Shameful. The girls are publicly fornicated by Papa Rooster, a self-appointed liaison between the spirit of the dead Papa Legba— the accepted intermediary between the *Loa* and humanity— and the people. His spirit stands at a spiritual crossroads that either gives or denies permission to speak with *the spirits of Guinee,* the necessary root of belief for the spirit-possessed rituals.

After Papa Rooster completes the first act, the girls are further seduced by certain elders who cast lots in a spiritual trance and are chosen for the special night. Isabelle scoffs, a bitter resentment in her heart. The whole ritual benefits the men in the village as they couple with virgins. Who prospers from such an ordeal but the males? After the night of depravity, the girls are respected as full women, and anything of a sexual nature is permissible and encouraged. She long ago determined she preferred death over participation in defilement of her body, soul, or spirit.

Tonight, she and Willy are escaping, never to return. She believes it won't be hard to sneak away once everyone starts drinking the gin Old Charley brought back from the city a few days ago. There will be light drinking, a bit of powder smoking, and plenty of excited gossip about the upcoming important consecration ceremony of Mam's firstborn, Isabelle, tomorrow night.

"Willy, not too close to that water. Stay away from the logs, too."

Willy turns to look at her. "My name is Judeson."

"All right, Judeson, come back over here by me and this willow tree."

Willy does as she asks, and Isabelle shifts her position with her eyes on the boy. She sighs and thinks of the preparations that will begin tomorrow afternoon when an enormous cauldron of water is put on the fire. Into the simmering water, the villagers sporadically throw frogs, a few live chickens—not so many as to damage their daily egg supply—rodents, bugs, and unimportant snakes. At dusk, the people start sipping *tafia,* a raw rum made from sugarcane juice. Later, the liquid from the cauldron is passed around in cups for the villages to drink along with more alcoholic drinks.

At a time determined by Papa Rooster, a black-cat blood sacrifice occurs in which the ill-fated creature is skinned alive, its blood drained into a cup. The cup will be passed to Mambo, Papa Rooster, and finally, to Isabelle. She is to remain in the special waiting shack dressed in a simple, see-through frock until time for the blood ceremony, at which time, she is brought forward by two village women dressed in long white robes with red sashes circling their waists.

Isabelle is then turned over to Papa Rooster. When she is given over to the elders, a living rooster is picked clean and nailed to a tree wearing a waistcoat, top hat, and a miniature man's tie looped around his neck. The crueler and more gruesome these acts, the more ferocious and powerful are the spirits who visit the people. Manifestations of spirit possession, wild hours of soul dancing, heavy drinking, and sinful copulation continue all through the night.

Isabelle watches the innocent boy laughing and playing a few feet away. Why was she born into this horrible life? Tears slide down her cheeks. She kneels, closes her eyes.

I beg you to strike me dead, and Willy, too, if we are caught leaving tonight. Please do not let these pagans damn our eternal souls to Hell—

"Whut ya doin, Isabelle? Ma boy be close ta da water! I tole ya no!" Mam's angry, broken Creole violently startles Isabelle from her secret prayers. She leaps up from the grassy bank.

"He's all right, Mam. I've been watching him. See, he just caught frogs and a jar of tadpoles. I was about to bring him home."

"No, dat no kay. Dem gators is jes woding for hem. Deh no kay with muh otra boy. No, dey vahn hem too. Judeson, cohm to Mam. We goin da home and et now." She finishes her tirade with a deadly glare at her daughter.

Isabelle shudders as she watches her statuesque mother grab Willy's hand and drag him along beside her. Mam doesn't give him time to retrieve his jar of tadpoles, but he clutches his little box of frogs under his free arm. One jumps out, and Willy turns to look at it over his shoulder. His small, bare feet barely keep up with Mam as she half-drags him away from the gators of the swamp and back to the village of the damned.

CHAPTER
Nineteen

Ruby

Denton, Texas
1905

*E*rnest can't put his finger on it, but something is different about the baby girl he and Arlene now love as their own. She's smart, no doubt about that. She keeps Arlene busy sewing her rag dolls and cloth animals with sewn-on eyes and smiles. Ruby adores the creations at first, giggling and toddling about the house in delight. Much too soon, she grows weary of them, casting them aside, never to pick them up again and becoming angry when they show them to her. She would be happy with a new diversion every single day, perhaps several times a day, Ernest thinks.

She has enchanted them from the moment Jack placed her in Arlene's arms that fateful day in Fort Worth. She is two now, and they have never seen a rosier-cheeked or brighter-eyed baby. Her smile lights up their world, and most certainly, heals their crushed hearts. Her silky dark curls circle her head like a halo, then spill luxuriously onto her neck. Her long eyelash fringe makes her blue eyes a wonder to behold. Like the sky. No, the sky can't compare to those eyes, Ernest believes. No one can see them without gasping.

She was six months old when they got her, and she began walking four months later. She started saying words, lots of them, soon after her first birthday, and rushed into full sentences—most profound sentences, really, many of which make the couple laugh with joy and surprise.

Of course, he and the wife are happier than they ever thought possible after the double tragedy of losing their precious children to illness, but, in the midnight hour, when Arlene and Ruby are tucked snugly into their beds, Ernest watches the dying embers in the fireplace and ponders his strange uneasiness.

He doesn't know what to call what's eating at him, but he might try to explain it thusly—Ruby has an over-abundance of *grit in her craw*. Sure, everyone needs courage and strength to survive, but Ruby's supply seems anchored in a willfulness that gives him an ache deep inside, a shade of worry that sits always on his brow.

CHAPTER
Twenty

Donnie Won't Tell

St. Louis, Missouri
1959

I suppose a frown has about frozen on my face ever since Momma told me I couldn't be friends with Mercy no more. I know I ain't going to quit being her friend so I've been thinking about how sneaky I can be from now on. I ain't talking to no one in my family about nothing except to answer Momma when she talks to me directly. She's gone all the time mostly, so that ain't a lot of talking we're doing. I used to tell her all my stories about school and ever thing when I saw her, but now I don't.

Back in school on Monday, I can't tell Mercy what happened at my house since I'm so ashamed of it. What if she don't want to be my friend no more with me having a Momma like that? I'm feeling so bad, I'm not a bit hungry at our dinner time at school.

"Why aren't you eating your lunch, Annie?" Mercy asks.

"I'm not hungry."

"You not hungry? Here, have half of my cold roast beef and potato sandwich Miss Etta made. You know you love them."

"No thank you."

Mercy stares in my eyes. "Something's wrong, isn't it?"

"No."

"Yes, it is. What happened?"

"Nothing." I look away because I'm about to start blubbering right in the school cafeteria.

"You have to tell me. We're best friends, aren't we?"

I nod and fix my eyes on a girl's brown anklets at another table so I don't bust out crying.

"Annie, Grandpa Grafton says truth and justice are the most important things we can own. Are you telling me the truth right now?"

That did it. Now, I have to get out of here. I throw my boloney sandwich and bag of tater chips and unopened chocolate milk in the paper sack and run out of the cafeteria. I rush to the bathroom and lock myself in one of the stalls. I throw my sack of food on the floor and lean on the door, covering my mouth with my arm. I don't even know if I can keep crying with no noise or if I'm going to start screaming out loud any minute. I drop my face into my hands making crazy snuffing and gurgling noises that means I need to cry out loud. I feel the gritty tightness in my chest that means I'll probably get an asthma attack.

When I take my hands off my eyes, there's Mercy staring up at me from under the door. I jump out of my skin and let out a loud holler.

"Now, will you tell me what's wrong?" she says.

Mercy on the floor—a bathroom floor—in one of her pretty dresses? I start blubbering louder than anything and can't stop. Mercy wiggles under the door and unwinds some toilet paper for me to blow my nose. She stands there without talking until I get okay to take it from her. She opens the stall door and tells me to come wash my face in the basin. Susan from our classroom comes into the bathroom.

"What's the matter with Annie?" she asks.

"She got stung by something on the playground," Mercy says quick as anything.

"Want me to get Mrs. Patterson?"

"Nuh-uh, don't bother her. She's having lunch in the teacher's lounge. Annie's fine now, aren't you, Annie?" I cover my face with my hands and nod big.

Soon as Susan leaves, Mercy says, "Let's go sit by the old fence on the side of the playground. No one will bother us there."

What happens next is the most surprising thing. I tell Mercy what happened Friday night after she and her grandpa leave me at the corner, how I go home and change my clothes, but Donnie thinks I'm lost and Momma comes home mad as a hornet and all that. When I tell her the part about how she said we can't be friends no more, she laughs.

"Oh, for heaven sakes, is that all?"

"What do you mean is that all? It's the end of everything!" I start crying again.

"Annie, no one can stop us being best friends. It's how we like to be, and that's that. I'll just have my mama call yours, and they'll work it out."

"No! Please don't do it, Mercy!"

Mercy looks puzzled. "But Mama can fix it, Annie."

"She can't fix it! My momma ain't going to be all right with us being friends no more, and your mother is so good to me. I c-can't take it if Momma says something bad or, or…"

Mercy sits back against the fence to think. "Okay, I get it. Grandpa says some people have too many years of bad thinking to get to the right thinking. Maybe your mom is like that."

That pains me like a face slap. Makes me embarrassed, too, since my family is so stupid. I drop my head feeling ashamed. A long, ugly wheeze comes from my chest and out my mouth. I cover my mouth with a hand and look at Mercy. She smiles sweetly at me.

"It's okay." She looks at her hands. "Do you want to stop being friends, Annie?"

I jump up from the ground so fast Mercy looks startled. "No, and I'm not going to stop, Mercy. I don't care. I'll sneak around and lie!"

"It's not right to lie."

"I know it ain't, but my momma leaves me no chance not to."

Mercy steeples her fingers and looks like she's thinking real hard. Presently, she says, "You know what? I bet you don't have to lie a whole bunch. Maybe just a little."

I sit back down beside her. "What do you mean?"

"Your brother Donnie."

"What about him?"

Mercy chuckles. "Well, I've been keeping a little secret, too. Jerome asked me to."

"What do you mean?"

"See, Donnie and my brother Jerome are almost best friends, too. Have been since they played gym together when school first started. They both got picked to be on the eighth-grade basketball team. We've been to all their games, and they're really good at basketball. About equal. They meet all the time and shoot hoops at my uncle's training gymnasium.

"They sneak in the movie show when it's all dark so they can watch war movies together, too. The Booker T. Washington Theater is easy for them to get in. You know where that is, but I have a cousin who helps work the projectors at the Park Theater on Minnetonka Boulevard. He sneaks them in the service door and lets them watch movies from private seating near the balcony. He even buys them popcorn and candy. I don't get it, but they're crazy about those boring war movies."

My mouth drops open. Donnie Blackburn, my brother, and Jerome Washington, Mercy's brother, are almost best friends? Is that where Donnie goes all the time, to play basketball and see movie shows with Jerome?

Mercy smiles. "Donnie won't tell if we stay best friends, Annie. No, he won't tell."

The bell rings for us to go back to our classroom. We don't talk along the way, but my head is jumping around with thinking. Learning about Donnie has near shocked me to death, but the way I see it, finding out about it has kind of saved my life. After all, me and Mercy can still be best friends, and who's better at helping me sneak around than a brother who sneaks around hisself?

CHAPTER
Twenty One

The Trade

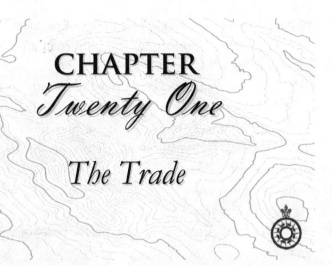

Lake Pontchartrain & Lake Maurepas Swamps
1905

The day is settling into a quiet hum of insects and faded memories of sunshine on the cypress and black mangroves thickly surrounding the village. Isabelle smiles pleasantly at her four sisters sitting with her for supper at one of the long outside tables. The table is hewn from rough wood with sanded-smooth benches along the sides. It isn't unusual for other villagers to sit among them or to sit as a group on the other end. Everything in the village belongs to everyone and to no one.

Because of the nature of their lives, neither Isabelle nor any of her sisters know who are their fathers. Many outsiders came from all around to join in the ceremonies—some White men, others Spanish or French, *mulatto*, or any combination of colors and races, both men and women. Such is life for this sect of Vodou followers, and the girls will never have a true father unless Mam decides to marry. So far, she hasn't bothered to wed any of her multitudes of partners.

Talek says, "Tomorrow, you be w'man after Zombi-Loa bless you, Isabelle."

"Oh, yes, sister, my day of freedom is truly upon me."

"What ya mean?"

Isabelle smiles, bows her head, and picks at her food. Talek, with no schooling at all, often struggles to understand her older sister's words. She stares at Isabelle with a look of defiance on her face. "You older tan me, but I a w'man before ya. I a w'man a year 'go."

"Yes, that is true, at a mere twelve years of age, my poor girl."

Talek frowns. "Why tell me poor girl? I full w'man. You girl. Whaaa! You cry like *bébé.*"

The sisters laugh. Isabelle good-naturedly mimics a crying baby, bringing more laughter from the girls.

God, help my sisters escape this madness.

She glances at her watch. Dusk is coming, and the adults and "fully mature" boys and girls, such as her sister Talek, will gather to drink gin, smoke, and lay bets about the ceremony tomorrow. The bets are about whether Isabelle will fight and scream when Papa Rooster molests her, or if she does what the villagers expect a virgin to do... submit without resistance and cry in silence.

Young children will be put to bed early tonight and tomorrow night. Isabelle prays she is given the job of watching over Willy tonight. When a child is allowed to view a ceremony, as Willy did on his first night in the village, it is only while being restrained on a lap or in an adult's arms. After that night, Mamba has let it be known she will kill anybody who harms her boy, and someone is assigned to watch over him at all times.

When much liquor is consumed, strong weeds or powders are smoked, or serious spirit ceremonies take place in the village, the young children are guarded by assigned women and selected older girls. They have been known to club a man half to death for trying to approach the children in profane ways if a bad spirit takes him over. It's a grave job—one the women take seriously.

Mam, who always eats supper in her shack with Willy, approaches the table where Isabelle and her sisters are seated with Willy in tow. She's dressed in a bright red sheath cut up one side of her long legs and belted at the waist with a wide, yellow belt. Isabelle is continually struck by the beauty and countenance of her priestess mother, but she has no regrets in leaving her forever. In her eyes, her mother is the devil's handmaiden, a sorceress bound for Hell's flames.

"Asefi, ya cohm to watch muh boy dis night. Isabelle, ya res dis night. Yer speshal day cohm tamar."

Isabelle's heart sinks, but she has another plan in her mind—something she and Mrs. Franklin thought up long ago. When the children and not-yet-mature girls leave the table to go to their shacks, Isabelle catches up with Asefi. "I have something I want to give you. I've been saving it," she tells her.

"Whut it is?"

"Something beautiful, Asefi. More beautiful than anything you've ever seen before."

Asefi clasps Isabelle's hands. Her eyes shine. "O cohm and give it ta muh, won't ya?"

"Yes! But I want to trade something for it."

"Whut?"

"Listen closely now, Asefi. I am to be consecrated to Zombi tomorrow night."

"Yah, dat truf, Isabelle." Asefi grins big. Haitian Village girls greatly anticipate the night they are inducted into the circle of adults and elders and blessed by the Loa gods.

"Asefi, I'm afraid tonight."

"Why for dat? Ya goin to be a w'man, Isabelle."

"Oh, yes, I am. A great honor, but, I'm still afraid. Our little brother makes me laugh. Trade places with me tonight, Asefi. Let me watch Judeson, and you stay in the house with blind Mama. She won't know it's not me. For this, I'll give you the prettiest jewel you ever saw."

A look of horror replaces the grin on Asefi's face. "O no, I can no do dat, Isabelle. Mam, she won like dis ting ya say."

She continues walking the path to Mam's. Isabelle follows, takes hold of her arm.

"Don't you want to see my treasure? Oh, it's prettier than the stars, Asefi. Once the gathering starts, I'll sneak over and show it to you. If you want to keep it, you can trade places with me and go stay in blind Mama's house while I stay with Judeson. Before the moon slides down on the other side of the sky, we'll switch again. Mam won't ever know."

Isabelle takes a step backward.

"Or... I can give it to Joenal tomorrow for fixing my hair for the ceremony. That's a good trade, too."

Asefi's eyes widen. She bites her bottom lip, pondering. At last, she nods her head and scurries off to Mam's. Isabelle watches her depart as darkness taps its baton to begin the night refrain, replacing the light of day with gusty fervor.

CHAPTER
Twenty Two

Café Coffee

St. Louis, Missouri
1959

The waitress tops off their coffee cups for the third time in the past ten minutes. "You sure you don't want some cherry pie? Fresh baked this morning." She smiles warmly at Dew.

"Guess you twisted my arm one too many times, beautiful. I'll give it a whirl."

"Heated or cold?"

"I like my women warm and my pie cold," he says. She giggles and practically skips off toward the counter.

"Oh, stop it, Dew. The poor girl is about to wee-wee herself," Zeenie says.

"Just spreading my charms to the ends of the earth, sis."

Zeenie rolls her eyes. "Yeah, I see that."

"Okay, back to business. I guess it's just a matter of if you want to go east, west, or head back to Texas," he says. "Who would have thought there'd be so many lonely hearts out there? The one in Texas sure sounds interesting." He laughs. Zeenie doesn't.

"I have bad memories from Texas. Besides, I don't know if... if, well, never mind. I just don't want to go back there."

Dew tips the cream pitcher and pours a generous splash into his coffee, stirs it, watches the liquid turn from black to tan to almost white. "I thought you said you were over that."

"Over what?"

Dew snorts. "This is me, sis. You can't tell me you aren't still carrying the torch for D.J. I see it in you every day. Look, he probably doesn't even live in Texas anymore. He's kind of like the wind. No telling where he's at—maybe punching cows in Montana, Colorado, or some such thing."

"Unless he drank his fool self to death."

"How old is he now?"

"Thirty-nine."

"Aw, he's still pretty young. Betcha he ain't anywhere near dead yet. Too old for bull riding anymore, but D.J.'s tough. Who knows? Maybe he beat the bottle."

The waitress places a saucer of pie in front of Dew. "I forgot to ask... you want a scoop of ice cream for your pie?"

Dew winks. "Nah, this is great right here. Thank you, now."

He keeps grinning as she walks away, then turns his attention back to his sister. "Hey, enough with the long face. Aren't we on the hunt for a good guy to rescue you from this hard life? You're from durable stock, Zeenie. Ain't one of us kids in our family been down or out for long. We're nine strong puppies. Just look at me and you. What kind of teenage knotheads take off for Texas to seek their fortunes by working at the Fort Worth Stockyards? Just pull up stakes and head out in a broken-down car not knowing a living soul out there?

Huh? Who does that?"

"Some pretty dumb ones, I'd say. That was terrible stupid what we did. You thought you'd be a cowboy or a rodeo star when all you ever rode before was Dad's mules and that slow-witted horse, old Dunder-Head."

She tips her head back and laughs, stops abruptly, looks serious. "I guess I thought... oh, I don't know. All I knew was there had to be better opportunities in Texas than what we had out in the sticks. The concession stands at the stock shows and rodeos seemed a good enough place to start changing our circumstances. Remember how Mary Lou told us they were easy jobs to get?"

"Not to mention fun."

"Yeah. Fort Worth, Texas. A dream place in my mind back then. Didn't work out, though, did it?"

"Well, it was 1942. How did we know all the rodeo shows were canceled that year so they could use the stockyard buildings for assembly plants for the War? Two little country-hick kids from Missouri wouldn't have known about that."

"We should have checked. Asked people. Done something."

"Like what? Momma died, and Daddy wasn't doing so good. Who could we ask... our older brothers and Vel? They all thought we should shut up, get working, get married and start spitting out kids. Well, you did that part, but five of our brothers wound up going to war. I tried to go, and James about had my scalp. He told me I had flat feet so they wouldn't want me anyways. Said I had to stay and look after Dad and you two sisters. Been doing it ever since."

The waitress brings the coffee pot, and Dew waves her off. She looks disappointed, moves on to the next table.

Zeenie blows out a weary sigh. "I suppose you're right.

You learned about horses and ranching at D.J.'s daddy's place those six years we were there. I loved everything about living on that little ranch, Dew. You know, I thought D.J. and me were the perfect couple. How did I lose him to that crazy rodeo life? He just didn't love us enough." Her voice trembles on the last few words. She looks down.

Dew feels a familiar ache in his heart. Nearly nine years passed and his sister still loves the damn guy.

"He loved you and the kids something fierce. He just had a... I don't know, some kind of personal vendetta that wouldn't let him settle down for long. It pulled at him—a restlessness. Tossing a rope at a steer or getting his brains knocked out by a mad bull seemed to calm him down. Try to remember the good times, sis. Didn't we have a bunch of 'em, though?"

"I guess so, but look what came of it. Driving an old Pontiac back to Missouri with my tail tucked between my legs and four little mouths to feed."

"Yeah, look what came of it. You fell in love with a handsome rodeo cowboy, married him, had six years on a ranch in beautiful Texas country, and got four great kids out of the deal."

"You make it sound almost, well... romantic."

"Good Lord, girl, it is! It's a Zane Grey novel starring D.J. and Zeenie Blackburn."

Zeenie cracks a smile, lowers her head, raises it. "You're a mess, Dew."

"Ain't it the truth!"

"Did you know you say *ain't* about half the time? Annie says it all the time, and so do the twins. You're a bad influence."

"That's my kiddos... doing everything like their

handsome uncle. Okay, now... fess up. Why's your bottom lip dragging the floor today? Lose your best friend?"

Zeenie shakes her head, checks her watch. "Oh, nothing. Listen, I don't have a lot of time. Show me the ads you think are best." She lights a cigarette and leans forward.

Dew opens a folder filled with neatly cut newspaper ads. "Well, let's see..." he says, taking a forkful of pie and savoring it before he answers, "... here's an interesting one in California. A widower with two teenagers. Must be pretty loaded. Says he likes taking romantic trips in his schooner."

"What's a schooner?"

"A big fancy sailboat, I'm thinking."

"Right, and he's wants to get involved with a tired-out, broke waitress with kids all living in a run-down apartment building."

"You never know. Keep an open mind now. Here's one in Arizona. A rancher in a remote mountain area. He needs a housekeeper and cook, and if romance blooms, he's says he's sure okay with that, too."

"Are you pulling my leg?"

"No. Look." Dew pushes the ad in front of his sister and focuses on his pie. "I found one here in St. Louis, too. Owns a thriving coffee shop and says he's lonely since his wife passed on a few years ago. One kid, grown, so he's probably older than you."

"He owns a coffee shop here in the city? He must meet more women than you can shake a stick at. Why advertise in the *Lonely-Hearts* ads?"

"A mystery. Guess you'll have to write and ask him. I mean, here you are looking in the ads, and you rub elbows with men all day long. Guess it's kind of unexplainable."

"No, it isn't. I've been too busy and tired to think of

starting something up. If I'm just writing to them, there's no hold on me if I don't like them. I don't want anyone trying to fence me in."

"Hmm, sounds pretty Roy Rogers to me, you know the song... *Don't fence me in?*"

"Oh, brother." Zeenie shakes her head, hides her smile behind her hand.

"Hey, speaking of Texas, I really like this one in West Texas, kind of in the Panhandle. He owns a large cattle ranch. Yes sir, that might be the winner, hon."

"Trying to get a second chance at *cowboy-ing*, little brother?"

"Why not?" It's never too late. Shoot, I'm a mere kid."

"You're one year younger than me, pardner, and I feel about a hundred years old right now."

"Which is why we're getting you out of this rat race."

"I don't know. It just seems odd meeting people through newspaper ads."

"It is, but ain't life full of oddities, Zeenie? What does it hurt to stick your toe in the water? Doesn't mean you have to dive in. Here, take this folder with you and look over all the ads. There's more where those came from. You find some you like, and we'll sit down and write them a few lines. Like I said, what's the harm?"

Zeenie takes a deep breath, exhales. "I guess you're right. Lord knows I got to do something about my kids. They're growing up like little savages with no adults around. No training. Rarely any home cooking, and I'm pretty sure they're pushing the boundaries in one way or several. Just a feeling, but I'm too tired to chase it down."

"Do I need to come over there and give them my serious talk?"

"Not yet, but stand by."

CHAPTER
Twenty Three

Aunt Viola

St. Louis, Missouri
1959

onnie wasn't mad when I told him I know about him and Jerome being good friends. He surprised me and said he was sorry he caused me so much trouble with Momma about cutting school. "If you'd just come and told me about it, none of this would have happened," he said.

I didn't know my big brother would take up for me like that. Seems like us kids don't know each other very good. I don't even know the last time we went any place together. Feels like a long time ago.

"Just so's you know, I ain't giving up my best friend Mercy, neither. Are you going to tell on me?"

"No. Just don't let Joey and Jackie know anything. Those little brats can't be trusted with a drink of water. They'd sell us all out for the price of a new model kit or a few baseball cards. Ornery little snots. I'm about to call Uncle Dew to give them a thrashing if they don't settle down."

So, there it is, and today, me and Mercy are going to eat at Chinaman Bill's after we go see Aunt Viola. Mercy says Aunt Viola called her at her house and asked her to please come by, so she is. Mercy's family don't know me and her go where Aunt Viola sings, and we mean to keep it that way. At least I don't have to worry about Momma seeing me from the Walgreen's or The Royal Restaurant no more since she works at that athletic club.

We ride the streetcar part of the way. It's crowded which means we can stand by one another holding the aisle poles and talk behind people's coats and dresses and big purses hanging in the crooks of ladies' arms. We know how to do it quietly so's no one hears us. After that, we take the bus and get off close to the Peacock Alley Jazz Club on Lawton Boulevard.

We knock on the door in the alley, and the same man with bushy eyebrows and the grouchy voice opens the door. This time, I get it right and tell him Momma is Miss Viola's marketing manager, and we have important marketing information for her from Momma. Mercy gives me the biggest smile when I do it right.

We step inside, and Aunt Viola tells the man in a soft voice he can leave just like always. As soon as the door is closed behind him, she tiptoes over and presses her ear to it for a few seconds. She puts her finger to her lips and says, "Shh. We have to talk low this time, girls. Mercy, Annie... I need your help. Can I count on you?"

You just know we nod big and proud that she wants our help.

"I-I can't... well, how do I say this? I love someone very much, but someone else thinks he owns me and is practically keeping me a prisoner here. He's having me watched day and night by goons like the one you always see when you arrive. This man, the one who tries to keep me for himself, he's, uh, he's a bad man, a kind of a crook, who thinks he can make anyone do anything he wants. Do you understand?"

Mercy says, "Mafia, right?"

"Yes!" she whispers, and her face looks like she just scratched an itch. "Oh, my smart little niece. How I shall miss you!"

"What do you mean? Are you leaving?"

"I'll explain in a minute, honey."

She steps to the wall with the long gold pole holding all her gowns. She scoots the hangers to the left until she comes to a dress so glittery gold it hurts my eyes. She reaches behind it and pulls to the front a bag with long strings that was hanging on the backside of it. It's the same glittery gold as the dress. She loosens the puckers on the top and reaches inside. She pulls out a small, powdery-pink envelope.

"I need you to take this to Bill for me. Right away. Tell him we have to change our plans. The rest is explained in the letter. See, Vincent—he's the manager of the club—thinks he's taking me to Las Vegas this weekend to marry him. We're supposed to leave tomorrow night in a private plane after my last performance. Oh, my sweet Jesus, I can't marry that man."

Aunt Viola crumples onto her little couch with the red top and buttons all over it that matches the stool she usually sits on. She covers her face and starts crying, soft like, but sad. Mercy goes to sit by her.

"We'll help you. Don't cry."

"Bring me a handkerchief from my dresser, honey. The top drawer. Left side."

After she dabs her eyes and blows her nose, she looks up at us. "Girls, I want you to remember something. Don't ever let anyone put you in bondage. People can put chains on you that no one else knows are there, and you mustn't let them. You understand?"

We nod, but I know I don't understand. I shore hope Mercy does so she can explain it to me later on.

"I wanted this gig, wanted to sing, more than anything in the world. I believed working in a famous nightclub like this, wearing beautiful clothes, being admired... well, I thought it was the key to happiness. Let me tell you something—it isn't.

"Sweet girls, when you're women, you'll understand what I'm trying to tell you. Sometimes you have to sell your soul to get anywhere in this man's world. And now... I feel like a pet, not a person. My freedom drains away more each day."

She shakes her head back and forth. "I-I love Bill so very much. He cherishes me. Treats me with love and respect. Did you know he's come every night to see me sing for two years? He says he has many connections for me to continue my singing career when we get to California. That is, if I still want to. He might even buy another restaurant out there."

"California?" Mercy asks.

"Do you want to keep singing?" I say.

"Maybe," Aunt Viola says.

"What about his restaurant here, Aunt Viola?" I ask.

"He sold it, sweetie. The very day I agreed to become his wife, he put it up for sale. Didn't take but two weeks for the perfect buyer to want it, it being so successful and in such a good location on Grand and Olive. We planned to elope to San Francisco in about a month, to quietly break the news to family... but now... it seems like Vincent has some sort of sixth sense. He told me we were 'getting hitched' this weekend and not to give him any lip about it. He never asked me. Just like everything and everyone else, he *told* me how it was going to be. I have no say in anything about my own life around Vincent."

I never heard so much growed-up talk in my life. All's I figure is we're going to help this beautiful lady, who happens to be Mercy's aunt, escape from a bad man so she can marry a good man and run away to California. Now I wonder if Mercy and me will ever get to eat Chinese food again.

It's like Aunt Viola is reading my mind 'cause she smiles at me with her swollen face and says, "The new owners know all about you two little darlings, and Bill made them promise they'd leave the special table in the kitchen for you. You can go any time and eat to your heart's content, and all they have to do is send him the bill every month. That's the dear man I'm marrying, girls, and now I think you'd better get a move on. I have an afternoon show to get ready for, and I don't want to arouse any suspicions."

Mercy throws her arms around her aunt. I'm standing here sniffing and trying not to cry out loud. Aunt Viola motions for me to come over by them. She wraps her good-smelling arms around us and hugs us both at the same time. She kisses the tops of our heads.

"My little angels of mercy, both of you. Don't ever let the world rip you apart, you hear? It's your destiny to be best friends forever. I feel it in my soul."

The look in her eyes digs right into my heart and stays there. I know I'll see Aunt Viola again someday, somehow, and me and Mercy shore are going to miss her and Chinaman Bill.

CHAPTER
Twenty Four

Suicide Bridge

Lake Pontchartrain & Lake Maurepas Swamps
1905

The cricket chirps echoing off the watery reed grasses sound like bells tinkling in a distant hollow box. An owl hoots above the two lone figures making their way in and out of the shadowy trees along the water's edge. Willy cries out. Isabelle crouches down beside him. "It's only an owl. It won't hurt us."

"I want Mam."

"I know. I know. Just a little longer till we find the frogs."

"Don't wanna find dem no more. Want Mam." He starts crying.

"Mam is gone tonight, but she'll be back in the morning. You know what? She said you can keep all the frogs we find and take them to the town cottage. Did you know it's time to leave the lake in a few days?"

Willy shakes his head. He rubs his eyes with his fists, sobbing quietly. He always cries like that, and it cuts her deeply to see the boy of seven so accepting of his cruel fate, whatever it happens to be at the time.

"Come brave boy. We don't want to miss finding all the best frogs, do we?"

Willy shakes his head, wipes his nose on his arm, takes Isabelle's hand.

Isabelle has imagined the escape path from the village to the road many times in her mind, but the darkness of this cloudy night distorts her perspective. Her heart beats erratically as she pushes on. The steady drone of the cicadas gives her a smattering of comfort on a night when she is committing a village sin for which, if caught, she will be punished severely, perhaps even poisoned.

A sudden loud buzzing at their feet stops Willy cold.

"Don't be afraid. That's the cicadas saying, "Please don't step on us.""

Willy giggles, only a half giggle, but it's something.

Above them, clouds whisper-glide past the pale moon. A grating *whau-whau-whau* makes Willy grab Isabelle's leg.

"That's a daddy frog calling out to his kids. We'll find some fat ones like that when we get to our frog place, Willy."

"Judeson," Willy says quietly.

"Okay, Judeson. It's just that I like that Willy name so much."

"Muh name be Judeson," he mumbles as they walk on.

Isabelle stops constantly to listen for more than night sounds. At times, she is certain she hears footsteps running quickly behind them. She ducks down or presses the two of them behind a tree to wait. Her imagination runs wild, creating images of the villagers jumping out from every dark clump of reeds or dropping from outstretched tree limbs to take them back to their hell on earth. Along with worry, her conscience pricks her sorely for lying to the boy to entice him from the village. What else could she do? She's the only one who would ever rescue him.

Thank God for the beautiful crystal brooch Mrs. Franklin gave her to use as a bribe when the time came. Asefi gasped when she saw it unwrapped from the dark blue velvet square. No, Asefi won't be telling on her for a while, but if Mam comes early to check on her boy, all is lost. The thought of Mam's wrath if she discovers they are running away makes her stomach hurt.

After what seems an eternity of making their way through the darkness, never knowing if a snake is coiled up like a rope or straight as a stick in their path, or if a hungry alligator is lying silently for them on the banks of the marshes or has ventured further out among the trees, they at last come to the large, dreaded clearing. Isabelle, quivering with the effort of keeping them safe while hurrying at the same time, stares at the far end of the tree-lined meadow.

There it is.

The bridge—the terrible bridge.

The moon has broken free of the clouds and shines a silver madness on the old, rickety structure that crosses over the last finger of swampy waters and feeds onto a well-traveled road. Isabelle has crossed the bridge many times. Never at night. Never alone. No one uses it at night. In the daylight, villagers cross it in groups of three or more.

Suicidal jumps, petrifying apparition appearances, normal minds dissolving into lunacy—such are the tales of Suicide Bridge. It is said that dogs have suddenly jumped off the bridge into the water, never to resurface. The infamy of this place lives in the gossip of the residents of New Orleans and spreads throughout the land in all directions. It is indeed known in all of Louisiana as a chilling place, a place one must avoid whenever possible, and one which a person should never venture near in the dark.

What faces her now is, by far, her greatest trial. Her eyes are hypnotically pulled toward the arch humped over the brackish waters dotted with cypress knees. Spanish moss draping over the tupelo trees like burial clothes beckons with evil resolve. She cannot see the foamy, green algae on the water at night, but she knows it's always there, suffocating the surface of the water below the bridge. Every natural or manmade detail standing before her has horrifying tales attached to it—stories she has heard for as long as she can remember.

Isabelle prayed fervently for months that the village would break camp again with her consecration put off for another year. It would have been easy to steal Willy away in the city. Alas, circumstances were not in her favor. Now, before her is the object and place she has most feared, where evil lives in every old graying board and rusty nail holding it together. Spirits must abound in the waters and even in the air surrounding it, she thinks. Where else might they go when not being conjured up by the disciples of the Vodou gods?

Isabelle forces herself to think of the friendly, clumsily painted wood sign with arrows just on the other side of the bridge. One red arrow points down south to New Orleans. The other arrow points up toward Baton Rouge.

Almost free, almost free, her beleaguered mind tells her as she stands at the edge of the clearing trembling.

"Whah ron wid ya, Izbelle?"

She looks at the boy she has come to love, noting his big, trusting eyes, the whites gleaming like cotton in the moonlight. She squats down and puts her arms around him, crushing him in a motherly hug.

Over his little shoulder, she bites her lip. Can Hell itself be more frightening than this task before her? And yet, and yet... the bridge signifies her freedom, a link to a new life for her and possibly the old life restored for the boy. It is a conduit to all that Isabelle hopes for the rest of her life—a life of freedom to openly practice her faith, to marry, to become someone different than the daughter of a Vodou priestess.

She releases the boy, stands and peers into the night sky. The raspy, croaking calls of a night heron, an eerie refrain, make her shiver. Willy presses into her leg. The delightful song of a whip-poor-will pushes against the fear in her heart, again making her feel the closeness of freedom. The paradox of both good and evil surrounding the two makes her light headed.

She takes a resolved breath and lets it out. Grabbing Willy by the hand, she breaks into a sprint. Willy stumbles. She picks him up and dashes across the clearing toward the bridge.

Almost there.

She pants as her foot touches the first board. Horror consumes her. Her mind reels, leaving her weak. She feels darkness surrounding her. Halfway across, she stumbles, goes down on one knee. Hyperventilating, she folds Willy tighter against her and rises to her feet. Her feet are made of iron, her legs of lead. She tries to make them run, to go forward. They are impossibly weighted. She sobs in frustration and fear.

A surge, a lightness like a breeze fills her body and spirit. She bounds into steps that feel enormously long. She is flying over the bridge, barely feeling her feet touch the boards. Willy is air in her arms, no weight at all. In moments, she is across the bridge and standing in front of the old painted sign with arrows pointing up and down.

She puts Willy down, puts her hands on her knees to draw a deep breath, and finds she is not out of breath. It is as if she never ran at all. Willy stares at her with open mouth and scared eyes. She glances back at the bridge, then steeples her fingers together, smiling joyously into the night sky.

CHAPTER
Twenty Five

The Accident

St. Louis, Missouri
1959

*J*ust 'cause I stay mad at my momma all the time now don't mean I want something to happen to her. So, when it does, I'm worrying inside myself while Uncle Dew drives all us kids to the hospital to see her. I do all right until we pull up to park. Looking at that big building with the Emergency sign in tall red letters and seeing ambulances pulling up one after another freezes me up. Uncle Dew and the boys get out of his truck and gallop off and don't know I'm still standing just outside the truck door not moving an inch.

Donnie and Uncle Dew look back at me at the same time, and Uncle Dew comes running back. He kneels down and puts his hands on my shoulders. "Honey, it's all right. Your momma has a slight concussion, a broken rib, and she's bruised up pretty bad, but she's gonna be fine. She needs you to be strong now. We all do."

He takes hold of my hand and takes a step. I pull back. I can't do it. I can't go see my momma like that. I want to cry, but now the twins have come back to the truck and are staring at me. I sneak a look expecting they're making fun of me or sticking their tongues out, but they ain't doing neither one. Fact is, they look downright scared.

"Come with us, Annie. Please?" Joey says. Jackie nods his head.

That surprises me so much I start walking, holding Uncle Dew's hand, and my three brothers are walking around us all close. I feel proud of us being strong together for Momma.

The shiny tile on the floors and walls inside the hospital are so white they hurt my eyes. Nurses with starchy looking hats standing up on their heads are going everywhere. Men wearing white pants and shirts with stethoscopes around their necks hurry in and out of doors and up and down the halls. People are pushed around on flat, hard beds with metal sides and wheels on the bottom, or they're sitting up in wheelchairs going here and there.

At a counter, Uncle Dew says, "We're here to see Ozina Blackburn, please."

"What is your name and relation to the patient?" the young, red-headed nurse asks him.

"I'm her brother, Dewey Hamilton, and these are her children."

"I'm sorry, sir, but only two visitors at a time. Looks like the young lady is too young for visitation. The younger boys might be, too. How old are they?"

Uncle Dewey turns his back to the girl and gives us *the look,* a kind of expression on his face we've seen before. He starts popping his gum in his back teeth real loud, pulls a piece of his dark hair down in the middle of his forehead, kind of bobs around while he's doing it. He smiles a lopsided grin as he turns around and leans over the counter.

"Sweetheart, let me explain."

He starts talking so low we can't hear what he's saying, and pretty soon, the nurse giggles, writes something on a little piece of paper, creases it, and hands it to him. He grins some more, keeping his eyes on her while he puts the paper in his shirt pocket. He's still kind of dipping around funny like he does around women. I don't understand it, but it shore does something to those gals.

"The elevators are down that hallway on the right. Room 214. Let me know if you have any trouble finding it, Dewey, or if there's anything else I can do to help," the nurse half whispers.

Uncle Dew keeps grinning at her over his shoulder when we start walking down the hallway.

"Now that was slick!" Donnie says, punching Uncle Dew on the arm. "Man!"

"All in a day's work, my boy, all in a day's work." The two of them keep grinning and punching at each other even when we get in the elevator. Me and the twins are smiling 'cause we've seen it before how our uncle changes women's minds like that.

For a minute, I almost forget our momma was hit by a car.

CHAPTER
Twenty Six

A Shadow on the Sun

San Antonio, Texas
1905

*J*ack's business investments in the thriving city of San Antonio have rewarded him in more ways than he ever thought possible. A friend and drinking colleague of most of the original entrepreneurs of the city, he listened with a good ear when they advised him to put a little capital in a certain enterprise, a little gold in another. Now, he is counted as one of the prosperous business elders of the city. Much of his investment money originally came from his knack — or is it luck? — of gambling, it's true; but once invested, does money know where it came from, or have a reason to exist other than for being invested or spent?

All in all, life is good, very good indeed. Jack is currently settled into one of the several slatted rockers on the long, covered porch contemplating life and puffing a cigar. The porch is a nice addition, he thinks, to the four-unit bungalow built to house the hired help once his two-story log manor is complete. For now, one of the bungalow units is where he, Selene, and Joseph are residing. He would build his beautiful wife a hundred mansions if she but asked, but as it is, she is in wonderment of each and every thing he has given her and her son, especially safety.

Ah, but there are the bitter times when she cries unconsolably and beats her fists on the mattress of the bed they share. Oh, what ghosts the mind is capable of bringing forth in the dead of night. The hellish regrets she whispers through her hot tears for not trusting Jack to keep both Joseph *and* Monique safe.

A shadow on the sun.

A tragedy.

Jack becomes so distraught seeing her in this state of agony, he has, many times, all but put a foot to the stirrup to ride into the darkness and snatch the girl away from Ernest and Arlene and bring her back to her rightful mother. Only the wholesome spirit of his young wife has stopped him from doing so. It is Selene herself who talks him out of it— explaining the cruelty of stealing Monique away from the tragically childless couple, people who have built their lives around her own baby girl for more than a year.

Morning always dawns afresh, and Selene, following one of her midnight fits, goes about her daily duties of pleasing her husband and loving her son with not a word of the sadness lodging in that particular dark corner of her heart.

What man would not gladly die for such a ravishingly tragic and logical creature as his Selene?

CHAPTER
Twenty Seven

Sleeping Candy

New Orleans
1905

"You gave him some of the sleeping candy, child?"

"Yes, ma'am. We were four days coming, what with hiding out in the tree lines to be sure no one was after us. I was as nervous as a rabbit the whole time. I had food supplies and water with us, but Willy was near passing out with weariness. I carried him a lot, and he cried most of the time—big old silent tears, ma'am. Never complained, he didn't. In my thinking, that makes it worse, he being carried this way and that according to the whims of whoever takes hold of him. This time, it was me."

Mrs. Franklin shakes her head in sympathy.

"I gave him one of the candies when that family picked us up yesterday and let us ride in the back of their wagon with the cows. I had to, Mrs. Franklin. Once he was in the wagon and the man geed up the horses, Willy got it in his head to start crying out for Mam. I got scared those nice folks would figure I'd stolen him. I gave him a candy and told him to hush since we were almost to the frog-catching place. I said Mam was waiting for him with good food, especially his favorite milk pudding. I-I'm sorry I had to lie, Mrs. Franklin, but I didn't know what else to do."

"Tut-tut-tut, darlin'. The Lord knows the burdens you been a' carryin'. Why, just look at how thin and drawn you are. You lost so much weight this summer, Issy."

Isabelle nods. "I've done my fair share of worrying, ma'am, I sure have."

"We'll get some meat back on your bones after we get Willy safe in Baton Rouge."

Mrs. Franklin's kindly ways are a comfort to Isabelle, especially now. She takes a deep breath and says, "Willy's not of a good mind, ma'am. He doesn't remember his real family or much of anything before he was stolen. He thinks he has to be with Mam. She's near kept him tied to her skirt for two years. I suspect he might be brokenhearted once he wakes up."

Mrs. Franklin, an attractive, middle-years woman a bit on the plump side with thick, dressed hair graying at the temples, stands with her hands on her hips. She looks down at Willy sleeping on a cot on the screened porch of the Franklin's lavish home where Isabelle has worked a portion of every year for eight years.

"My, my, such a beautiful, sad little boy, and what tragedy he has suffered in his young life! Yes, I agree we must get him to my cousin in Baton Rouge in all haste. Dr. Franklin said we can leave this afternoon. It's a few days journey, child. What shall we do with him when he awakens?"

Isabelle looks down. "I-I think we are beholden to give him the sleeping powders in a drink of water until we get there, ma'am. I don't like it. I sure don't."

"I shall leave that up to your discretion, my dear. I have given Jenny and George the day off and did so as soon as you showed up and told me you'd hidden the boy in the boat house. They have no idea he's here."

"Thank you, ma'am. Nowhere in New Orleans is safe from the gossip of its hired workers. Baton Rouge gives me cause to fret, too, but we must trust the Lord that it is too far from this city's prattle to spread any word of him."

"Yes, we must trust the Lord, my dear child."

"I will try hard to find his daddy, that Simon St. Clair Willy told me about two years ago. Thing is, I don't know what town he's from. Right now, Willy's memories are all jumbled up."

Mrs. Franklin clicks her tongue. "Poor little thing, and that poor mama losing her dear boy to witchery."

CHAPTER
Twenty Eight

Food, Lots of It

St. Louis, Missouri
1959

A loud knock on the door sends Joey flying across the room.

"It's my turn!" Jackie hollers.

The two boys crash into each other just past the couch Donnie sleeps on. They go to scuffling to the floor.

"Boys! That's enough!" Uncle Dew calls out in his *I mean it* voice.

The boys untangle and scramble to their feet.

"He did it last time. It's my turn," Jackie yells, giving the evil eye to Joey.

"Last time was just old Mrs. Braxton from down the hall checking on Momma. It don't count," Joey argues.

"That's enough. Go sit down before I tan your hides. Last time I'm gonna tell you." Uncle Dew glares in their direction.

Donnie and I grin at each other. The twins are right on

the edge of getting in some bad trouble with our uncle. He's been here since morning when he brought Momma home from the hospital. It's Saturday, and it's raining, which means we're cooped up inside. Those brats have been in so many arguments, I can't hardly count them all. Some of them are about who gets to read a comic book first or which cowboy show to watch on the T.V. Most are about who gets to answer the door. People have been bringing fruits and all to our apartment all day.

Momma's manager from her work drove hisself here and left a sealed card and a whole box of chocolates for her. Uncle Dew won't let us have even one candy from it until Momma sees it and chooses the first one. The pretty red and gold box is sitting on the counter in the kitchen, and I keep going in there and rubbing my finger over the ribbon on top. My mouth waters ever time.

Another knock on the door, and Uncle Dew dips his head at me. When I open the door, I see a teenager boy holding an almost-closed, dripping umbrella. He looks a few years older than Donnie. He's got on black pants, a white jacket with black buttons down the front, and shiny black shoes. His hair is all combed back, and he's carrying some kind of a covered metal thing with a handle on top of it. It must be heavy 'cause his left shoulder is drooping a little.

"Are you the Blackburns?" he asks.

"Yes."

"Special delivery lunch from the Diamonds Restaurant."

"Lunch?"

"Yes, ma'am."

By now, Uncle Dew has come to the door. He says, "Diamonds Restaurant on Route 66? Ain't that kind of far away?"

"Yes sir, but my manager says he packed it all real good to keep the food warm."

"We didn't order any food."

"No sir. Someone else ordered it for you."

"Who?"

"Uh, I don't know, sir. I just do whatever my manager tells me to, and he don't tell me who or what."

"Do we pay for it?"

"No sir. It's all paid for."

"Well, that's mighty fine. Here…" Uncle Dew pulls a dollar out of his wallet and a fifty-cent piece from his pocket and gives them to the young man. "… a little something for you. Thanks, now."

Uncle Dew takes the metal thing from the boy and closes the door. Delicious smells come out of the top vents as he carries it to our table. We follow behind him like we're Mary's little lamb and watch him slip the cover off. He snoops all through everything, and we're leaning towards him and those good smells.

"Would you look at that, kids? Fried catfish, and… what? A whole half of a ham? And just lookie here, fried frog legs!" He keeps moving things around inside the box. "Say, when's the last time you kids had steak?"

We don't say anything.

"Is it cow meat?" I ask.

Uncle Dew laughs. "Boy-oh-boy, you-uns are turning into little city rats. It's time to get back to the country. Okay, well, you're gonna have some steak today. Looks like we got a mountain of boiled red taters, gravy, slaw, corn muffins, and bread rolls, too. Who can afford stuff like this? There's enough here for a couple of days, I'm thinking. I'm gonna go tell your mom. Time for her medicine, so she needs to eat something."

Before he goes to check on Momma, he points a finger at us. "No grubby fingers in the grub, hear? My belt is warmed up and ready to go. In fact, it's itching to go."

All of us smile, but not too big. We know Uncle Dew is our fun uncle, but he can be strict, too. When we go see Momma in the bed a few minutes later, she says, "Kids, I have no idea who's being so generous, but I sure want to thank them when I get my strength back. Probably..." she yawns "... folks from work."

Uncle Dew takes her a plate of food in the bedroom, puts it on the dresser, and tells us to bring all the pillows in the whole apartment to prop her up. He helps her sit up, and she's groaning the whole time. Her broke rib is so sore, she has to slump to the side all crooked. We're standing around watching her like she's a television show. She forks a few pieces of red-skinned taters and two bites of steak and eats them since Uncle Dew says she has to. He hands her a glass of water and some pills she brought home from the hospital.

"Everybody out," he says, and we march single-file down the short hall. I don't know what to think of having Momma home like this. I'm still mad at her, and that may never change since I know now how she is about Mercy and all. Still yet, I don't like seeing her hurt and bruised up. Course, there's that other thing I worry about, but I keep shoving it out of my mind.

Someone knocks at the door while we're eating our hearts out at the table.

"I'll get it," Donnie says.

In a minute, he brings a big white box in and puts it on the coffee table in the living room. "The guy says this is from Lubeley's Bakery. No charge."

"Open 'er up, son," Uncle Dew says. "Hey, this is like Christmas!"

"There's a card scotch taped to the top. It says, 'To Mrs. Ozina Blackburn. May God bring you back to health in record time.' It's signed, 'Friends of the Family,'" Donnie says.

We leap out of our chairs to go look while Donnie opens the box. Inside is a tall, round cake with white icing. Pink icing designs outline the top edge like I line my coloring before I fill in the color, but fancier.

"Are those toy swans and rabbits on top?" I ask.

"Naw, honey, they're made out of sugar. You can eat 'em, but not until your momma wakes up and sees how fancy this thing is. Man, she sure is liked at that athletic club. I'm kinda wishing I worked there, too."

On Sunday, we get a whole pork roast with mashed taters, green beans, corn on the cob, and a peach cobbler delivered to us from a restaurant downtown. Everything tastes almost as good as how Momma makes it. Later on, I'm coloring in my coloring book outside the apartment near the sidewalk and Miss Ettie, the cook for Mercy's family, comes walking up carrying two square pink boxes. I'm so glad to see her, I jump up and throw my arms around her waist.

"Why, my goodness-gracious!" she says. "You okay, sugar?"

Now, why should I feel like bawling? I don't know, but I do, and lots of tears fall right out of my eyes. I wipe them away quick, and when I breathe out, a big wheeze comes out too. It makes me ashamed. Miss Ettie ain't never heard me wheeze before. She puts one of the boxes down and feels my forehead.

"Is you frettin' yerself sick about your mama, honey? Ain't she doing well? We shore been a'trying to keep her, and all y'alls, good and fed so she mends fastly."

And now I know who's been sending us all the good food. If my whole body could grin, it would. Miss Ettie is watching me. "There now, you looks better already, chile."

"What's Mercy doing today, Miss Ettie?"

"She's been lolling round the house all weekend sportin' a big frown on her little face. It aches me to see her like that. I thinks she's missin' you, Annie girl. You oughts to go see her. Cheer both y'alls up."

I lead Miss Ettie inside the apartment and tell everyone who she is. "Hi," they say, and "Umm" when I tell them she brought us her homemade chocolate-chip cookies and some peanut butter ones, too.

"Uncle Dew, is it okay if I walk Miss Ettie to the bus stop?"

"Sure, kiddo. Just leave us the goodies."

He and Miss Ettie grin big at each other. "Awful nice of you to think of us, Miss Ettie. I'm sure Zeenie will love these. I know we will."

Miss Ettie dips her head.

"Uh, Uncle Dew, when I come back, I'm gonna play outside for a while. Is it okay?"

Donnie gives me the eye for a minute, and I know he knows what I'm up to. Uncle Dew waves a hand at me. He and the boys are digging into the cookies, not paying much mind to me at all.

I smile up at Miss Ettie with no thought in the world of letting her get on that bus to go to Mercy's house by herself.

CHAPTER
Twenty Nine

Auntie Dove

Baton Rouge, Louisiana
1905

untie Dove brings a silver tray into the room laden with an ornate silver teapot, a small brown cake, and bone-white china sprinkled with floral clusters in cobalt blue. She sets the tray on a low table in front of the couch where Dr. and Mrs. Franklin are perched.

Isabelle can't help but stare at Mrs. Franklin's distant relative, a woman who loves to be called Auntie Dove and who she has heard mentioned many times over the years. To Isabelle, Auntie Dove looks to be floating inside a shiny underdress covered over by a layer of blushing peach embroidered organza. Short, wide sleeves move like airy waves around the attractive woman with vivid green eyes. Her golden-streaked brown hair falls in loose waves past her shoulders.

It nearly feels as though Mrs. Franklin has been telling her an untruth all these years, yet she knows Mrs. Franklin wouldn't lie. She thinks of how her benefactress describes her relative as *perhaps quadroon, maybe somewhat less than that, but still a negra, don't you know?*

After settling the tray, Auntie Dove rises to her full height, and she is quite tall, Isabelle notes, and looks Isabelle in the eyes. "Dear, please sit down. Nobody stands in my home unless everybody else stands. If they sit, you sit. We're all God's children here."

Isabelle smiles timidly and glances at Willy sleeping in one of the pretty chairs against the wall in the richly decorated sitting room. She looks at Auntie Dove. "Thank you most kindly, but I'll watch over the boy from here if it's all right."

Apparently, it isn't all right, and Auntie Dove smiles at the girl until she squirms. Isabelle sits down awkwardly on the edge of a small French Provincial chair beside the couch. She feels self-conscious, so she studies the room. On the wall behind the Franklins are matching frames containing photographs of seven males, five are young men, and two are boys. Isabelle has heard about Auntie Dove and her husband, Jacque—a wealthy French merchant—taking in ill-fated boys who have no chance in life without the benevolence of loving patrons such as they.

Auntie Dove takes a seat in a chair opposite the Franklins. She places four delicate tea cups onto saucers. As she does so, she says, "I always say we're a family the angels put together, and that, of course, includes the master of the house and me, along with Moses, Pierre, Billie Joe, Edward, Charlie, Frederico, and José Luis. If the Lord is willing, and Isabelle doesn't find his own family, Willy will join our proud roster of accomplished young men."

"Gracious, Dovie, a whole passel of boys! Are you and

Jacque raising all of them?" Mrs. Franklin asks.

Auntie Dove smiles at her cousin. "We are very blessed, Matilda. We prayed for our own babes, as you know, but it was not to be. I ask you, were we to remain only the two of us with all this love in our souls and no way to share it? I think not." She slices the brown cake with a pearl-handled knife.

"But-but where are they, all those boys?" Dr. Franklin asks.

Auntie Dove laughs softly. "I'm afraid you've touched upon a subject very dear to my heart, John. Now, I shall have to shamefully brag about my brood." She raises her eyes to the wall beyond the Franklins. "Please, take a look behind you, if you don't mind."

The doctor and Mrs. Franklin pivot in their seats. Mrs. Franklin cries out in a small voice and rises to go inspect the photos up close. Dr. Franklin coughs in his hand as he turns back toward Auntie Dove.

"Dovie, you and Jacque aiding so many young men over the years? Why, this is nothing short of… of incredible," Mrs. Franklin says, taking her place back on the couch.

Auntie Dove smiles demurely and fastens her eyes on the pictures. "And now, if you shall allow, I will tell you about our sons. Let's see… Edward, our fourth son, is now a musician studying back east. Oh, what a pianist that young man is! A natural. Charlie, son number five, married when he was eighteen, and his wife is a fine girl. We love her deeply, and the two of them live quite close to us. Charlie helps Jacque with the tallies and books at our Baton Rouge office.

"Frederico and José Luis, our sixth and seventh sons, are still at home with us. Their nursemaid Cecelia took them for an outing before you arrived. I didn't want them to meet their new brother until I had a chance to consider what state he is in. You see, they are merely nine and eleven years old—still babies, actually."

She clasps her hands together. "I save this for last because I am prone to cry when I speak of it." She takes a deep breath and lets it out with a smile on her face. "Matilda, John... our first three sons have enrolled in Oberlin College in Ohio! They are studying diligently, all of them, as we knew they would. And the most wonderful thing—Moses believes he will pursue law."

"But... I don't understand. Aren't they all, uh, somewhat of the dark race, Dovelle?" Dr. Franklin asks, his brow furrowed.

Isabelle barely breathes as she studies Auntie Dove's face. Is it amusement she sees there, or pity? What new world is this?

"John, since you ask, Moses is fully Negro. Pierre is French and Spanish. Billie Joe is a mixture of everything good and decent. Jacque and I don't concern ourselves with those particulars."

"Dark men, uh, mixed-bloods, attending college?" Dr. Franklin says.

Mrs. Franklin pats her husband's hand. "Dear, you have been so busy the last several years. Many things are changing in this country, especially up north."

"*Dark men,* as you say, John, have actually been graduating from open colleges for quite some time. Some become lawyers, educators, proprietors, even doctors."

Dr. Franklin coughs into his hand.

"Have you ever heard of George Boyer Vashon, John?"

He shakes his head.

"Oh, my goodness, he was one to *montrer la voie.* He spoke and taught many languages, and he graduated from Oberlin

College in 1844. Yes, before the Civil War. Among other professions, Mr. Vashon was a university professor. He also holds the honor of being the first, um, *dark man* to practice law in New York state. Isn't that simply delightful?"

"Dr. Franklin stands and clears his throat. "I believe I shall have a smoke."

"Of course. Would you care for a glass of water, as well?"

"Yes, I-I surely would."

"I'll have Nellie bring you one right away. If you go through those French doors, you'll find comfortable chairs on the veranda. There's a lovely view of the pond and the pecan grove from there. The birds will lull you into contentment, no doubt about it."

He bows. "Would you be so kind as to excuse me, ladies?"

Mrs. Franklin dips her head slightly.

"Most certainly," Auntie Dove says.

Isabelle doesn't understand all the particulars of what she just witnessed between her employer, whom she truly respects, and Auntie Dove. Though she knows she is by far the dearest girl to the Franklins' hearts out of all their other household help, and in spite of the fact that they have no children of their own and often treat her as if she is their daughter, Isabelle knows she is and will always be *household help*, she is still Colored, and the Franklins are still wealthy non-Coloreds.

The invisible lines of the New Orleans social strata were drawn long before Isabelle was born. Heretofore, she has had no intention of crossing those lines, and she has been comfortable with the way things always seem to be. Yet, Auntie Dove has opened a new window in her mind through which a refreshing breeze is beginning to blow.

She smiles to herself as the two adult women chatter

politely about the recent heat and humidity, taxes and Brazilian coffee. She glances at the sleeping boy. How magnificent that he will reside in a home such as this. That is, if Isabelle cannot find his family. Perhaps it is best that she not? No, she determined long ago she owes the child and his family at least a truthful try. If she can't find them, it is gratifying to know what kind of life Willy will have.

She will leave the sealed envelope she has hidden so long and now has on her person listing Willy's family names and all that he told her before the potions confused him. At a time when Auntie Dove and her good husband deem proper, they can share the written account with him. Oh, how she will miss the little boy she has come to love and has felt so protective of for so long.

"Can he hear us right now?" Auntie Dove asks, noticing Isabelle staring at Willy.

"No, ma'am."

"I know much of his tragic plight from Matilda's letters. After tea, you can tell me all about what state of mind he shall be in when he awakens and how the two of you managed to escape such a place as my cousin has explained to me. My, how brave of you, Isabelle! Obviously, you are a very special girl."

Isabelle feels as though a lit candle is making her glow from the inside out hearing praise from Auntie Dove. She resolves in that moment to be the kind of woman sitting like an angel on earth before her this day, one of service and self-sacrifice.

CHAPTER *Thirty*

Zero Balance

St. Louis, Missouri
1959

All of Momma's brothers—my uncles—came to see us this Sunday morning. Two of them live in St. Louis, and the rest are scattered in towns around Missouri. They work on fixing and painting houses and stores and city bridges just like Uncle Dew. I didn't want them to leave, they're so much fun. They teased us kids something terrible and ate from the big box of doughnuts they brought us. Uncle Dew brewed three pots of coffee while they were here.

When they left, an upside-down ballcap of cash was on the coffee table in the living room. When Uncle Dew counted it, it was one hundred and fifty-five dollars. He looked happy and worried at the same time.

"What's the matter?" I ask.

"Oh, uh, nothing, honey. Just you kids be careful and don't get in any accidents. Getting laid up costs lots of money, especially when you have to miss work."

"Why did Momma run out in front of a stupid car anyhow? She's always yelling at us to look both ways and look again before we cross a street." Joey says.

All of us turn to look at our uncle.

"I guess she was just too tired, son. Your mom's been tired a long time. She didn't even see that damn—, I mean, that danged car. You know how she is about being at work on time. She said she was hurrying across the street and forgot to look."

"Why doesn't the man who hit her pay for her doctor bills?" Donnie asks.

"Son, not too many people have insurance."

"It's the law."

"That doesn't mean folks can afford it. Besides, your mom says it was all her fault and not his. She ran right out in front of him. He couldn't do anything but hit her. He's a young guy with a wife and three little kids. Barely makes enough money to keep his own family going. Anyway, it's being off work for four to six weeks that hurts the old pocketbook."

"I'm getting a paper route, Uncle Dew," Donnie says.

"Now, that's real fine, son. Proud of you. That'll put some bread on the table for sure."

I stare at the floor so nobody guesses my secret. I've been hiding my feelings about it, but talking about money when I know we ain't got much of it has me feeling guilty as sin. What I haven't let myself think about is how all this trouble is probably my fault. Momma maybe wasn't thinking right when she crossed that street 'cause we had an argument right before I left for school that morning.

I couldn't stand not knowing the answer to my

question—the most important question in the world—so I walked right in the bedroom and asked if I could go to Mercy's house sometimes this summer since school's about out. I been worried sick about if me and Mercy ain't in the same classroom next year and we can't see each other any other way neither.

So, that's what I did, and Mama told me no. I just up and threw another fit, and she got mad. She said if I didn't stop this behavior, she was sending me on the Greyhound bus the day after school was out and I could stay with Aunt Vel the whole summer, and how would I like that? I told her I liked it fine 'cause then I wouldn't have to look at her no more and that would suit me real good. She jumped out of bed and grabbed the strap to give me a whooping, but then she started bawling. She said I should be ashamed of myself, and she went back in the bedroom and closed the door.

I stood there mad as I could be and feeling bad at the same time. I never talked to my momma like that before, but I never seen her so mean about something, neither. Specially about the best friend I ever had in my life.

The twins had already headed out the door to school, and I ran to catch up with them. Before dinner time, which Mercy calls *lunch*, Uncle Dew came and got us since Momma was in the hospital from that car hitting her.

That's why I'm thinking everything is my fault. I sit down at the eating table and put my head on the top of it. I stare at the wall with the Chinese lady pictures.

"What's wrong, Annie?" Uncle Dew says.

"Oh, nothing, I guess."

"Listen, this here money from your uncles plus what your Momma already had in the till will pay the rent this month. Don't worry none about that. I'm taking it down to the manager in just a minute. I'll fill up the cabinets and ice box with food, but it won't be steak, that's for darn sure," Uncle Dew laughs.

"We'll make out okay. I got some extra work lined up, so all we got to do is keep our heads down and walk straight ahead. One step at a time. Soon's your mom's up and around again, everything's gonna be fine."

"What about the hospital and doctor bills?" Donnie asks.

"Well, now, you can't squeeze water out of a rock, can you? We're going to get those bills tended to, but it won't be right this minute. Main thing is to survive and get your momma well. We've already made it to week number three. See how fast time passes?"

I feel a little better about things and watch Uncle Dew straighten all the cash money from the ballcap so's the bills face the same way and the big ones, like twenty-dollar bills, are on the bottom. He goes down the hall and knocks light on the bedroom door, waits for Momma to tell him to come in, goes in and closes the door. When he comes out, he has a white envelope in his hand. He takes out more money bills from the envelope and adds them to the stack he just made. He puts it all together in the envelope, folds the whole thing in half, and shoves it in his back pocket.

"Okay, I'll be right back, kids. No fighting. Donnie, heat up a couple cans of that Campbell's chicken noodle soup. Sprinkle some black pepper in it. Sis, get out the saltine crackers and put some on a plate. Oh, and get the Tabasco out of the ice box. Livens up that canned soup pretty good. Joey, Jackie... you boys set the table."

"Uncle Dew!" both boys whine at the same time.

He points a finger at them. "Hey, everybody helps around here now. Get a move on."

Uncle Dew is back shortly with our mail from the mailboxes in the lobby. One letter is already open and in his hand. He sits down in a chair at the table and keeps on reading whatever came out of that ripped-open envelope. He stands up, takes the bended envelope out of his back pocket and throws it on the table. He sits down. The envelope is still fat.

"You didn't pay the rent, Uncle Dew?" Donnie asks.

"I, uh, no, son, I didn't."

"What happened? Was Mr. Greer gone?"

"Oh, he was there all right."

Donnie pulls a chair out from under the table and positions it facing our uncle. "I don't get it."

"Neither do I, Donnie, neither do I."

"What's that letter in your hand, Uncle Dew?" I say.

"It's the bill from the hospital."

"Oh."

"And here's one from Dr. Ellsworth. Let's see what it says." He rips the envelope open with his finger. He takes the folded paper out, reads it quick, and throws it on the table. He stands up and sticks his hands in his pockets. He walks into the living room and back to the table. Us kids look back and forth at each other.

"What's wrong?" Jackie asks.

"Kids, I wouldn't have believed this if someone told me, but something crazy has happened. Yes, indeed-ie, something crazy has happened."

Donnie picks the doctor bill off the table. "What's got you worried, Uncle Dew? It says nothing is due. Zero balance."

"That's right, son, now look at this." He holds the hospital bill up for Donnie to read."

"Holy cow! Another zero balance? How did that

happen?"

"I don't know. Get this… when I tried to pay the rent, the manager said it was already paid for this month and the next one, too."

"How?" Donnie asks.

"Don't know. He doesn't either. The money was delivered by a delivery service a few days ago. No other information, he said."

We all go to the living room and sit down. None of us know what to say. Finally, Uncle Dew slaps his knee and starts laughing.

"Hey, Donnie-Hot-Dog, turn the fire off that soup and let's all go down the street and get us a hot dog from Maurizio's stand. Ain't nothing better than one of those dogs with slaw and hot peppers. We'll bring your momma something when we come back. If we come back. See, we's rollin' in the dough! May have to cut out for Old Mexico."

He does a little dance while we laugh our heads off. Donnie doesn't even get mad about Uncle Dew calling him Hot-Dog. Grinning like crazy, we race to the door. We shore have a mystery on our hands, but at least we get to eat good and have some fun.

CHAPTER
Thirty One

Snake Skin

St. Louis, Missouri
1959

Another flash of lightning tints the trees and grass of Forest Park a white-blue. Loud claps of thunder follow, rattling the windows in Dew's 1953 Chevy pickup. Heavy rain pounds the metal cab.

"Are you sure we won't wash away in this thing? I mean, we're sitting here parked and rivers are gushing by. It's kind of scary." Zeenie says.

"This *thing?* This *thing* happens to be my solid little honey that gets me anywhere I go, come rain or shine. Your kids love it, you know, even when they have to sit double stack up here in the seat with me when we're city driving. Yes sir, she's proud of her beautiful maroon paint, too, so don't go hurting her feelings." Dew grins and lovingly pats the dashboard. "Now, you were saying…"

Zeenie twists the tissue in her hand, flattens it out, folds it into a fan shape, then twists it again.

"Zeen?"

"I-I just don't know. Everything I thought I knew seems ridiculous now. *I* feel ridiculous."

"What is it you thought you knew?"

"You know what I'm talking about. Everything I been thinking about the human races might be wrong now, and I don't even know why I thought what I did think anyhow.

Dew twists in the seat to fully consider the state of his sister. She's a mess. Her eyes are swollen from crying, her lip keeps quivering, her hair is windblown to high heaven from their careful dash through the storm to the pickup from the apartment a quarter of an hour ago.

"Would you like to translate that? Sounds like a foreign language or something."

A fresh gush of tears starts down her cheeks. "My children are better people than me, let's just say that."

Dew senses he has to let Zeenie figure this out on her own. It's a door in front of her, and she's the one who must twist the knob. Whether she turns it right or left, it will have to be her own thinking. She watches him, wishing he would say something to sooth her anguish. Instead, he picks up a folded rag just underneath the seat and starts polishing the steering wheel. Blows on it. Polishes it some more.

Zeenie blows her nose into the tortured, twisted tissue she has in her hand. Without looking at her, Dew hands her a fresh one. She says, "I mean, *why* did I think what I did before? What is the reasoning behind our behavior in this world? Did Mama and Daddy think like that? Did they ever say they did? Seems like it's been a feeling born in me—in everyone—and for what? To be hateful? To be high and mighty? Why aren't we judging people by their actions and that's all? Is this poison in our blood?" She tilts her head sideways in her hand and watches the streams run down the side window. "I'm miserable, Dew, just miserable."

He leans back into the seat. It's all he can do to keep from expressing his own opinions, but he keeps still. Zeenie sits up straight and looks at him with her eyebrows raised and her eyes wide.

"Wait a minute, didn't I... didn't we get these ideas from the Bible? Is that where it comes from, Dew, this idea that races shouldn't mix?" Hope springs into her eyes, but Dew shakes his head.

"Sorry, but I have my own opinions on that, sis. Not everyone believes it like I do, but I know what I know."

"What do you mean?"

"I mean the Good Book, as far as I understand it, says to be good to one another. You know... kind and all. That's just great for most folks walking around doing their lives, maybe going to church on Sundays, helping their neighbors sometimes. Then, here comes someone of another skin color or who believes differently and they forget all about their good behavior and not judging everyone and treating everyone like they want to be treated themselves, you know?"

Zeenie looks at him a long time. "I didn't know you were such an avid reader of the Bible."

"Aw, I'm not really, but I used to read it when we were growing up. Remember how Daddy wouldn't let us read anything but that on Sundays? Well, I couldn't give up my reading habit for a whole day, could I?"

She smiles. Dew was always the big reader in the family. "So, this separation of the races doesn't come from the Bible?"

"Not the way I read it. I mean, dang, Moses himself had a beautiful Colored wife."

"What? He did?"

"Yep. A Cushite. That's an Ethiopian, in case you don't know. Those were dark-skinned people, hon. Before that, there was ol' Solomon, the smartest man who ever walked the earth."

"Nuh-uh."

"I can show you where it talks all about it. He fell in love with the beauty queen of all beauty queens, the Queen of Sheba."

"She was of the dark races?"

"Sure was. Hey, you were in church all those years just like me. Mama and Daddy wouldn't have had it any other way. After they passed on, sister Vel took up the gauntlet. I guess you really did rebel against your raising, didn't you?"

Zeenie stares through the rain-drenched front window. In a small voice, she says, "Yes, I suppose I did. I wanted to get out and taste the world. Shake off those backwoods' ideas of religion, the way we spoke, how we thought. Look where that got me. I didn't pay a lick of attention to most things, Dew. Maybe that's why I've turned out so stupid."

For once, Dew doesn't correct his sister's self-depravation. If she's going to get to the bottom of herself, he figures she has to suffer a little in the process.

Zeenie wipes her eyes with her fingers. "Did you know Mercy's parents are highly educated? Look at me... a high school dropout. I didn't even finish my senior year. Why I didn't, I have no idea. Just stupid. Annie told me Mercy's whole family is full of heroes, educators, business people, nurses, a lawyer or two. All that. Why would I ever think those two little girls shouldn't be friends? Know what else? Annie says Mercy is teaching her the proper way to speak. Imagine that! I never bothered to correct her language. Figured she'd grow out of it soon enough. But, here again, was I doing what I was supposed to with my own kids?"

Dew raises his hand. "I'm partly responsible for that, Zeen. As you know, I'm partial to our country roots. I like to revert back to our hillbilly raising, and the kids pick up on my talk and such."

"But you know when to turn it off and speak correctly. Annie and the twins don't."

"Guilty," he says.

"Anyway, after Donnie told me who our benefactors were, he confessed something else I didn't know," Zeenie says.

"What's that?"

"He said Mercy's brother and he have been playing basketball together all this school term, and they've both been contacted about playing on the team at high school next year. I-I didn't even know Donnie was good at basketball. Did you?"

"Yeah. Sorry, sis, but I've shot some hoops with those boys at Jerome's uncle's gym, too. Nice place. Guess I forgot to mention it." He ducks down like Zeenie may slug him. She ignores his slight attempt to be funny.

"See? I never know anything! I'm a complete failure!"

She starts crying again. Dew fidgets. It kills him when Zeenie cries. He peers out the windows at the swirling trees and changes the subject. "Hey, that wind gets any worse and I'm gonna predict a twister. Conditions are pretty ripe right now."

Zeenie blows her nose and sniffs. After a few minutes, she says, "Donnie said he and Mercy's brother have been going to war movies together and slipping into certain backdoor restaurants that don't care about color so they can eat together, and-and, oh my Lord, Dew! It's all so much to take in. What kind of person am I that my kids have to hide their lives from me?"

She slams her hand on the dashboard.

"Hey, take it easy. You'll hurt my truck and that almost-healed rib."

"Then-then… those folks just out of the blue pay for our rent and the doctor bills, send us gourmet meals when I got hurt, and why would they do such things? I honestly don't know what to do about it. You know I don't accept charity.

"Oh, hogwash, sis. Don't get all righteous."

"I'm not. It's the way I am, and you know it. I didn't even let my father-in-law know where we were all these years because I didn't want him to pay for his son's bad behavior."

"I never agreed with your thinking on that, Ozina. Not at all. You took his grandkids away and never looked back just because of your silly pride."

"Dew!"

"Sorry, but that was a pretty rough thing to do to the man. Real rough."

Zeenie covers her face, rocks back and forth. Dew didn't know he was going to say what he did, but it was high time. He clears his throat and continues. "Mrs. Washington told me when I called her… called her for YOU, I might add… that you shouldn't think of this as charity, that she has some favors she'd love to ask of you when you're completely well. You'll hear all about them when you get the backbone to call her back and talk to her yourself."

"Setting up hors d'oeuvres for a couple of her spring garden parties on my days off? That will never be enough to repay them for all they've done."

Dew leans back in the seat and sighs loudly. "You don't

get it, do you? They don't expect a single thing in return. They did all those benevolences because they care. They care about their kids' friends, and they care about you and your circumstances. That's the kind of people they are—good, honest, and kind enough to reach out to others. I'll bet they've been through more than most of us will ever know."

Zeenie stares at Dew. She bows her head. "I'm quite the fool, aren't I? I guess I've been so busy feeling sorry for myself and trying to keep me and my kids afloat for so many years, I got blind to everything else. I'm selfish, silly, and—"

"And exhausted and skinny. It's time you got those love letters written, gal. You hear me? This constant workload with four kids is too much. You're wasting away and going a little crazy besides. Remember, you've just recovered from being hit by a car. A car, for heaven's sake! Something that never would have happened if you weren't so bleary-eyed weary all the time. We gotta find you a man."

"That sounds terrible, like I'm a loose woman on the prowl."

"Well, you ain't, and if I have to write those letters myself, we're getting it done."

"But I don't know what to do about all my confusion, Dew. My feelings. I'm so conflicted—"

"You know what you're going to do with those feelings?"

Zeenie, big-eyed, shakes her head.

"You're gonna shed them, that's what, just like a snake sheds its skin. Underneath that old, dirty skin is a fresh, new one, and that's what you want... a fresh, new way of thinking and living."

The rain suddenly stops, leaving a strange silence inside the truck cab. Zeenie gazes down at her hands for several long moments. Finally, she looks into her brother's face.

"Then, that's what I'll do. I'll shed that old Zeenie and get us a brand new one."

Part Two

CHAPTER
Thirty Two

The Lure of the Track

Baton Rouge, Louisiana
1913

Auntie Dove dabs her eyes with a lace-edged handkerchief and picks up the handwritten letter from the table beside her, touching it to her cheek. A mockingbird perched in a magnolia tree trills forth a repertoire of songs just beyond the veranda. She gazes out over the landscaped lawn spreading from the house to the pecan orchard. Fresh tears fill her eyes. She puts the letter down and weeps silently, her slender frame shaking.

"Come now, my dearest, you must not be overwhelmed. You shall make yourself ill. Our William will find his way back to us. We must be of good courage."

"But, Jacque, Willy is too young to be alone in this unforgiving world."

Jacque leans forward conspiratorially in his chair. "My sweet, fifteen was measured as manhood in my youth. William has overcome more than most boys twice his age. We must give him credit for having more than a childish, whimsical mind. *Petit a petit, l'oiseau fait son nid."*

Auntie Dove moans softly, takes in a delicate breath of air. "I do think, and not that I blame you, my dear husband, as you were merely adding to his intellectual knowledge of the world… but I have a tendency to believe that pen drawing of a portrait you gave him when he was a boy of eleven has… has… influenced him so very much." She dips her chin as she speaks so her words will not be taken as a reprimand to her husband.

Jacque chuckles. "Oh, my, he did so cherish that, didn't he? Did he not carry it with him everywhere? To school, to church, even on picnics. I say that boy loved it with a majestic heart!"

She looks evenly at her husband. His exuberance is somehow exacerbating the sorrow in her spirit. She watches him tamp out and refill the darkened meerschaum pipe, one of many he imported from Turkey on one of the merchant ships. He lights it and settles back in the cushioned rocking chair.

"I remember that day as though it were yesterday. All the men at the racing club were jockeying—if you'll excuse my use of the word—to purchase drawings made from the photograph of jockey Jimmy Lee. A high time we had doing it, too! *Zut alors!* The bidding reached a crescendo to equal a Saratoga race!"

"I often wonder if any other child had such a reaction as our young Willy did to those sketches," Auntie Dove says flatly.

Jacque stares intently above the ornate spindles of the veranda banister. "That picture." He shakes his head. "That picture, indeed. There was Jimmy—in fine stature—standing proud at the Coney Island Jockey Club. And, oh, that mirthful calm in his features. It was as if he carried the secrets of life behind those eyes. Proud, indeed he was proud, and he had every reason to be so. *Mon dieu!* Already a winner in Clipsetta, Latonia Derby, Latonia Oaks, and the Kentucky Oaks, the lad went on to win all six races at the Churchill Downs! But was that to be all to his acclaim? I should say not! He rode Dorante to the win in the Travers Stakes at Saratoga the very next year.

Jacque is moving in rhythm as if he himself is riding Dorante to the finish line. He rocks back and forth for what Auntie Dove deems must be a full half-minute, perhaps longer, his shiny eyes gazing at remembrances in his mind.

"Oh, I do miss those gaieties with the gentlemen at the tracks and the grand race horses, my love!" he declares. Sighing, he leans back puffing contentedly on his pipe, rocking slightly, his heels tapping gently against the painted wooden boards below his feet.

For the first time in their many years together, Auntie Dove feels a deep separation between them, almost as if her heart and that of her husband's are made from a different fabric altogether. She is in grief—he is lost in memories of good times. She takes a bird-sized sip of water and clears her throat.

"Yet, I cannot help but think... well, Mr. Jimmy Lee's occupation seems to have, um, most certainly convinced our son to abandon his studies to embark upon a premature career for which he has no affiliations. Nor is it even a valid choice for him since he will have to leave the state of Louisiana, horseracing being unlawful here now, and—"

"Ah, it is true that our Colored jockeys disappeared from the great race tracks more than a decade ago. I told Willy all about it, and how many of those men traveled to England, France, and Russia to ride to victory on foreign soil. Yet,

Jimmy Lee came out of Louisiana and lit the fires once again. He showed them, yea he did!"

"Yes, but I cannot see how pursuing a vocation in something that no longer—"

"My dear, the strict discipline of working with track trainers and groomers will be good for the boy. Heaven knows, he needs a way to rid his soul of the troubles he carries inside himself."

"He does have a lovely way with horses, I admit, but—"

Again, her husband interrupts her. "Oh, does he not! The boy rides as naturally as if he cut his teeth on a saddle. You recall how spirited Madoon's horse was when he wintered him here last year, how William rode him fearlessly and, I might add, faultlessly?"

"He was forbidden to go near that horse."

"But he did go near, my dear, he did, and what a horseman our boy is! The two moved as one."

Tears cascade down Auntie Dove's cheeks.

Jacque stops rocking and clasps his wife's delicate hand. He captures her eyes with his and holds them there. "Dovelle, our son will be under the watchful eye of all the Saints. You must have faith."

A fierce desire to trust those words, along with an abhorrence for the present giddiness of her mate, gleams from Auntie Dove's wet eyes. She swallows the pain spreading through her like black ink and nods.

"I shall do my best," she whispers.

CHAPTER
Thirty Three

Joseph

San Antonio, Texas
1913

Fourteen-year-old Joseph sits in a chair against the wall watching the ladies scurry back and forth carrying rags and blankets to rinse, emptying basins, and whispering among themselves. His mother has given birth to another son—her third in the ten years since she married Jack.

The winter wind blows outside the darkened window panes, and Jack rises from his chair near the fire to tend to the logs in the massive river-rock fireplace in the great room of the luxurious log manor. He inquires often of the ladies as to his wife's condition and smiles contentedly when they tell him she and their new son are faring most excellently. He lights up a cigar and sits back down in the rocking chair awaiting Doc Adams to emerge from the bedroom to give him further reassurance.

Joseph follows all the movement in the room with his

eyes, leaning forward, hands folded in the vee of his open legs. He has no complaints about the life Jack has given them. Jack dotes endlessly on his mother and has been kind to Joseph, teaching him how to ride and hunt and making sure his schooling has been of the highest caliber. Yet, Joseph feels a loss he can't come to terms with. Once, he tried to speak of it to his mother. She became so distraught, Jack asked him not to broach the subject of Monique anymore, if he didn't mind.

Joseph did mind, but out of respect for Jack, he refrained from mentioning the girl again. That didn't stop him from wondering about her privately. That wasn't all that was on the young man's mind these days. As more children were born to his mother and Jack, Joseph began feeling, at first, slightly estranged. Now, he feels the odd man out, even though he has no actual reasons other than bloodline for it. It's a feeling of drifting through the sky unanchored. He is, after all, the only step-son in a house of sons.

He is at odds with his mother, and therefore, with his step-father, on another subject as well. Joseph wants to be a Texas Ranger like Jack was, but his mother is dead set that he must attend a fine college and become a professional… a doctor, a lawyer, or a banker. She is more determined that he follow a life course of education toward a high career than are any of the mothers of his friends. He doesn't understand her persistent and dogged need for him to better himself.

He has a faint scar of a memory of a terrible evening when he was a young boy in which a man beat his mother until she ran with him and Monique from their home in desperation. No one talks of it, and Joseph simmers with curiosity about his past and his missing sister, and he wonders more and more about his rightful place in this family.

CHAPTER
Thirty Four

What Love Isn't

St. Louis, Missouri
1960

Somewhere between her feisty teenage years and her twenties—a time that was forged in ungrounded and, therefore, surface wisdom that led to one mistake after another—and now in her exhausting thirties—which are but a blur of work and habit and guilt—an unfinished concept lies hidden in the back of Zeenie's mind of what love *isn't*.

Love isn't something you turn on and off.

Love isn't walking out the door with tears in your eyes but a jaw set like iron, never to return.

Love isn't found in the bottom of a bottle.

Does she love Thomas, then?

She doesn't *not* love Thomas.

After all, he's a pleasant, lonely widower who frets if Zeenie is ever slightly sad or worried. He's a hard-working owner of a busy coffee shop here in the city, and no one did him any favors on the way up. He started as a dish washer, just seventeen years old, became a waiter, manager, and wound up buying the coffee shop from the owners a mere decade later. He married, had a son he sent to two years of college, and still built the café up to one of the most bustling, popular ones in St. Louis.

Zeenie flops over in the bed. She hears Annie's even breathing, and it comforts her. Sleep has eluded Zeenie lately, most likely because she can't seem to stop second-guessing herself. If she marries Thomas, does it mean she doesn't love D.J. anymore? Why has his memory stayed so fresh—so agonizing—for almost ten years? Is he dead or alive? Has he ever tried to find them?

Memories of her life with D.J. on the Texas ranch flood her mind. So rich with love, so full of expectation and adventure. Everything in her was satisfied in those years except for the aching dread that increased each year, the fear that he was drowning his deepest feelings in liquor, that he would never be tied down for long.

And she was right. Dammit, she was right!

She sits up in the bed. Regret as tangible as her own face courses through her. Look what bridges she has burned! What foolishness she has wrought. Her parents are dead, and the kids don't even have a grandfather because of her pride.

The fact is, Dew was right. Her pride is the main reason she broke off all ties with D.J.'s father—another of those "wise" decisions she made in their twenties. At the time, she figured if D.J.'s love for her and the kids wasn't strong enough to bind him to them, she never wanted him to return because of guilt or a sense of obligation, let alone because of his father's reproach.

Her face heats at the thought of D.J. staying with her for

anything less than undying love. She scolds herself for thinking so much of the past. Time to make a clean break.

In fancy scroll, she writes D.J.'s name on a chalkboard in her mind. She pins a photograph of his handsome image— white cowboy hat, piercing sky-blue eyes, and rakish smile— on the cork strip above the board. She sees herself step up to the board with an eraser. She scrubs the board clean until dust flies everywhere, filling the room like a cloud, and finally settling on an imaginary floor. She takes the photograph and tears it into tiny pieces, scattering them on top of the chalk dust.

Now think about Thomas, she commands herself.

For one thing, he dotes on the kids, and isn't that something? His only son is in the Marines, and he misses him being near and especially their times together when he took his son fishing, played baseball with him in the yard, went camping. Imagine her kids having a dad like that, one for them to count on, to grow to love, to fish with, and to be there to talk to when they had a problem.

She smiles in the darkness thinking about how Thomas worries about her work schedule at the Athletic Club, and he fears something will happen to her getting off the streetcars alone at night when she works overtime. She worries about that, too, and didn't tell him she carries a switchblade knife in her hand after work.

She lies back in the bed. It's nice having him care so much about her wellbeing. She assumed she would go to work in the coffee shop if they married, but he said if she must work, it could only be part time, no more. In fact, he wishes she would stay home and be the mother she cries about not having time to be. In short, he wants to cherish her and take care of her—no outside job required.

What in the world is wrong with that?

Who else besides her own brother ever cared that much?

How rare are such men!

Just like that, she makes a determination. The section of her heart deeply bruised by the man she has never gotten out of her system will no longer rule her life and break her spirit. She will marry Thomas, and she will make him happy. D.J.'s memory will wither like a discarded rose on a hot summer sidewalk.

CHAPTER
Thirty Five

Here Comes Thomas

St. Louis, Missouri
1961

*O*ur crinoline petticoats make our dresses flare out like starched cones. I turn this way and that admiring myself in the full-length mirror in Mercy's bedroom. The dresses are identical, and Mrs. Washington picked them out for us to wear to Momma's marriage to Thomas today. They're white with yellow roses sewn on the skirt, wide yellow sashes, and they have a line of green satin buttons on the bodice.

"This is the last year I'm wearing a full skirt when I dress up," Mercy says. "Mama thinks we're still little girls."

"I think they're pretty."

"Oh, Annie, you're so quaint. Don't you realize we're teenagers now?" She sighs loudly and arranges the crystal clasp in the top of her hair. "Our moms sure don't. We're thirteen years old, for heaven's sake."

I don't answer. I stare out the upstairs window at the oak

trees lining the street with their yellow and orange leaves fluttering lightly against the black bark. I'm thinking how Mercy and I are the same age within a few months—our birthdays are both in the spring—and yet, from the first day I met her, she seems so much older than me. The gap widened when she started going on summer trips with her parents and grandpa. Twice, she has visited France, and when she returns, she talks about things and places I've never heard of in my life. Things I can't pronounce. She spouts off the history of that country like she's lived there. She says her favorite places, besides Paris, are Séchault and Hâteau-Thierry, Aisne, France.

She takes French lessons and speaks the language enough to sneak us into French restaurants and order for us and talk to the staff in all French. I'm doing well to speak our own language properly with all her careful tutelage of my grammar these past few years.

Ever since Momma got to be friends with her mother, Mercy and I have had the best times. We get to go wherever we want with each other, and even the twins behave when Mr. or Mrs. Washington is around. Jerome and Donnie run around all the time, too, and nobody gives a care about it. They're both popular basketball players at the high school.

Everything changed in our lives after Momma got hit by a car. Seems like she and Uncle Dew were always having private talks behind closed doors, or they'd leave for an hour or two. I thought she sure did miss her job to be so upset all the time. One day, she got all dressed up and went to see Mrs. Washington in the *Ville*. I thought she was going to visit her friends at the Athletic Club.

When she came home, she hugged and hugged me and told me she was sorry for her foolish behavior about Mercy. She told me I could be Mercy's best friend forever if that's what I wanted. Donnie and Jerome, too, it didn't matter because there sure wasn't any room for foolish-thinking people in our home. Us kids all about died of shock. I told Donnie it looks like that car knocked some sense into Momma's head. When he quit laughing, he said I was getting pretty smart for a squirt kid.

Soon after that, Momma started getting lots of letters in the mailbox in the apartment lobby. Uncle Dew would come over, and they'd leave to go get coffee, even if there was a full pot in the kitchen. Sometimes, she'd ask us if we'd like to move to Indiana, or Florida, or some other place. We'd all holler out, "No!" She'd smile and go on her way, not telling us a thing about what she was up to.

Some more months went by, and Momma told us she had a date coming to pick her up at our apartment. She said he owned the Sunrise Coffee Shop right here in St. Louis and for us to behave and act like we had good sense. We had to take early baths and dress up like we were going to church. The boys had their wet hair combed and neatly parted on the sides, and Momma warned us not to mess up a single thing in the living room, which I'd cleaned spic and span earlier. What could we do but sit on the couch and wait like we were little kids instead of teenagers?

When the knock on the door came, Donnie made a crossed-eyed, crazy face and stuck his tongue out. That started us off laughing like hyenas just as Momma, all dressed up, opened the door and stepped into the room with a tall man wearing a long overcoat and a hat. She made a face at us that said *stop acting like heathens or else,* but we couldn't stop. The twins fell on the floor giggling, and then Joey broke wind. That set us off worse than anything. I had my hand over my mouth snorting and snickering.

Of course, Donnie... he caused this, and now he was fine... walked over and shook Thomas's hand. He turned back around to us, shook his head and said, "Momma, I tried. They just can't act civilized for more than fifteen minutes."

It was terrible bad, and we expected Momma to lower the boom when she got home. Actually, she never mentioned it again. We were in bed when she got home, but the next morning, all she talked all about was how Thomas took her to the Crystal Palace in the Gaslight Square over by Olive and Boyle streets. She said she saw some funny guys called the Smothers Brothers and a young woman who sang really good named Barbra Streisand. I've never heard of any of those people, but Momma was so excited about seeing them. I guess because she never went anywhere for years and years except to work and back home.

On the counter in the kitchen the next morning was one wilted red rose with the stem wrapped in pink tissue. When I asked Momma about it, she said, "Oh, Thomas bought it for me while we walked around Gaslight Square."

So, Momma started dating Thomas, and we all liked him. He was nice to us and took us out to eat at different places and his coffee shop, too. Once, he took us to a theater to see real people singing and acting in *The King and I,* and the boys all hated it. I loved it. If Mercy hadn't been in France, she sure would have gone with us. She left a few weeks before eighth grade was over with special permission since it was considered educational to travel to a foreign country. I missed her so much I felt sick a lot, but at least we got to do a lot of things with Thomas all summer.

Thomas took all the boys to the St. Louis Cardinals games and went with Donnie and Jerome to shoot hoops, they called it. He went to the twins' league baseball games, too, so he was okay in their eyes. I rode the streetcar sometimes to his coffee shop on Grand at Washington, right next door to the fancy Fox Theater, and ate whatever I wanted, just like Mercy and I did at Chinaman Bill's.

Mercy and I stopped going to the Peach Garden after one or two times because it was too lonesome with Chinaman Bill and Aunt Viola gone. We were glad she escaped that manager trying to make her his wife. Sometimes we wondered what he did when he found out she was gone, like maybe he went wall-eyed crazy and sent men all over the city looking for her. Mercy says Aunt Viola has written them that she's married and very happy, and the return address is a post office box in San Francisco.

Anyway, when Momma sat us all down at the table and told us Thomas wanted to marry her and move us into his nice, two-story home with five bedrooms, we all looked around at each other's faces. Momma started looking really worried until Donnie said, "I think that's fine, Momma," and the rest of us nodded our heads.

And that's why, after dating him for all these months, Momma decided to marry Thomas Boswell today.

CHAPTER
Thirty Six

Can't Beat No Righteous
Sense in 'Em

Kingston Stables, Kentucky
1914

The knuckles hurtling toward his face are calloused and scarred. That's all Willy has time to notice before they plow into his jaw, slamming his head into the boards of the horse stall wall. He slides downward, is jerked by the collar from the hay-covered floor, and is tossed through the open stall door. He lands crumpled on his right shoulder in the alley of the stables. Dizziness clouds his mind as he dimly counts the horse legs showing underneath the other stall doors.

"Get off and stay off this property, boy. Come back, and I'll chop you up and feed you to the pigs. You hear me?" snarls the large lout straddling Willy's long, lanky body. A dilapidated boot covered in horse manure and straw is planted near Willy's head. The man raises it and brings it down on the side of Willy's face. Everything goes dark.

Rain. Dripping off his nose onto his hand wedged under

the side of his face. Willy is lying on his back. He stirs. Agony shoots through his head and settles back as tiny torches behind each eyelid. He attempts to open his mouth, but it feels unhinged. His lips don't fit right. He tries to rise. Too raw. Tries again and makes it, clenching his lopsided teeth against the effort. Stabbing pain in one shoulder and fire in his chest. What happened? Was he thrown off a horse? Stomped? He tries to reason but can't.

Thirty feet below him, the friendly lights emanating from the Kingston-Farm barn and stables create a halo in the wet darkness. He is underneath the massive fiscus tree on the hill overlooking the barn, but it doesn't make sense to him.

"Glad you ain't dead, Willy."

It's Jedediah, the elderly groomsman for *Lightning Rod,* the horse Willy was assigned to as an exercise boy several months ago. His ability to handle and calm the horses had not gone unnoticed, and he was up for promotion to assistant trainer. His height disqualifies him from becoming the jockey he always dreamed of becoming. He learned that the first week he ran away to Kentucky. To his dismay, he continues to shoot up, probably almost six foot by now.

"That damn 'ol Murdock woulda stomped more'n your face and chest if I hadn't stirred the horses up. Made him think 'bout something else, Willy-boy. That shore was a bad thing happened tween them horses, but it ain't no call for him to snap your bones like a tree limb, no sir. That don't solve nothing, I say. Can't beat no righteous sense in 'em, you boys, that is. No, we gots to learn you young'uns how to be with horses since yer just beginnin' in this bizness. Show 'em, don't hits 'em. That's what I say."

Willy's critical error happened when he led *Lightning Rod* inside a pen, pushed the gate closed but didn't turn around to secure it while he went inside the tack room to get the exercise leads. *Magic Night,* the newest and youngest pride and joy of the stable owner, was in the process of having his halter switched to a bridle by a new groomer when he spied his opportunity to challenge *Lightning Rod.* He broke free and lunged through the half-open gate. An instant and ferocious fight broke out between the two thoroughbreds with the younger horse coming out the loser.

As *Magic Night* was led away severely limping, Murdock sent Jedediah to take over the still proud and snorting *Lightning Rod.* He called Willy inside the barn, fired him, beat him, stomped him, then made some of the men drag him out of his sight to the top of the hill.

"*Lightning Rod,* uh, he, I…" Willie moans, his head throbbing.

"Don't you try using no words, son. No sir, you be still whiles I gets you a wet rag for that poor face of yorn. I gotta get you to Doc Ravensport soon's you can walk. You been out cold for hours, young'un. *Lighning's* fine, don't you worry none 'bout him. Whatcha doin' there, boy, you passing out on me again?"

Deep within the darkness, Willy hears a voice singing.

Danse Calinda, boudoum, boudoum.

Danse Calinda, boudoum, boudoum.

"Mam!" he shouts. "Mam, I got ya some frogs."

"Sha-hush, boy. Yer in our hands now. Old Big-Bob and me, we's getting you to the doctor quick as this wagon'll take us. There now, try keeping that rag on your face. Law, if you ain't a sight," Jedediah mutters.

"Mama, mama, mama, take me home! Daddy, where are you? Zeke?"

"Big-Bob, this boy's gone teched in the head, he has," Jedediah says. "Best to hurry this wagon along fast as it'll go."

CHAPTER
Thirty Seven

Doctor John

St. Louis, Missouri
1962

I squeeze a quarter of a lemon into my glass of iced tea. "But why do people think it's so special and magical?"

"It's steeped in superstition, Annie, and things like that get rooted in a culture and become as natural as breathing."

"Speak normally, please, for us peons."

Mercy laughs. "I am, you goose."

Mercy is spending the night with me to catch me up on everything she's been doing recently. She returned yesterday from New Orleans after a trip to Florida with her dad and grandpa to see where the *Freedom Riders* had stayed when they were there last year. Mercy loves anything to do with squashing injustice, and she said the *Freedom Riders* were the best kind of heroes. From what she's told me, I agree.

She said all they were trying to do was make it possible

for Colored people in the South to ride on buses or trains or streetcars and sit where they wanted to. They wanted the normal privileges of eating at a lunch counter or using a restroom like everybody else. I have no idea why they can't, and it was horrible learning what all happened to them. One man had fifty stitches on his head after Klan guys got hold of him.

She met a friend of her grandpa down there named Martin Luther King, Jr. She said he's the most wonderful, dedicated man she's ever met, and that surprised me she'd think he was the *most* anything since her family has so many special people in it.

A big rally was happening the next night, but her dad and grandpa wouldn't stay and let her attend it. They said she was too young for that kind of dangerous heroism. It made her so mad, she didn't speak to them the next day, just rode along in the back of that beautiful convertible of Grandpa Grafton's with her headscarf on and her nose in the air all the way to New Orleans. It was, she said, the first time she ever wished she wasn't obliged to anyone on this earth, not even her family.

"Someday, I'll join the fight and no one can stop me," she told me.

I believe her. I really do.

"Once we got to New Orleans, I saw shop after shop with windows crammed with the crazy candles and powders and whatnot like we saw that time in the New Awlins Candle and Magic Shop when we were in the fifth grade. They put fake human skulls and lots of black, white, and purple material in the shop windows."

"Tell me again what that *gris-gris* is used for."

"Pronounce it like *gree-gree*, Annie. Anyway, to understand it, you have to think about Vodou, black magic, spells, all that. Basically, it's a little bag stuffed with an assortment of things like herbs, stones, small animal bones, powders. I saw one advertisement saying their *gris-gris* bags had graveyard dust in them."

"No!"

"Yes."

"Remember the *gris-gris* that weird shop man gave you in your sack that day?"

"Sure. We opened it on the bus sitting in the very back seat. It had that little bird amulet, a tiny statue of Saint Peter, and a strip of paper saying Jesus and Doctor John would bring me good luck if I kept the bag under my pillow."

"That's spooky. What did you do with it?"

"What do you think? I put it under my pillow."

We both laugh, and I pour more tea into Mercy's glass.

"Then Mama found it when she was changing my bedsheets because I forgot to hide it that morning. She and Grandpa Grafton had a big talk with me that night about the dangers of messing with the black arts. They made me throw it in the fireplace."

"You never told me."

"I didn't think it was that important. I mean, I don't believe in any of it, so what was the point?"

"Who is that Doctor John guy, anyway? That little paper in your *gris-gris* bag said *Jesus and Doctor John*."

Mercy rubs her palms together like she has a great secret to share. "Well, while Daddy and Grandpa were in our hotel, the Royal Sonesta, having lunch, I said I wasn't hungry. Earlier, I had noticed a bookstore just down from the hotel, and I snuck down there and read about Doctor John. I kept hearing his name mentioned, saw some shops named after him, and I was curious. I remembered that slip of paper in the *gris-gris* bag from so long ago, too."

"Did you learn anything about him?"

She rolls her eyes. "Really, Annie, you know me well enough to know I'm always going to find what I go after."

I nod.

"Anyway, Doctor John, also called *Bayou John*, was a big deal in the Vodou world in the 1840s—a man of color, a witchdoctor who claimed to be a Senegalese prince. Apparently, his face was full of awful scars that he said his father, a king, had carved on him because it was a royal tradition in their country."

"Hmm. That's kind of hideous."

"I know. Anyway, Dr. John hated mixed-bloods for some reason. He owned slaves, but they had to be pure-blood Coloreds. He married lots of them and got so much money lifting curses and doing ceremonies that he built a house on Bayou Street. He sold *gris-gris,* conducted healings, did astrological readings. And, listen to this… wealthy White ladies wearing veils so they wouldn't be recognized came in droves wanting advice about lovers and love affairs. They bought little bottles of his very expensive concoctions to use for capturing beaus or leaving them or whatever they needed it to do."

"You know what?" Mercy smiles wickedly. "I'll bet it was nothing more than old swamp water in those vials. He was probably just one great salesman, you know? One book said his house was full of snakes, lizards, embalmed scorpions, animal skulls, and human skulls stolen from graveyards."

"That's just plain evil, Mercy."

"Yeah, I suppose so, but you have to admit… it's interesting!"

She giggles and slips out of the chair to sit cross-legged

on the floor of the screened-in porch. "I really like Thomas's house, Annie. It's nice. I love this porch, too. It's the best for keeping mosquitoes and June bugs away, but it's still like we're sitting outside. I wish our porch was screened in."

"I know. My brothers and me getting our own rooms was like a miracle, and Momma loves the kitchen. She cooks all the time now."

"Does she work with Thomas at the coffee shop?"

"She likes to go help sometimes when it's really busy before holidays and some weekends when there's special events in town. He's lets her do whatever she wants."

Mercy smiles and looks down at her hands. "There's something I never told you."

"What?"

"Mama's mother, my grandmother, lives in New Orleans, and Grandpa Grafton goes to see her a few times a year. That's why we went there after going to Tallahassee. Sometimes, Mama and I go with him, but he always goes off by himself. Other times, Mama takes Jerome instead of me. We see my grandmother for maybe a half an hour, that's it. Mama and her two brothers go occasionally. She's their mother, after all."

All I can do is stare at my friend. She smiles. "Anyway, the first day Grandpa's in New Orleans, he goes to see her by himself and stays all day and night. When we see her, it's the second day, and, as I said, we never stay long."

"But I thought she was dead. Are they divorced?"

"No, they just don't live together."

"Why not?"

"Mama says there are two reasons, and she won't tell me either one. One definitely has to be because my grandmother had a torrid affair with someone after she married my grandpa.

I mean, I'm not stupid. How else would Mama have a half-sister—my very own beautiful Aunt Viola?"

CHAPTER
Thirty Eight

Dearest Auntie Dove...

A Letter
May 1916

*D*earest *Auntie Dove and Uncle Jacque,*

I humbly apologize for not writing to you these past many months. It isn't because I don't think of you. You are in my thoughts each and every day in one way or another, and always in a most joyous and sentimental way. How I cherish the years of my youth spent with you!

I trust and pray you are doing well. It is hard to believe that I am soon to be eighteen! Of course, my dreams, as I expressed some time ago, of becoming a race jockey were dashed very soon after I left home. Foolish simpleton that I was, I didn't consider my height as a negative nor as a positive when planning my entire life at that rich age of fifteen! So many things I didn't consider, and isn't that the reality of a youngster planning his own bright future with the total experience of a field mouse? I have to stop and laugh at my own ignorance sometimes.

I am neither sad nor happy to announce that I am now six foot, two inches tall, and I may not be finished attaining height yet. I am taken by surprise that I am this tall, but perhaps it will serve me well in life. That, naturally, remains to be seen.

These past months have been very happy and quite unique. After leaving the Kingston-Farm Stables in Kentucky under rather precarious circumstances, some of which I will share with you when I return home, I found myself under the tutelage of a great man who was stern in the right and proper ways and lenient in others, much like you, Uncle Jacque.

I had a recuperation period after leaving Kentucky for reasons, as I said before, I shall share with you later. My recovery time continued the good part of a year. No, don't worry, I'm robust and healthy now. Afterward, the most extraordinary thing happened because of another slight mishap, and I shall explain it toward the end of this letter.

Let me take a few steps back and tell you about the renowned horse trainer who took me under his wing for no other reason than he is a good man, a man of ethics, and perhaps because he saw something in me that, though underdeveloped to the point of pitiful, was still something of good fabric. You will understand that, won't you, Auntie Dove, more than most? You always told me that when the smoke cleared, I would be standing there tall and dignified, made of fine cloth, and ready for any challenge life might bring to me.

Well, it took a while, but here I stand with none of the old demons of the past making me restless or dimwitted, which you never let me call myself, but it was true. I remember it as a kind of diminutive fog that came over me in the old days, a collapse into my own mind, even a darkness, and it led me down many paths of foolish uncertainty.

A confession: Remember that letter you promised I could read when I was a man, Auntie Dove? I must admit that I sneaked into your sewing basket, dug under the spools of thread, found it, and read it. Yes, I knew of your hiding spots, pernicious imp that I was! Please forgive me for my childhood nonsense.

Did the facts in that letter confuse and agitate me? Oh, my heavens, yes! I think they made me nearly idiotic for a while learning of my corrupted and superstitious past. Those truths written down for me were a great part of my decision to run away at age fifteen, and that's what I was doing... running.

Do not put your hand to your chest and swoon upon hearing these things, dear Auntie Dove. Please! I am more than over any ramifications from learning of how I was stolen at the tender age of five and lived for two years as the ward and substitute child of a Vodou priestess. Good Lord! Writing those words even now shocks me anew, yet somehow cleanses me even further.

From those times I know I gleaned gems of life I find both worthy and essential, for what is a man if not a totality of his experiences, good and bad, that constitutes what he is as he stands in the present, thereby always contributing to his total mind and spirit at any given time? I embrace that stormy past now, and I will spend the rest of my life paying homage to you dear guardians who took me in and gave me love and a solid foundation on which to stand.

I wish to describe to you another guardian with whom I have been so fortunately associated in the recent past. He is Mr. Benjamin Allyn Jones, Ben Jones, he goes by—a trainer of famous thoroughbred racehorses. You see, finding out I could never be a jockey was heartbreaking to my young soul, but I never realized how intrinsically more satisfying it was to train the magnificent horses of the track. Oh, Uncle Jacque, you won't believe the horses I have been privy to touch, to calm, to work with under Ben's watchful eye.

I have had a glorious time of it, and what do you suppose else happened to aid my future? Ben insisted that I continue my studies with a friend of his, an internationally known professor who happens, out of a passion for horses and the track, to invest in and to travel with our training team. I am proud to announce that I am completely ready for the university whenever I decide to attend. I am probably more than ready since I have had such disciplined and focused care. I'm certain you already suspected as much with my greatly improved vocabulary, Auntie Dove!

How hard you worked with me to drop my old patterns of Creole speech, and I know I was not always a willing student.

In the event you need to catch your breath and read about my finally rising to the high standards you set for me long ago, I'll wait, ha ha!

On to my other news, and in my heart, I believe this experience points vividly to the Divinity of God Himself and how our lives are but small shares of something so grand it is difficult to imagine. You see, all that has happened in the past few years, and even before then, led me down a path to a person from our past. I can't wait to tell you, so this is how it transpired.

A month ago, I traveled with Ben to North Carolina to meet with a horse owner recently moved over here from England. We dined in lavish style at the man's home, and yes, he made no difference about the color of my skin, nor does Ben—not at any time. Later, while viewing the man's fantastic cache of thoroughbred horses in his stables, an incident happened that is, actually, quite humorous and definitely providential.

As we walked throughout the paddock, a maverick wind stirred. A heavy door, partially open, was caught by the gust. It slammed closed, which, in turn, jiggled loose a bucket that happened to be hanging from a nail on the wall. The bucket, which contained special pellets for a certain horse, flew off the wall and struck me in the side as though it had been specifically aimed at me.

It was painful, but not really serious. Believe me, I have been horse kicked a hundred times more painfully than by a mere flying bucket. However, the gentleman insisted that I go to the St. Agnes Hospital, located nearby, a hospital and nursing school for Coloreds, to have my injury diagnosed. I protested, but Ben silently indicated that he wanted me to placate our new business client. Of course, I complied.

Now, you will never guess whom I encountered at that hospital! I believe you should drink something soothing before you read further. Perhaps a lemonade, Aunt Dovie, and a cognac, Uncle Jacque?

Are you ready?

I found myself being assisted by a kind Colored nurse I guessed to be in her mid-to-late twenties. She tended to me, but she kept glancing at me in an odd manner. The poor thing became quite beside herself, and, at last, she asked if I would be so kind as to show her the inside of my left wrist. I found that odd indeed, but noting her distress, I acquiesced. When I showed her the scar that I had gotten sometime before my memories allowed, she cried out and grabbed me in a tight hug. I truly didn't know what to do, it was so surprising. I submitted, but I must admit, I did so most awkwardly.

At last, she recovered enough to tell me that she was Isabelle, the girl who had saved me—"her Willy"—so many years ago from a village of Haitian Vodou followers. Thank God I already knew of those things from reading the secret letter, Auntie Dove, else I should have thought her completely mad.

As it was, we had a bit of a reunion. She explained that my wrist scar was the result of my tripping and breaking a jar of tadpoles I was carrying. Apparently, I fell onto the broken glass. It was a serious cut and occurred my first year in captivity. She also told me the terrible facts about that fateful night when she risked everything to steal us away from that hellish place deep in the swamps.

There was much crying, laughing, and raising of hands toward Heaven on her part. She said "Praise Jesus" and "Hallelujah" over and over in the most heartfelt manner. It was quite engaging and sweet, I admit. She said that you, Auntie Dove, are the reason she had the courage to become a nurse and to dedicate herself to the service of others. She sent you her love, and we promised to write one another.

And now I will tell you that I am coming home for a wonderful reunion with the two people I love most in the world. God willing, I shall be home in a few weeks, and we shall renew all that has happened with my dear brothers and their families since last I heard.

I will have other important news at that time, but for now, I remain…

forever your William
May 1916

CHAPTER
Thirty Nine

Wild Heart

Denton, Texas
1917

*A*rlene, sweet and frail, closes her eyes for the last time on a snow-covered day in February. Ruby doesn't cry, at least, not that Ernest ever sees. It feels like a knife in his heart watching the death harden the girl even more than she already is in small, unshared ways. How he would gather her to him to console, to share their grief as a family, but she will have none of it, won't even speak of her mama's passing. That hurts him almost more than losing his dear wife.

He has never felt like Ruby was truly theirs, whether it was the quick flame that ignited in her eyes when she was angry, or the fact that she wasn't his bloodline—only his whole heart— it didn't matter. Somehow, he knew early on that she would never be satisfied by the ebb and flow of an ordinary life.

The one thing he truly has in common with the girl is horses. Ruby takes to them as a retriever takes to sprinting after a fallen bird, and for that, he is grateful. Together, they have trained a multitude of horses for the surrounding ranchers, and even some from afar, after word of her gentling ways and horse sense spread. Now fourteen, Ruby has entwined Ernest's heart as surely as it beats in his chest, yet it beats with pain and pleasure both, never simply the joy of a doting father.

If only he knew more about her, this beloved, beautiful girl of his—who her parents were and why she questioned or balked at every rule he and Arlene ever gave her, no matter how trivial. He fears only life and its cruelties will chip away his daughter's sharp edges. Lord knows his praying and explaining, wishing and hoping hasn't changed anything. Truly, she harbors something wild he can't put his finger on, and it breaks his heart.

Jack never told them how he happened upon Ruby, how this girl came to be taken from another life and placed into his and Arlene's care. Jack doesn't come for his yearly visits anymore, but Ernest hears from him twice a year—in July and December. The letters always start with questions about how Ruby is faring, which Ernest thinks somewhat peculiar, but certainly a nice gesture.

He owes Jack more than he can ever repay. If not for him, he and Arlene wouldn't have had their precious Ruby. That would have an unbearable life spent only yearning for one thing—death's bony hand.

CHAPTER
Forty

Brief Forms

Trois Fontaines Restaurant, St. Louis, Missouri
1963

The white escargot shells arranged in a circle in the dish before me are striated with blond streaks. The steamed snails inside are covered over by a parsley garlic butter. The smell of garlic and the freshly baked loaf of French bread in the center of the table makes my mouth water as I wait for Mercy to stop conversing in French with the waiter. I take my hundredth sip from my crystal glass of ice water. Mercy flails her hands dramatically as she speaks. I tear off a hunk of bread and butter it lavishly. Taking a bite, I sigh loudly and turn pleading eyes on my best friend.

Mercy ends her conversation with the waiter and waits until we're alone.

"Good grief, you're impatient, Annie."

"Me? Look who couldn't wait five seconds while I tried on a few dresses at Famous-Barr's this morning."

"Well, I didn't like that prune-faced saleslady turning up her nose at us."

"She was old-fashioned and ridiculous, and I intended to ignore the old grouch. I really wanted to try on that navy-blue dress, the maroon and white one, too, but no, you had to start talking like a Southern Belle's waiting girl. 'Oh, yhas ma'am, missy Annie. Let me's take that dress offen the hanger, missy Annie. My, my, this dress shore-en will be purdy on you, honey-pie.' That was a horrible thing to do, Mercy. I was so embarrassed. God, it's too much."

"But, did you notice how she brightened up when she thought you had your own 'girl' to assist you—a little servant?" Mercy puts her head back and cackles.

I shoot up straight in the chair. "I'm sorry, but I don't find that funny at all. Your sense of humor sometimes is, well, it's off the wall. I've been playing catch-up for five years trying to be in your league. You've re-trained my speech patterns, ignited my fashion sense, made me read mountains of books, hauled me everywhere it was possible or impossible or feasible to go to *change my perspective,* you said… and that kind of belittlement nonsense you just pulled isn't amusing at all. In fact, it hurts."

I look away to hide the tears that spring into my eyes.

"Okay, okay. It's not your fault or mine that old habits die gradually for some people. I know there will always be intransigents who act like her. My way of handling it is to turn the tables and make a joke out of it even if they don't realize what's going on. In my demented sense of humor, it makes a joke out of them instead of us. That's all I was trying to do."

She makes a crazy face to lighten the mood. I dab at my eyes with the white cloth napkin.

"Let's eat our escargot before it gets cold," she says.

I stare at the food that looked so tempting earlier, but not so much now. "A lot of things are getting to me lately," I say.

"Which is why we're going to take that shorthand class together this coming year. High school sophomores... can you believe it?"

I know her tactics. She's changing the subject and trying to invest me in something interesting to make me cheer up.

Mercy the counselor.

"What does my being annoyed have to do with us taking shorthand this year?"

"Have you ever looked at that shorthand code? It's incredible! No one will ever be able to read our notes or lists or anything we write after we learn it. I skimmed through one of the textbooks in the library, and it's like learning a new language. We need something like that to learn together. My favorite thing about it are the brief forms."

"Brief forms?"

"Yeah, the whole shorthand thing is just a series of strokes representing how a word sounds phonetically, not using any of the silent letters in that word. Long words break down into a few strokes. For example, *trans* has its own little symbol, so *transit* is that symbol and a little circle attached to a slanted line underneath it. Then, there are those crafty little brief forms—they go even further. You memorize them because they are continually used in speaking or writing, and they consist of almost nothing. The word *government* is just two connected lines! Also, 'a' and 'an' are a mere dot raised above the line of the paper."

"I'm not sure I understand."

From her purse, Mercy pulls out a tiny notebook and a fancy gold ink pen with sparkling crystals on the pull-off top. Without even looking, she knows I'm staring at that pen. "Got this at the Eiffel Tower last year. It's actually your gift, and I forgot to give it to you."

She makes a dot a little above the pale blue line on one of the pages of her miniature notebook paper. She flips the book around so I can see it.

"That's it. That little period represents 'a' or 'an' when it's above the line. Isn't that something? One more I remembered so I could show you is a slightly curved line to the left that stands for 'be' or 'by'. Think of the time saved when we're taking notes in class," she says, drawing the symbol on her pad. She flips it around for me to see. "What do you think?"

I stare at the marks. "I think I'm ready to sign up for the class this very second."

Mercy chuckles under her breath. She did it again, and she knows it. She took me out of my mood and got me excited about a new plan. She puts the cap back on the pen and hands it to me. "Take it. I have one just like it at home. It's yours."

I smile and put it in my purse. I spear an escargot with my snail fork and dip it in the melted butter, blot it on a piece of bread. Thoughts swirl inside my mind as we eat daintily, which is how Mercy insists we eat in fancy restaurants. "You know, I like that name *brief forms*. I think it's symbolic of our lives."

"How so?" Mercy asks.

"I'll be putting it together as I talk, so bear with me. It just hit me, and I think I know what I mean. See, we are born on this earth through no fault of our own, right? We get the family, the station in life, even the color of our hair, eyes, and skin through nothing we've done or contributed to. It merely… is."

"That's right."

"Later on, we can take our talents and improve them and use them to attain success, but there is nothing we can do about how and why we're here in the first place. We are forms, or lines, surviving and living. Though we may be forms or, should I say, breaths?... we are always so much more than what we look like or what people see when they glance at us, or even when they talk to us.

"Just like those brief form characters, the one or two strokes you see on the paper may stand for ten more strokes below the surface. You see some lines, but what is the actual word they represent?"

I dip a small chunk of bread in my melted escargot butter and pop it in my mouth. "Then, too, we are here in this world for a brief time, and then we are gone. We, us... we're the brief forms of this life, Mercy."

Mercy takes a long drink of water, pats her lips with a napkin. "Annie, I... uh, girl..." She looks down.

"What?"

She shakes her head. "That may be one of the deepest things I've ever heard."

I sigh. "You see what you've done to me? I'm not normal anymore because of you."

"What did I do?"

"You took this little twig of a country girl and chiseled the *backwoods* off her. I'm afraid you've carved me into a dadgum philosopher."

"Dadgum?"

"Sure. I'm not giving up all my old country-bumpkin ways, Mercy."

CHAPTER
Forty One

To War?

Aboard the Panama Limited Train to Chicago
1917

Scenery passing in green and brown steaks outside the train window between New Orleans and Memphis goes unnoticed by Auntie Dove. She absently rubs a finger over the locket lying open in her lap. One side of the locket holds a picture of a young man in a uniform, the other side, a photo of a young boy.

"S'cuse me, ma'am. You need anything before we pull into the next station?"

She doesn't look up. "No, thank you."

"I, uh, have this extra pillow, ma'am. I could leave it with you for your comfort."

Auntie Dove glances at the Pullman porter, a Colored man dressed in white tunic and black trousers. He smiles. She smiles back, and without warning, starts to cry. She drops her head and picks up her purse to retrieve a handkerchief. She dabs at her eyes and nose, aware that the man is still standing beside her day seat.

"Begging your pardon, ma'am, but can I bring you a cold drink of water, or maybe some lemonade?"

She doesn't look up. "Water would be nice, thank you."

The man hurries down the aisle after softly dropping the extra pillow in the seat beside her. She scolds herself for letting her emotions spill over, and publicly, too. That is against the strict protocol of her upbringing. Why did that child, well, young man now—her Willy—evoke such raw emotion in her?

It had been true ever since he was left in her and Jacque's care more than twelve years ago. All of the boys they had taken in had been, and were presently, as loved as though she had borne them herself, including Willy. Somehow, though, deeper emotions overtook her when it came to him. His actions or moods created a sensitivity in her that rendered her as vulnerable as a blanket of fresh snow on a sunny day.

Perhaps it was the fact that his past was so truly shocking. Stolen on a dark summer night? Kept as an icon, a symbol, of another child... never left to be a normal little boy for two years and perhaps witnessing every kind of evil behavior? Uprooted yet again and added to a whole new family? All those events had left the poor little boy emotionally wounded, and his pain elicited Auntie Dove's most protective maternal feelings—feelings that were as real and tender as was physical injury.

When Willy came home from his horse training adventures last year, she was ecstatic. There he was, her young man, her last child, so fine and educated, tall and handsome, with a radiant smile that lit up any room. How wonderful had been their time together reflecting on the best experiences when he was young, catching up on the ones in which he had been gone from her, and discussing subjects of world importance, even academic matters. No mother could have been prouder than she!

Alas, her joy was short lived, for the other news he had referenced in his letter in May of last year had, when revealed, left her breathless with panic. He waited a week into his return to tell her and Jacque. Now she understood why he had sidestepped any questions about further studies at the university. When she discovered the nature of his future plans, she had pleaded with him, teased him, offered him alternatives to his choices, as had Jacque, but Willy was not to be dissuaded. His visit with them consisted of a mere two weeks. Afterward, he left for New York to join the 369th Infantry Regiment, a regiment of Colored men who had their hearts set on serving in the United States military.

That was frightful enough for the poor woman, but when President Wilson declared war against Germany in April of this present year, it was pure anguish. Willy's infantry was called into Federal service a few months later at Camp Whitman, where he said the men learned formal military practices.

In a letter, he told her there was much *inside chatter* that the men would be relieved of their "lady" duties of guarding construction sites, rail lines, and other camps throughout New York and might be traveling to Camp Wadsworth in South Carolina to receive authentic combat training. More talk suggested the men were likely to be shipped to France to fight the Germans.

Oh, his delight! Each word of his lengthy explanation in his letter pierced more deeply Auntie Dove's wellbeing. Her Willy engaged in war? Would he ever return to her?

Without a heart's beat of delay, she had made her plans to travel to Chicago, by way of New Orleans on the Panama

Limited, and, from there, to New York on the Twentieth-Century Limited to see her son.

God help her... her favorite son.

CHAPTER
Forty Two

A Mane of Golden Curls

Magnolia Manor, San Antonio, Texas
1918

Her beguiling, deep southern accent, her beautiful sapphire eyes, that mane of golden curls... Joseph can barely keep his eyes off the young lady accompanying her parents to Jack and Selene's home, now known to all as Magnolia Manor, that crisp afternoon in November. Home from the university for the holiday, he had dreaded the annual gathering of the high-brow families of San Antonio to celebrate Thanksgiving.

If not for the fantastic news that the horrendous war had ended merely weeks before in Europe, he might have begged off this year with one lame excuse or another and stayed in his room at Harvard's Claverly Hall. No one was staying this holiday with that kind of news in the air, but he had longed for the solitude.

Thank God I didn't, he thinks as he watches the angelic girl engage in sporadic conversation, sip hot cinnamon cider from a china cup, delicately gather her shawl about her shoulders as she glides between her parents on the now-brown lawns of the immense front yard.

Oh, how his younger brothers try to hide their stolen glances at her, especially fourteen-year-old Jonathan. *Was I ever that obvious and clumsy?* Joseph muses as he views the maneuvers of his brothers. First… Jonathan, now Michael, and even five-year-old Stephen making excuses to crisscross in front of her or step aside quickly as she passes.

After discussing his wishes with his mother, he knows, despite there being many other eager *stallions* at the gathering, he is the one who will be seated beside Julie at the long dinner table when the outdoors socializing moves inside.

Not that he's avoiding most of his other friends right now, both male and female. He isn't, but he knows beyond a shadow of a doubt he had to quickly gain the advantage when it came to that ravishing vision of a woman he has been eyeing; ergo, the first step being the upcoming seating arrangement. Otherwise, he knows his debonair, wealthy friends will trail her like bird dogs on a first-day hunt. He sees them plotting from the sidelines even as he is doing the same.

"Joseph!" calls a familiar voice behind him. He turns slowly.

"We ladies have been trying to get your attention for ever so long. Won't you come join us over by the smoke pit? We're all dying to know how you're faring as a college man. From the looks of you, I'd say you are faring very well," says a young woman with tight brown curls capping her head. Her batting eyelashes and thin tight lips when she finishes talking sends a wave of disgusted panic coursing through Joseph.

Doris.

That female has been trying to harness him since he was

paired as her escort in a series of etiquette classes their mothers put them in when they were ten. From that time forward, she has acted like she owns him, even telling her girlfriends she and Joseph will marry when he finishes his education, and they will have at least five children! It was this kind of gossip among the giddy socialite females of San Antonio that propelled him out the door to the university last year, much to his parents' relief.

"Oh, hello, Doris. I, uh, promised Mother I'd oversee the pouring of the dinner wine. I-I'll try to get over there after that."

"Of course, Joseph. I'll be waiting, dearest."

Joseph hurries toward the house shaking his head. When the time comes for a woman in his life, it will be his choice, his way. But for now, a glass of sherry awaits as he anticipates the summon of the dinner bell on this now most stupendous Thanksgiving Day.

CHAPTER
Forty Three

The Visit

Denton, Texas
1919

uby pours more cream in her mug of coffee, stirs it, stares sullenly out the sheer-curtained kitchen window as dawn drags the sun up over the horizon.

"Penny for your thoughts?" Ernest says.

"Don't waste your money," she snaps, then, seeing his face, adds, "I mean, I'm just thinking about those yearlings we put in the back pasture Tuesday. I thought I'd ride Galahad over today and check on them."

"Well, you just go right ahead and do that, honey. I'd appreciate it, and I'm sure they will too. By the way, Mr. Carlton sent word that stallion of his is acting like a puppy dog since you been working with him. You want to ride over to his place with me and check on him later... say around two?"

"I guess. Yeah, that's fine."

She sighs loudly, walks over to the sink. She takes the cloth dishrag and holds it under the pump to wet it, then wipes off the tops of her boots, something she would never do if her mother were still alive. She knows Arlene didn't allow boot cleaning or fish gutting around her kitchen sink. Ernest watches Ruby in his peripheral vision, feeling the customary uneasiness flickering in his belly.

Outside, the dogs start barking their *visitors-are-coming* bark. Ruby and Ernest step into the living room and peer around curtains. A rather large car with white on the wheels and a covered top with open sides drives up the lane and parks out front beside the blooming redbud tree. Ernest cries, "Jack!" and moves quicker through the front door and over the porch than Ruby has seen him move in a long time.

Is this the mysterious Jack that Ruby has heard so many stories about?

She eases out the door and wraps an arm around one of the porch poles. The man stepping from the car is dressed in store-bought finery the likes of which she has never seen before. She suppresses a chuckle as he bends to retrieve a jacket that matches his loose city slacks and takes care putting it on and smoothing out any wrinkles. He reaches into the back seat and brings out the strangest hat, nothing like the cowboy hats all the males in her part of the world wears. He dons the hat with a flair.

"Jack, you old son-of-a-gun! What brings you to our neck of the woods?" Ernest exclaims, quick-stepping to greet his old friend. The two of them shake hands with gusto, embrace enthusiastically, and shake hands again, grinning so big their faces look like they might slide off into the dust.

"Why didn't you let me know you were a'coming? I'd've put the big pot in the little pot, if you know what I mean!"

"Aw, I didn't want to put you to any trouble. Had to try out my new Maxwell 25 touring car, and I thought why in the blue blazes don't I drive myself up to Denton to see Ernest and Ruby as a test to see if this thing has any loose screws."

"Well, does it?"

"Nah, drives like a blue-ribbon thoroughbred and gets the best fuel mileage you can imagine. Built to last and fun to drive. It certainly outdoes the old days when it took days to get here on horseback, but, honestly, nothing beats the squeak of the saddle on a fine horse and a long trail to ride, you know?"

"I hear what you're saying, Jack, I shore do. When did you head up our way?"

"I left early the day before yesterday, spent the night in Dallas, and here I am."

"Well, um, I gotta ask… what in the tarnation are you wearing, son?"

Jack grins mischievously. "What? You don't like my summer sack suit?"

"Sack suit? Hell's bells, why didn't you just get yourself a gunny sack and cut some holes in it?" Ernest laughs heartily, and it's the first time he's done so in a very long time.

"Hey now, I'm quite the fashionable gentleman these days, old friend. Have to look good driving a touring car and sporting around my fancy woman, don't you know?"

"But that hat…"

"It's called a straw boater hat. Latest thing." Jack does a little turn around.

Ernest stands with his feet apart, arms crossed, shakes his head with amusement playing on his features. Ruby isn't used to see her dad so pleasantly engaged.

"So, how have you been, Ernest? I'm awful sorry about Arlene."

Ernest drops his head. "It was rough, Jack, I'm not going to lie, but the Good Lord knows best, I reckon."

Jack and Ernest are quiet for a short time. Ruby becomes aware of Jack peeking at her around her dad's shoulders.

"Can that beautiful young lady be Ruby?"

Both of the men now turning to stare at her makes her one nickel short of giving them a tongue lashing, but she holds herself in. She dons a demure smile and watches them climb the three steps up to the porch. The closer Jack gets, the more his eyes widen. As soon as the introductions are over, Ernest says, "Come on inside and have some coffee, Jack. It's strong and black like you always like it. Ruby, honey, would you get us some of that good sorghum cake you made yesterday?"

Ruby does the cooking for one reason… Ernest is terrible at it, and they would starve, she thinks, if it was left up to him for long. She does enjoy eating, so it's an act of survival, nothing else.

Once inside, Jack twists his head looking all around. "When did you build this new house, Ernest?"

"Aw, I guess when Ruby was about four or five years old. I was so proud of her and the missus, I figured I'd make them a better place to fix up."

"It's sure nice, and it has Arlene's touch everywhere, doesn't it?"

Ernest nods, steals a glance at Ruby. The look on her face is unsettling. Not a speck of love or a sense of belonging does he see. Without a word, she walks out the door. He knows she's gone to saddle her horse, but couldn't she at least try to act like she's part of a family that has loved her unquestionably and asked for nothing in return?

Embarrassed by Ruby's brusque behavior, he says, "Bring your coffee mug, Jack, and I'll show you the place. Lots of changes since you were here last. Got another new horse for Ruby the other day—a quarter-horse sorrel. She's an expert horsewoman, you know."

"Is she now? Well, isn't that fine! Say, where did she run off to so fast?"

"She's about to go check on some of our cows near the old Skilley place. She pretty much sticks to herself. Always has."

The men make small talk walking around the sheds and horse stables. With Galahad saddled and waiting for her inside the east corral, Ruby wonders if she'll be cooking for two or three people for supper and, already mad about it, decides to ask. She walks soundlessly up behind the men as they lean into the corral boards conversing.

"I should have told you the truth about Ruby's mother before, but there are many circumstances. Trust me, it's a hell of a story."

"Sounds like we need to have a seat, Jack. Let's go sit in the barn."

Ruby freezes. Her mother? Why would Jack know anything about her real mother? Does he also know why she was given to Ernest and Arlene sixteen years ago?

CHAPTER
Forty Four

The Power of the Pen

Forest Park, St. Louis
1964

As long as I've known Mercy, she's never been in trouble with her parents. Oh, a little for having that Vodou *gris-gris* stuff when her mama found it under her pillow, but not too bad. That's why I don't know what to do now that she's crying like this. I've brought her water from the drinking fountain in a little collapsible cup I carry in my purse, a device she endlessly teases me about. I walked on a parapet next to the park bench doing my best Charlie Chaplin side-to-side walk. I didn't even get a smile.

"Hey, let's go see *Marnie*, that new Alfred Hitchcock movie. Sean Connery's in it… you know you can't resist him. And, did you know the Beatles are coming out with a movie? Couldn't you still just die we got to see them live at Carnegie Hall this past February? Boy, I still can't believe the strings your grandpa and my step-dad pulled for us to get in.

Remember how all the girls at school were so jealous?"

"Oh, Lord, Annie, don't you know you can't use my own tactics on me?"

"Why, whatever do you mean, Miss Mercy?" I ask in a feigned southern accent.

"You know what I mean—bringing up stuff so interesting it doesn't let me wallow in my own misery."

"You mean I can't *con a con man?*"

In spite of herself, Mercy smiles. "Something like that."

"Well, honestly, Mercy I don't understand why you're so upset. You know your parents will get over what we did. Momma already has."

"It's not that."

"What then?"

"Anger, Annie. I'm so mad that I'm too young to jump in with both feet, and furious that Black people in St. Augustine, Florida, are being treated so bad. I'm crying out of frustration."

I plop down on the park bench beside Mercy.

"I know it's bad, but we did something and not nothing, right? Isn't that what we heard over and over at the rally? How many sixteen-year olds secretly hop a bus to Florida to join in a Dr. King march? I mean, yeah, we both got in hot water later, but I think it was worth it. Gosh, when he was speaking at the church rally, I thought I'd die with, uh, I don't know... excitement and something else. Actually, I think it was pride. I was so proud of him and the others and what they're trying to do for everyone, especially the Coloreds.

"Don't say Coloreds anymore, Annie. Say Blacks."

"Oh, yeah, I forgot. Anyway, as long as I live, I won't forget following him as we made our way downtown to the *Plaza de la Constitucion.*"

Mercy jumps off the bench and plants her feet. "That's what I'm talking about. I want to do a lot more. You remember those two girls our same age, sixteen, who were arrested in that Woolworth lunch counter sit-in and sent to a so-called reform school for six months? My eye! It was more like jail. *The St. Augustine Four.* I would give my right arm to be part of something that important."

Mercy stares up at the afternoon sky with clenched fists.

"It *is* infuriating, and it makes no sense," I say. "I'm glad we live in St. Louis. It's better here than lots of other places. Thank goodness we have people of all races joining in to try and stop this crap."

"Annie, don't say crap. It's socially low."

I stand up, frowning at my friend. "Are you really going to correct my language when I'm lost in a moment of passion and compassion about the subject of equality?"

"Yes, I am."

We stare at each other for a few moments and break out laughing. We laugh so hard we struggle to catch our breaths. A small wheeze comes out of me, then several more.

"Hey, I thought you'd outgrown that asthma."

"It comes back sometimes when I laugh too hard and long. Stop changing the subject. I want to talk about that woman, the mother of the governor of Massachusetts. What was her name?"

"Mary Parkman Peabody."

"Right. You'd think her arrest in an integrated protest group would turn the tables on those disgusting Klan guys. I swear, those guys aren't even human."

"Well, her doing it brought international attention to the movement, so, yes, it helped a lot. Hey, did I ever tell you how many Black people here in St. Louis were also against school desegregation at first?"

"Why?"

"I guess it's the flipside of the *separate-but-equal* ruling. Previously, some of it was because of in the *Ville,* we have our own schools, hospitals, and banks, and some people felt those institutions were great the way they were so why mess with them?"

"Interesting."

We sit there a few minutes not talking. I'm relieved Mercy has calmed down.

"I thought you were crying your eyes out a while ago because your parents came down on you too hard. I mean, I know you cry when you're too mad to do anything else, but this seemed like it was more than that."

Mercy sighs and leans forward with her elbows on her legs. "It's Grandpa Grafton… he's against my joining protests or being physically involved now, or even when I'm older. He's a real peacenik these days. Funny how old people forget how important certain things are to the younger generation. He, uh, wants me to write articles and books and enlighten people. He thinks the real reform comes from the power of the pen. Now, isn't that a big deal? Guess I ought to go join the beatniks in New York City and spout poetry in the park. Maybe he'd like that."

"I can just picture that," I chuckle. "The truth is, none of us want to see you get hurt or put in jail, Mercy. What's wrong with fighting the good fight from a distance?"

Mercy smiles an odd smile at me, and I don't miss the hint of condescension that flits briefly across her features. That one second feels like the biggest separation between us in all our years as best friends, and it blows a cold wind through my soul.

CHAPTER
Forty Five

Simon St. Clair

New Orleans, Louisiana
1919

illy pulls the folded paper from his pocket and reads it, then glances at the houses along the narrow street. The structures on either side, wide and imposing, are in a state of architectural decrepitude—a collection of homes, both low slung or three-stories high with rusted balconies and peeling shutters, which money has previously built and polished, but where time and neglect have now assaulted and withered.

Upon each home seems to reside a decaying ghost, grinning broadly, declaring what has been shall never be again. The sinister spirit permeates the stucco and brick walls and the bleached, corrugated red-tile roofs and drifts onto the dusty leaves of the foliage lining the street, there to linger as nonchalantly as a lounging lady of a defunct royal court.

At a residence fronted with an enclosed carriage porch, a *porte-cochère,* Willy spies the numbers 3737 on a rust-eaten nameplate partly obscured by dark green ivy vines. He pushes on the slightly open wicket, steps through, and gasps as he beholds a thriving parterre in a most intricate pattern at the far end of a wide bricked courtyard. The pavement below him leads to a carriage house on the right, circles the formal garden in front of him, and goes left in two paths—one to the door of a palatial home; the other to a lavish open-air veranda.

How can this marvel of an estate even exist behind the decrepit face displayed to anyone passing by on the street?

Finding himself literally beguiled, and hearing the melodious sound of splashing water, Willy walks slowly toward the veranda with its Greco-Roman arches and pillars. The interior of the enclosure has an open-diamond shape formed by low, well-pruned shrubs. A layer of flourishing rose bushes stands taller behind the flat-topped shrubs. A gently bubbling fountain in the center exudes an air of opulent peace. He turns unhurriedly in a circle. The entire courtyard is decorated with strategically and proudly planted pomegranate, fig and banana trees, palms, blossom-laden crape myrtles, blooming jasmine, and lush green grasses.

He checks the piece of paper to affirm he is at the correct residence.

In all my searching, I found only one Simon St. Clair in this part of Louisiana. Can he truly be my father?

"Sir! May I ask what business you have here?" states a deep voice to his right.

Willy spins and sees a man, not old, but certainly not young—a tall, lean, graying man with an air of dignity matching the beauty of the residence and grounds.

"I-I, well… the wicket was ajar, sir, and I, please excuse me, showed myself in."

"Ajar, you say?"

"Yes sir."

"Blast that Benny's hide! He's getting too old, that's his sin."

At the look of puzzlement on Willy's face, the man says, "My manservant. Benny's been with me since I was a boy. He can't see, can't hear, and he forgets everything before he even knows it."

Willy begins to relax. "Yes sir. Uh, he or someone does a grand job as your gardener, I must say. I've never seen more beautifully kept grounds."

"My rascal Benny keep these grounds?" The man puts his head back and laughs a rich, hearty laugh. "No, young man, I am the gardener and groundskeeper for Florentine Estate. Merely me. In fact, if you had come an hour earlier, you would have caught me, alas, in my soiled gardening clothes."

"You do all this, sir? Why, it's a great deal for one man, especially of, of… your station."

"Perhaps, but it is my salvation." He casts his eyes around them. "A medicine sorely needed for my wounds." He nods, unsmiling, as if confirming something important to himself. He turns to face Willy, sticks out his hand.

"I am Simon William St. Clair, born and reared in this city, a son and grandson of a freeman and a freeman my whole life. A man of many sorrows and many stories."

Simon *William* St. Clair.

Willy silent absorbs the man's middle name and shakes the hand offered to him. The two men are of the same height, which is six feet and four inches.

"I am William Boyer of Baton Rouge. Pleased to make your acquaintance, sir."

"Likewise, William. To what may I attribute your social call today?"

"Sir, if we could perhaps sit somewhere for the briefest time, I would like to speak with you about a matter concerning my very life."

"Your very life, you say?" Simon rubs his chin and looks thoughtful. He's enjoying the young man and wishes to drag out the visit as long as possible. "Well, now, that seems a weighty matter. If you will step into the veranda…" he nods his head to the left "… just beyond the jasmine, you will see a small table and chairs. Pardon me while I fetch Rema to bring us some refreshments."

"Please, don't go to any trouble, sir."

Simon waves a hand in the air and proceeds to walk the brick pathway leading toward the entry of the house. About twelve feet from the massive double doors, the path is inlaid with marble tiles in the design of a spectacular peacock. A dark blue awning stretches out past the marble entry.

Willy walks trancelike to the afore-mentioned place of seating, his breath coming in shallow rasps, his mind consumed with how the entire faded façade along the street showed nothing of the grandeur inside the walls. Might there be a mistake about this man Simon being the Simon he is looking for? What if Isabelle made up those stories she penned about his youth so long ago and borrowed the name of an established, wealthy businessman to use as his father? Would she commit such a folly? If so, why? What if—"

"I see you have found my favorite spot. I do so love sitting here and enjoying the smell of the jasmine."

For the second time since he entered this unreal world, Willy has been startled by Simon's voice. "It's very beautiful, sir. Easy to see why you enjoy it so much."

Simon settles into a chair and offers a cigar to Willy, who shakes his head. Simon trims the cap, lights it, blows out a cloud of smoke.

"Please excuse my bad manners, but the older a man gets, the more outspoken he becomes." Simon takes another draw. "You see, I noticed you have a slight limp, and it has aroused my curiosity. Would you mind indulging an old man?"

Willie lets out his breath slowly and smiles. He is glad to delay his true purpose for the visit, which will undoubtedly be awkward in some or several, ways.

"Not at all, sir. I got in a little trouble during the *Meuse-Argonne offensive* in Lachalade."

"Lachalade?"

"Yes sir. The Forest of Argonne in France. I was part of the Harlem Hellfighters, the 369th, an all-Colored Infantry. We shipped out December 1917, and returned February of this year to the New York Port of Embarkation."

Simon clasps his hands together. "I heard of the parade for the 369th Infantry when they returned from Europe."

"Yes, thanks to our Colonel Hayward. He saw to it we had that honor. This..." he points to his leg "... caused an early release for me. It had been my desire to serve a few more years, maybe even make it a career. My fellow soldiers who stayed are being reassigned as part of the National Guard again."

Simon shakes his head in wonder. "Young man, William... I have never had the honor of meeting someone of our race who served in that war. Would you mind letting me shake your hand again?"

The two men stand and shake hands vigorously over the top of the small table, grinning profusely. They sit. Simon says, "The Hellfighters, you say? You know, we were all cheering and praying for you brave men. Not the whole world, of course, because it wasn't well known, but many of us. I'm very proud of you all. You know, son, I ache to hear a little about the action. Is it true what I heard, that the French soldiers were eager to have you there?"

"Oh, yes, sir. They treated us most kindly. We wore their helmets and used their gear, but we proudly wore our own uniforms from America. You know, we called ourselves the *Men of Bronze*."

"That's dandy, isn't it?" Simon's eyes are luminous. He leans forward to hear more.

"That Second Battle of the Marne… you may have heard about it, we had terrible losses, but our Allied counteroffensive was incredible indeed. Together, we whipped a bunch of air out of those German shirts, yes sir we did!"

Simon sits back in his chair smiling.

"Unfortunately, we sustained even heavier losses during the American drive in the *Meuse-Argonne,* but our unit captured the village of *Séchault,* which, thankfully, was an important victory. That's where I received…" Willy touches his thigh "… this."

Simon looks down at Willy's leg, then straight into his face. The admiration in his eyes almost startles the young man. The afternoon breeze wafts around the pillars, gently curling the leaves of the foliage surrounding them. Rema, a matronly Colored woman in bright, cheerful clothing brings a tray with a pitcher of lemonade, two glasses, a small jewel-encrusted bucket with tongs, and cookies. Willy watches her serving the glasses with chipped ice and wonders when the appropriate time will present itself to broach the subject most on his mind. Perhaps now? He clears his throat.

"Uh, Mr. St. Clair, sir, if I may venture to be somewhat curious myself, do you abide in this beautiful estate with your missus and children?"

The momentary darkness that crosses Simon's face is chilling. Simon doesn't speak for a time, just stares at the fountain, and then down at his hands. "No, lad. There is none but me to loll around this museum of my life and wrestle with the ghosts of regret."

So sad is the tone in Simon's voice, Willy feels he has trespassed onto a private matter that shouldn't be trod upon. Perhaps he shouldn't have come at all. Is his mother alive? His brothers and sisters?

Simon sits up straight, back not touching the back of the chair, and looks at Willy. "I had a son once, William, and two families. What's that… you wonder how I had more than one family? Well, you're a good man, and you've served our country at risk of death, injured in the cause, so I think I feel like telling you all about it. Would you have some time to sit with an old man this afternoon?"

Bewilderment and pain lie ahead, perhaps even anger. Old wounds shall open. Willy knows all those feelings are possible. Yet, he cannot miss this opportunity, this unsealing of the mystery of his life. He returns Simon's solemn gaze.

"I have all the time you need."

CHAPTER
Forty Six

The Truth

Denton, Texas
1919

Ruby knows if she wiggles so much as a toe, she risks a flurry of loose hay falling between the wide-spaced board flooring high above Ernest and Jack. She never met Jack before today, but she always felt a curious air fill the room when his letters arrived or when her parents mentioned him in any context. Whispering, yes, she had caught her parents whispering on the subject of Jack more than once. Less than ten minutes before, she had overheard him talking to Ernest about her real mother, and now she is bound to hear what he has to say.

She had backed quietly away from the men at the corral and hid quickly behind a mesquite tree on the side of the chicken house. She watched them make their way to the barn. Once they entered the barn, she took the back stairs on the outside of the barn leading to the loft and swiftly wiggled over the floor to her spying position just as the men sat on two hay bales facing one another.

She had heard the stories of when her dad and Jack were young and galloped the plains and mountains as Texas Rangers. They had seemed closer than brothers back then, and she found it peculiar that Jack stopped coming to see Ernest sixteen years ago. Not that she really cared, but it did hold a bit of interest when barely anything in her life—save for horses—did. Her dad told her Jack used to come see him and Arlene every year, sometimes twice.

In July and December, they received a letter from him. He always started the letters asking if Ruby was faring well before writing the latest news of his beloved wife, the stunning log manor they built close to the San Antonio River, and of his growing family of sons. She wondered why he specifically asked about her at the beginning of each letter, and why he would care anything about how she, Ruby, was faring.

She presses her ear close to a floor crack to listen and wills herself not to itch or make a sound. She's used to exercising self-discipline when she works with horses. The slightest movements or gestures can spook a wild or sensitive horse, and she has always had all the right instincts and maneuvers to quiet them and make them trust her. The wilder and more ferocious they are, the more she likes working with them. She calls now upon that discipline so as to silently eavesdrop on the men's conversation.

"She's exquisite, Ernest. I thought I was seeing her mother Selene, but with blue eyes. They look like sisters. What an extravagant beauty she has grown up to be!"

"Jack... you kept in touch with Ruby's mother?"

Jack looks down at his interlaced fingers. "I married her, Ernest."

Ruby almost screams in surprise. Ernest stands, his body

askew. "You married her? When? How did that happen?"

"It just did, my friend. I met Selene, her son, and her baby daughter in the St. Charles Hotel in New Orleans. They were on the run from a most horrible character, a Bradford Livingston, who had beaten Selene and had every intention of sending her son upriver and selling her daughter to a ship merchant to re-sell on the international open market. Dreadful how that nasty business still happens on the high seas."

Jack stands abruptly, puts his hands in his pockets, strides back and forth. Ernest slowly sits back down on the bale of hay and studies him.

"You see, the most extraordinary thing happened when that vision of a woman, my Selene, told me of her plight, how she had been the, uh, *charge* of a wealthy businessman in New Orleans. They had two children... Joseph, whom I have raised as my own son, and Monique, whom you renamed Ruby. When the older gentleman—Mr. Livingston—died, his son... oh, that most pernicious beast! How I have wanted to return to New Orleans to, well... anyway, that creature took it upon himself to obliterate all traces of his father's life with Selene."

Ruby's heart thumps wildly. Will the men below hear it? Dizzy, angry, she commands herself to be still.

"Selene was terrified he would find her wherever she went, he being of high wealth and family connections, as well as having political aspirations. A wicked man perfectly suited for politics, I should add."

"Jack, I, uh, hold on. Your wife... Ruby's mother was the, um, girlfriend of a rich man in New Orleans who died, but they had two children together?"

"Oh, look, Ernest, I know how it sounds to our puritanical senses, but in the deep South, especially in that particular city, prejudices are stilted... deep tracked. Going back for centuries."

"Prejudices?"

"That's right. And what is a young lady to do if the cards are already stacked against her the moment she takes her first breath, and because of what? Foolishness! It is common in New Orleans for such a woman to have a… a benefactor… a guardian, especially when said woman looks anything like my wife."

"I'm sorry, Jack, I don't follow you."

Jack sighs. "It's not like in the West where men and women are taken at face value—not judged for some drop of something running through their veins."

Ernest scratches his head. "I guess I'm dense, old friend, because I still don't know what you're getting at."

"Selene, my wife, had a full-blooded Colored grandmother. A slave. That makes my wife what they call in the South a *quadroon,* but we don't use those words in our household. In fact, the children only know they have the most kind and beautiful mother in the world. It matters nothing to me if they ever know or think anything more."

"So that makes Ruby, uh, what?"

How dare anyone classify me? thinks Ruby far above them, holding her breath for Jack's answer.

"It makes her one-eighth Colored, Jack. What some would deem an *octoroon* in those rigged southern societies back there. Hell, man, who knows what blood runs through our own bodies? I always heard I had a Choctaw grandfather, but who's around to prove it or even care? What difference can it make to our humanity, our lives?"

Jack's face is angry as he paces back and forth with his hands laced behind him. "Because she had folks on both sides, that is, former slaves on one and wealthy White people on the other, Selene had an abnormal fear of bondage… of not being in control of her own destiny. She begged me to help her hide her precious baby girl, even though it was a shattering tragedy to her. So great was her fear of enslavement for Monique, uh, Ruby, that no amount of persuasion convinced her I was capable of protecting all of them. Ernest… that's when I thought of you and Arlene."

Ernest is silent. Bent forward, one hand over his mouth, he watches Jack with red-rimmed eyes.

"I know it sounds ludicrous, but I fell in love with Selene the very night I met her. I would gladly have walked around the earth as many times as she asked, but safety for her family was all she wanted. She has been a flawless asset to my life, Ernest, and I pray you will forgive us for not telling you the whole story before now. She swore me to secrecy, and as I said before, her every wish has been my sole desire since I first beheld her."

Ernest's voice is shaky as he asks, "Why now?"

"Unfortunately, Selene has not been of the best of health the last few years. Oh, not to worry. We believe some time away from Texas might be helpful since the doctors speculate it's the damp greenery and living in such close proximity to the river that may be the root of her problems. She has been turning ill when the weather warms every spring, fully recovering after the first norther hits.

"We're planning a sojourn to the French Riviera to spend some time as a test for my wife's health. The coast, we hear, has been the answer for many ailing folks. For the first time, Selene urged me to come here and share the whole story of Monique—Ruby, that is—before we left in the off chance of an unknown catastrophe befalling us.

"Something else you must know… this woman, my

beloved, has cried a thousand bitter rivers over losing her little girl. I am here to ask—no, to beg—that when you someday tell Ruby of her legacy, you will be so kind as to impress fully upon her that she was deeply loved by both her mothers."

Ruby rolls onto on her back in the dust and hay, legs and arms splayed. Her breath slips in barely discernable streams from her open mouth. Her belly muscles constrict painfully. Her lips quiver violently, making her teeth chatter. Curling onto her side, she weeps silently and bitterly for the first time since she can remember.

CHAPTER
Forty Seven

So Final

Basilica of St. Louis, King, St. Louis, Missouri
1965

Zeenie sits on the church pew with all four of her children, her youngest brother Dewey, and Thomas's own son and his family alongside her. Seated behind her are Mercy, Jerome, Mr. and Mrs. Washington, Grandpa Grafton, Etta, and three more of Zeenie's brothers—Arthur, Ralph, and Wayne, and their wives. Row after row of people fill the pews of the Old Cathedral, the oldest building in St. Louis, and Thomas's favorite place of worship. Thomas lies at rest in front of the alters and the raised platform surrounded by two shops' worth of floral arrangements, green plants of several varieties—predominantly lilies—wreaths, and standing displays of vigorous flowering plants with buds not yet opened.

The massive pillars and beautiful architecture of the church somehow comfort Zeenie. Thomas would be so proud, and quite surprised, what with his humble demeanor, at the number of people who turned out for his farewell. She herself wasn't surprised at all. Thomas was loved, and his sudden death had shocked one and all.

Only a few nights before, she and Thomas were holding hands before the flickering fireplace in their bedroom discussing the renovations Thomas wanted to do to the coffee shop. Without notice, he sat up straight giving her the most startled look. His hand dropped from hers.

"What's wrong, you don't like my idea of adding a little private room for parties?" she'd teased.

He slumped forward in the Queen Anne chair. She leaped up, shook him slightly, took his pulse. There wasn't any. She backed up in horror. This was the man she had come to need in a thousand different ways, as had her kids. He couldn't leave her. Couldn't leave *them*. No, not her dependable, sweet Thomas!

Another flood of tears grips her now as she puts her face into her third handkerchief of the last half hour. She wishes the priest would hurry and stop talking about Thomas's patronage, his faithful ways, his goodness. It's all true, but the tribute is ripping her apart. He has been her tower of strength, her rescuer, her wonderful friend for these past five years, four of which she spent as his wife. He left her his lovely home, a thriving business, and money from good investments over the years in city land. Thomas had given her everything, even prosperity, but he couldn't give her *him*.

Death is so… final.

Deep loneliness overshadows Zeenie, the likes of which she has not felt since her first husband and father of her children made the rodeo life his first choice and walked out the door. A hand pats her on the shoulder. She turns and looks into the sympathetic face of Hope Washington, Mercy's mother. A shared look of pain passes between the two women. Zeenie turns back around, reaches up and clasps the hand on her shoulder, holding it tight.

CHAPTER
Forty Eight

Buried Anguish

New Orleans, Louisiana
1919

Suffering rests on the brow of Simon St. Clair as he summons memories from the hallowed ground of the heart's locked chambers to share with the young man he doesn't know but who has somehow touched him in some unusual way.

"Do you remember hearing about the hurricane that hit Ruddock back in 1915, William?"

"Yes sir. Terrible thing. Wiped out a town or two, didn't it?"

"That it did. Ruddock and Frenier, too. At least fifty-eight people died in Ruddock alone. Killed the town and my heart along with it."

Willy sits rigidly stiff, not moving, and breathing more shallowly with every word he hears. What will this man say that may affect him? Is he ready to hear it, to bear it? A familiar dread comes over him. He briefly puts his hand on his forehead and rubs it. He ignores the whining sound of bombs whistling through the air, explosions, bullets hitting their fleshly mark. Sounds that live in his head since the war... the smells, the sights that pull him back to those horrendous moments when his fellow soldiers were blown to pieces, losing limbs, screaming in pain and horror while their entrails lay in the trenches beside them.

Simon, lost in his own reflections, does not see the changes playing on the young man's features. "... my woman, Flo, and her daughters were preparing to move to New Orleans..."

Willy, unnoticed by Simon winces visibly. *Flo* is the name Isabelle wrote down for the woman she said was his real mother. He shakes his head to clear it and leans closer to the narrator.

"... but Zeke and Eli, those were Flo's oldest boys, they had moved off and married with a young'un or two and weren't in town when that storm hit. Both of them live up North now, and bless their little hearts, they write me a long letter every year. They do that, William, though they owe me not a thing. When I pass to the hereafter, they shall have a piece of my life to feather their nests good and proper, yes, indeed they shall. I already send them benevolences, and my heart loves to do so.

"It was my mind to take Flo and the three girls out of Ruddock. The logging business had tapered off so much in the whole region and, she, being a tailor seamstress, wasn't making much money anymore. Many of the residents had turned to cabbage farming, and that wasn't something my Flo could do. Not something I would let her do. So delicate and sincere, that sweet woman! So, I bought her a little sewing-tailoring shop on Canal Street here in the city. My, but that woman could take any fabric and whip out a suit or a dress after church on Sunday before lunch was served!"

For a moment, pure joy shines in Simon's eyes. The look quickly vaporizes, and his face glazes over with gloomy remembrances. He stretches out his legs, leans back, and folds his hands over his chest. "Most wonderful woman God ever made was my Flo, and her kids were good as gold. She was a widow with four little ones, working her hands to the bones, when I met her."

In the lapse that follows, Willy asks, "How did you meet her?"

"Well, sir, I happened to travel by train to Ruddock one or two times a month to cut deals between certain lumber companies and the sawmills. Daddy owned stock in some of them and put me in charge of overseeing the outreach operations from the time I was twenty-five years of age. There was a little place in town called the Owl Saloon. A merry place, it was, and no bother if a man of any color came in to imbibe or eat pickled eggs or sausages. Such a rarity, as you most certainly know. After I'd been going there for a time, a year or so, the new owner of the saloon, Shorty, noticed my city suits and told me one of the best little suit makers in all of Louisiana lived right there in Ruddock. I decided to pay this suit maker a visit, and that's how we met."

Willy doesn't comment. He has successfully swept the acrimonious memories of war back into their locked place and finds himself more interested than upset at hearing about the woman who is possibly his real mother. Still, his face bears a tragic residue that inspires Simon to say, "Sir, I believe you look famished. Let us move into the house and ask Rema to fix us some cold pork sandwiches."

Simon ignores Willy's mild protest, and they walk from

the veranda onto the bricked path to the impressive doors under the awning. Settled into large armchairs in a spacious room with a raised ceiling and luxurious furnishings, Simon resumes his tale.

"As I was saying, William, that hurricane took my Flo, her other two children and my own daughter, as well."

"I'm not quite following you, sir."

"Let me explain. Flo had four children, and she and I had two children together."

"I take it that Flo became your wife after you met her in Ruddock, sir?"

Simon looks down at his hands. "No, William, Mrs. Simon St. Clair and our two daughters lived right here in New Orleans in this family estate. I had two families at the same time. Flo and I never lawfully married though we had children." Simon rests his head in his hands and rocks back and forth. "Oh, how terrible I must be in your eyes now."

Before Willy can respond, Rema enters the room with a tray bearing sandwiches cut into small squares, gherkins, sliced cheeses, and iced tea with mint sprigs. She sets it on a small table in front of a heavily draped window overlooking the courtyard.

"Thank you, dear Rema."

"Will there be anything else, sir?"

Simon shakes his head and rises wearily from his chair. "Let's have a bite, William."

He waits for Willy to approach the table, then points to the chair facing the fireplace. They eat in silence for several minutes until Simon leans forward and points a fork at Willy. "I said this before, and I'll say it to my dying day. I didn't intend to have two families. I've had to live with God's judgment because of my sins. He has dealt me many sorrows for what I did."

Not quite sure of his feelings in this matter, Willy says, "I can't help but discern that your woman in Ruddock was named Flo, and that this estate is named Florentine. What a coincidence."

Simon looks a little taken back. "I'm afraid not. I changed the name of this estate to Florentine Estate after... well, after everyone left me. Florentine was my love's full given name, son."

"What was the name of your estate previously?"

"My daddy named it *Villa de la Liberté.*"

"I see," Willy says.

"Oh, I've paid for my wrongdoing, but the trouble is, the payments never end. Flo knew the truth when our beloved little son was stolen from us."

Simon doesn't notice the widening of Willy's eyes or his clenched jaw.

"That was the first cat-o'-nine-tails lashes on my back. Flo understood from her Biblical insight that losing him was a punishment for our sins. What would God do next? I waited, and everything went well for a long time.

"Did I end my secret life with Flo after losing little Willy? No! I thought, in my blind love for her, that the price was now paid. What folly! That hellish hurricane of 1915 took the woman I loved more than my own life, along with three innocent young women, one of which was my own flesh and blood.

"So great was my grief, William. So great. I thought perhaps I might die of wretchedness, and how could I hide such inner torment from my legally-wed wife? In the end, lost and destitute of spirit, I confessed my carnal sins to her, and, of course, as I knew she would, she left me. She's been gone now these four years, and I fear I shall never see my other daughters again. All of them find me worse than an infidel."

"Where did they go, sir?"

Simon lets out a ragged breath. "My wife originally came from up North, and that's where she returned... to a fine family that wouldn't walk across the street to shake my hand after what I've done. She's a good woman but never held my heart."

The man stares out the window wearing a crown of grief on his head. Willy sees him brush away tears, and both men work to conceal the act. Willy sips his iced tea looking as calm as a sapphire sea sporting gentle ripples; but the truth is, he's a churning storm inside. He urges himself to take that one and only important step that lies before him. He dabs his mouth on a napkin, runs his tongue over his teeth and submits privately to the questions arising inside his inner squall.

Will he judge this man as have so many, with the cruelest accuser of all being his own self? Can he overlook the sins of the father to get to the seed of truth that has yet to be disclosed between them? He momentarily closes his eyes and sees Auntie Dove's sweet face before him— Uncle Jacque's kind and jolly one. What fortune it was to have the Boyers in his life! Was he, Willy, not only a wealthy man, but also in the process of obtaining an exclusive education that only connections and money could ever provide? Perhaps his life would have taken a turn he would now find utterly deplorable had he not been stolen from one place, whisked to another, and then to another. Or, would he have died in that terrible hurricane of 1915?

What was it that Auntie Dove always proclaimed, that every person in this world needs to be forgiven? This man, more than any Willy has ever met, is in desperate need of forgiveness.

His mind made up to stand in no judgment of Simon St. Clair nor any other, Willy moves forward with his inquiry into the truth. "Sir, you mentioned you felt that God took your son from you for a punishment. Did he die of a disease, or an accident, perhaps?"

Simon rises from the table and treads heavily back to his comfortable chair, signaling for Willy to follow him. He opens a cabinet and removes a jar of tobacco. He opens a drawer and selects a pipe from a rich assortment laid into slots lined with velvet. With his eyes, he asks if Willy wants one also. Willy shakes his head. While Simon fills and tamps, Willy studies him. He believes he is looking at his own nose and forehead. Of course, the two men's heights match as well.

Simon settles himself back in the chair with a cloud of blue-gray smoke surrounding his head. The delicious aroma of wild cherry and vanilla tobacco floats in the air. A clock's pleasant ticking spreads a quietness over the room that feels natural. Willy finds himself enjoying Simon's presence though the man is reliving both their painful pasts. While he waits for the older man to speak, he glances out the windows and watches birds flitting blissfully from tree to bush to flower in the courtyard.

At last, Simon turns to face him again. "William, what do you know about the practice of Vodou?"

CHAPTER
Forty Nine

Different Paths

St. Louis, Missouri
1966

*J*ust because we can't go to the same college this fall doesn't mean Mercy should replace me as her best friend and confidant. Lately, it seems like she wants to. She's busy with that new friend of hers... a lot. Her name's Dottie, and I realize how impressive it is that she has an uncle or someone in her family who was part of the *Little Rock Nine*. That puts her in high status with Mercy, and it should. I'm awed, too, but I'm still the girl who has been Mercy's best friend for eight years and who considers her closer than a sister.

The only time we get together now is to study for a big test that makes a difference in our final grades since it's important to keep good grades for college next year. We don't go to the movies, bowling, the park, eat out, or shop together as we used to do all the time, at least one or two of those activities every weekend.

I've become a lover of art, especially that of the classic artists. Mercy used to be. In fact, she's the one who introduced me to art and museums in the first place. I probably never would have known about it if not for her. When I ask her to go with me now, she says she'll take a rain check.

I started doing local teen modeling early last year, and Mercy came with me on every assignment. Now, of course, she doesn't. I got into modeling by answering an ad in the paper. I didn't want to, but Mercy said I fit all the qualifications of height, weight, and with my long blond hair, I would be a shoo-in. It turned out to be true, and I went through runway and photography training right away. It's fun and earns me good pocket money. Mercy thought it was cool beyond words until she became too involved to be excited about anything but *the cause.*

She's totally into writing scathing papers about equality and fair practice. I'm with her one-hundred-percent on those subjects; in fact, I write about them from my perspective and have had some of my opinions printed in the editorial section of the St. Louis Post Dispatch, as well as a few of the underground newspapers Mercy writes for all the time. I'm with her on *fighting the good fight,* as she calls it, but why is she pushing me away at the same time?

I was upset when I found out she was to attend Harris Teachers College—which her mama calls Stowe Teachers College—and I was going to the University of Missouri. Of course, her enrolling in U of Mo as a female Black student, if we could even accomplish it, would have been a significant statement and a way to garner attention to her personal campaign. Her mother was dead set on her going to the same college she attended, so that was that. I get the feeling her family worries a lot about Mercy's fiery crusading these days.

Since Harris is a Black teaching college, it seemed ridiculous for me to try to sign up, especially with my major in art history. Mercy kind of sneered when I told her about my intended field of study, and I asked her why. She said it was okay, but art couldn't reach people and open their minds like writing and teaching. I strongly disagree. Art is the universal language, isn't it? Who can deny anything so obvious? Why has she changed so much?

She's so charged up with her causes that she's forgetting about everything else. It's the first time we won't be in the same school since we met. That's a big deal for me, but I'm not sure it's bothering her. With her energy and brain, she'll probably get into some highbrow school back East in a year or two.

I admit, I'm feeling lost.

CHAPTER
Fifty

Broken Man

Denton, Texas
1919

*E*rnest picks Flame's hooves clean, curries his coat, brushes his glossy red mane and tail. He dips his rag into the bucket of water and washes the sorrel's face, nose, and eyes. He takes a soft brush and brushes away the dirt raised by the curry comb. The horse whickers and backs further into the stall when Ernest finishes. He flings his head, asking.

"I-I'm sorry, Flame. She isn't coming."

Ernest latches the alley door to Flame's stall and repeats the process with Galahad. He, too, watches for Ruby. Ernest can't yet face the ache building in his chest. Taking care of her horses seemed the best thing to do after... after. Sweeping the barn aisle, he suddenly crumples like a wad of paper. He places a hand on the wooden half-door to Galahad's stall. Is he having a heart attack? He runs from the barn, his boot soles thudding on the plank floor.

He stumbles into the house and pours cold coffee from a metal pot into a mug with a shaking hand. In a small closet by the front door, he pats the pockets of several coats until he finds an old pack of Lucky Strikes. His hands shake so violently, he can't get a cigarette out. He fumbles for a pair of scissors from a drawer and cuts the pack down the side to retrieve a flattened cigarette. He bends down and lights it from a stove burner. He takes a deep draw, stands, then collapses in a fit of hacking. Old, dry tobacco, and he hasn't smoked in years. He takes a gulp of the coffee and runs to the sink to spit it out. He throws the lit cigarette into the discarded coffee and listens to the slight sizzle as the orange and gray end extinguishes.

He walks unsteadily back to the kitchen table where yesterday morning he and Ruby had early-morning coffee, eggs, biscuits, honey. He gingerly picks up *the note* as though if he handles it just right, it will magically say different words. He sits down holding his forehead in his hand as he reads it.

Dad, I overheard you and Jack talking last week. I know who I am. I'm not cut out for this life. I'll leave the pickup in town at the café. I have enough money to make it from there. Thanks for everything. Ruby.

The words are as cold and shocking in this fifth or sixth reading of them as they were the first time. She had left in the night. Quietly. Stealthily—like the thief she is. She stole his heart the moment he laid eyes on her. Now, she has stolen his very breath, his life, his future.

Arlene gone and now his beloved Ruby.

The room swirls. Ernest stands to his feet and exits the house through the back door, not noticing he leaves it open. He goes down the little pathway and through the gate. Bob, their cow dog, tries to come with him, but Ernest nearly shuts the gate on his nose.

"Stay, Bob," he mumbles.

He staggers down the cattle path toward the forest of mesquites and live oaks lining the wash, a place he has always gone to think things out. He slides down the side of the wash, his shirt sleeve hanging on a protruding dead stick from one of the trees. He rips himself loose, continues to slide to the bottom of the sandy draw. He sits there in shock on a day that marks the end of any joy or hope he has ever felt or hoped to feel again. Hours pass as he sits staring at nothing. The top of his head and the backs of his hands burn from the unforgiving Texas sun.

Trauma eventually gives way to bitter anger as Ernest stands to his feet, moving side to side, his gait unsteady. He makes his way through the wash as it deepens into a small canyon. He stops to wipe his forehead, then his caked lips, on what is left of his torn sleeve. The sun is setting, yet the day's heat clings to him like a shroud.

He kicks an eroded can sneering at him from the sallow sand, kicks it so hard his other leg turns to powder and drops him to the ground. First pain—then rage—charge through his body like a dark stallion. His anguished screams bounce off the canyon walls and straight into his private hell, filling him with hopeless despair.

CHAPTER
Fifty One

Not a Priest

New Orleans, Louisiana
1919

Simon's question about Vodou has rattled the younger man. Willy leans forward coughing, covers his mouth, stands, walks to the window coughing some more.

"Are you all right, William?" Simon asks, scooting forward in his chair, a look of concern on his face.

The young man nods and takes a cool swig of tea from his glass still sitting on the luncheon table.

"I can pound you on the back if you need it. That's what my daddy always did when I got choked."

"I'm fine now." Willy returns and sits in the chair separated only by a small table from the one Simon is sitting in. "You-you asked me what I know of the practice of Vodou. My answer is *some*... I know some about it. You, sir?"

It felt right to turn the tables at this point in the conversation to give Willy more time to collect himself.

Simon blows his breath out in a weary sigh, almost as if he's been holding it in for a long time. "I know more about it than I should."

Both men study their own hands, spreading their fingers, flipping them over, falsely inspecting them as if they held answers to questions they are seeking.

"My daddy was a righteous man, William, but he was a man of flesh and blood. No angel, it's true. One fateful day, a comely *mulatto* beauty caught his eye. Daddy became more entrenched in the affair as time went on. He stayed out later at night, drank more spirits, even dabbled in wagers and gambling. Deeper and deeper he fell under this... hold on now... Vodou woman's spell.

"I'm sorry if that surprises you, lad, but this is New Orleans, a city of prodigious mystical history. Certain women practitioners use their beauty and tricks to lure men with money into buying them cottages, jewelry, clothes, trinkets, whatever they want. Thus, my Daddy fell prey to this woman's bewitchment and bought her many expensive things, even a place of her own."

Simon sighs heavily once again. He looks past Willy out the large window behind him. "You know, William, Vodou has been a part of Louisiana history ever since slaves were imported from the Congo, the West Indies, Haiti, and other places. Most of those folks went on to become Catholics and Protestants, but others clung to their ancient religions.

"It was discovered that if the slaves could get together once a week, their attitudes and work were better. The ones still trying to practice dark arts began to meet along Bayou St. John and along the shore of Lake Pontchartrain for their dances. The meetings continued on a regular basis in various places, but Lake Pontchartrain was by far the most popular. They would hold their tame dances on barges in the water when the outside world and newspaper journalists were watching. When they weren't watching, all hell broke loose, and I'm about to tell you exactly what I mean.

"One terrible night in 1881 when the moon was full and my mother was visiting her ailing aunt in Lafayette, Daddy took me in a carriage to the Pontchartrain River. I was excited because he said we were going to a party. I was seven years old at the time, and I remember a beautiful woman seemed to be waiting for Daddy. I'll never forget her appearance—a vision of a woman in a tight dress made of every color in the rainbow. I thought I could see her breasts through the top material, but I was so young, you know, and not yet attuned to such things.

"She and my daddy were soon hanging all over each other. I was confused seeing him with this strange woman who wasn't my mama, but I had my own worries to think about."

"Worries?"

"Indeed. Something about the sound and rhythm of the music in the air had already caused a cold fear to creep like a tarantula up my back and perch its hairy legs on my scalp. And, too, that woman kept throwing her head back and laughing in the strangest way. She gave long kisses to my Daddy and put a silver flask to his lips again and again.

"William, he changed before my eyes… threw off his hat and shoes, had an unnatural grin to his face. The people were drinking all manners of liquids from bottles, jars, cans— dipping their cans into pots set along the edge of the dancing grounds. They were singing, shouting, smoking pipes and papers, but, most of all, they danced. The more they danced, the more extraordinary they acted.

"I tried every way to get my daddy to take me away from that place, but, oh dear Lord, son, he wasn't himself. I pulled on his sleeve, tugged on his coattail, even threw my arms around his waist. That woman gave me the evil eye for trying to coax him so ardently. I tell you, boy, I shrank back under that woman's glassy-eyed gaze."

Willy realizes his scalp and back are covered in goosebumps. A whisper of wind blows across the back of his neck. He reaches behind and slaps it, weakly smiles at Simon, half embarrassed, but feeling oddly uneasy. Simon notices the changes in the young man's demeanor.

"William, this is a long tale. Are you sure you still have the time to sit with me?"

"I most certainly do, sir."

"Splendid! I'll have that old rascal Benny make us some of his chicory coffee. That'll revive our souls."

Simon steps to an arched doorway leading into a long hall and loudly rings a bell that sits on a narrow table. In minutes, an elderly Colored man with gray hair ambles into the room with a friendly demeanor.

"What can I do for my little Simon boy?" he drawls in a deeply southern accent. He smiles affectionately at the man whom he has watched grow from a tot to a middle-aged man with graying temples.

Simon raises his voice several levels, almost to a shout. "Benny, we are in need of a pot of your wonderous chicory coffee. Please make us some right away, and don't forget the warm milk and cane sugar. Tell Rema we'll have some of her honey-cinnamon buns from the pantry, as well. Hurry now. My friend William and I are in dire need of refreshments."

The old man nods his head. "Yes sir, Simon-love, that's just fine. Coffee and buns. Yes sir, honey." He shuffles from the room.

Willy finds himself smiling as the old man leaves the room. Something about this place and time comforts him. Here they are discussing the evilest of things, a Vodou dance ritual, not to mention the flashes of uncomfortable suppressed memories he's experiencing as Simon talks, but he somehow feels like he's at home.

"Please, Mr. St. Clair, continue."

"Oh, no, you must call me Simon. I insist."

Willy nods good-naturedly and postures his readiness for Simon's story to continue.

"So, there I was… a lost little soul standing back from the crowd. I watched in horror as people began to disrobe, but none of that compared to seeing my own daddy do so. People were shaking and falling to the ground in spasms. I screamed until I was hoarse, but no one heard me above the music and shrieks of the revelers.

Out of nowhere, a man grabs me and runs to the center of those merry makers where a huge black cauldron… oh, I'd say almost as big around as a carriage… is bubbling over a fire. Another man, then another, joins him. They jerk off my shoes, then my socks. A man violently pulls off my pants and shirt so that I'm merely wearing my underthings. I never fought so hard to be free! I couldn't fight or scream enough as they lowered me closer and closer to that boiling water."

Willy jumps to his feet. "My God, man! Don't tell they meant to boil you in the cauldron?"

"I'm afraid so. You see, children weren't allowed at those particular rituals. The men mistook me for one of their *gifts* whom they periodically sacrificed, along with hapless cats and whatever else their demented minds thought of to offer to their spirits."

Willy paces up and down in the room shaking his head, his soul deeply troubled. Snatches of memory float into his consciousness. *Mam.* He sees her face, sees her standing on a table with a snake coiled around her bare body. He feels her dragging him along stretches of soggy green moss, frogs hopping from a box he carries under his arm. He hears beating drums. He covers his face with his hands and turns to lean his forehead against the cool marble mantle above the fireplace.

"Are you all right, my boy?"

Which is worse, Willy wonders... the bloody war memories or the ones now tumbling through his mind like unwelcome shadows? Heart pounding, he takes slow draws of air to reestablish his deportment. He hears the sound of a tray being placed on the long table behind him, turns in time to see Rema and Benny leaving the room.

"Come and have coffee with me, William. Perhaps I should not have told you this awful incident of my past? I admit, it is difficult to comprehend—unholiness in its worst attire."

Willy inwardly chastises himself for letting his memories overtake him. He gives Simon a broad grin that he himself knows is entirely counterfeit. "Oh, not at all, sir. I merely had to settle myself after hearing what you went through. So very awful for a young child to experience such a gruesome affair. Please, I must hear the rest of the story."

After fixing themselves mugs of coffee with generous amounts of milk and sugar, the two men sit once again in the large chairs. Willy nods at Simon, who accepts the signal and begins talking right away.

"Well, my daddy rescued me, William. I saw him running toward me, desperately running. Just as the toes of my foot touched the scalding water, my daddy snatched me away from the men. He punched one square in the mouth, turned with me in his arms and bloodied the other chap's nose with his elbow. He had his arms around me, holding me tightly against him. The sounds coming from his mouth were that of a wild animal—a roaring lion protecting its young. I have no choice but to believe it was God and the Saints who brought him to his senses in time to save me from death.

"How did you escape out of there, the two of you? I mean, they... those people obviously were insane."

"Truly they were. Daddy fled with me hanging on for dear life, both of us sobbing and wearing nothing but our undergarments. The pretty woman ran to join us, and he screamed at her to get back. Within earshot, he shouted out to our driver, who jumped down and threw open the carriage door. In mere seconds, our horses took us from that hellish place of depravity. Undeniably, Daddy and I saved each other that day."

"You saved each other?"

"Oh, yes. You see, that event marked the end of his affair with the Vodou woman. Daddy had lost his way, and it took the shock of seeing his only son nearly sacrificed to bring him back to Mama and me. Mama found out about it, as we knew she would, from the servants. They were, are, and always will be a web of unstoppable, rich gossip here in New Orleans. She forgave my daddy, and, henceforth, if any of it ever came up in any manner of conversation, she explained that he had been bewitched and was completely unable to help himself."

Simon chuckles. "He was a perfect husband and father from that day forward until his death, don't you know?"

Both men smile.

"Mama, before she died, made me promise on his grave to flee from any kind of paganism, especially Vodou, and to remain a good Catholic who served only the true Lord and saints. I promised her, William, and I've tried to live up to that promise even though I failed so miserably as a man."

Outside, the afternoon shadows slant into early dusk. It is silent inside the room save for the ticking of the standing clock. The men, lost in their thoughts, are quiet for several minutes.

"Begging your pardon, sir, but you haven't yet told me how you lost your son."

Simon pours more coffee into both their mugs, adds the extras, and asks Willy if he wants a honey-cinnamon bun. Willy declines. Simon sips noisily from the top of the brew as he sits down.

"I lost my son because of my sins, William. This, too, is an appalling story. Are you quite sure you want to hear it now? Perhaps you could come back tomorrow and—"

"I beg you to finish!" Willy says with a passion that surprises the older man.

"Then... by all means, I shall." He takes another drink from his cup, puts it down, and folds his hands in his lap. "My Willy, my sweet boy. We were taking a short drive in the buckboard close to the swamps outside Ruddock before I departed the next day back to New Orleans. All the children, Flo, and me. We'd had a lively time at her little church that morning, so different, you know, from my Catholic church, but I always enjoyed it. All that gusty singing and happy clapping of hands filled me with joy. We had fried chicken for lunch and watched the children play all afternoon.

"Not long before dusk, Flo got it in her mind to go for a drive with the mules and buckboard. Oh, the songs we sang as we drove around! All the kids loved to sing, and it was a most pleasant sound.

"A woman… she seemed to appear out of nowhere. She pretended to be in distress, and my Flo wanted to help her. That woman always helped the most helpless, she did." Simon slams a flat hand on the arm of the chair. "William, we were deceived! The minute I looked in that woman's eyes, I knew. See, once you've truly encountered evil, you know it from then on. The slightest hint of it chills your very soul.

"She started up one of those Mumbo-jumbo dances, chanting, trying to beguile all of us. They have a way, son, so never let your guard down around them. My blood was running cold when, in the twinkling of an eye, she reached out like a striking snake and stole our Willy! She ran swiftly, more swiftly than a deer, straight into that swampy water with nigh a fear for her life from snakes or alligators. Why? Because she herself was a devil!"

Willy pinches his jaw with his fingers to keep from crying out or speaking. Simon, lost in his remembrances, has no idea what effect his words are having on the younger man.

"How we searched for our boy." Simon lowers his head to his chest. When he continues, his voice is edged in pain. "We brought all our friends and anyone else who would come with us back to the place where he was taken, but we found nothing. After searching and calling for hours, we went back to Ruddock without him."

"Flo and I were sick with grief for the good part of a year, William, but, Flo… she helped us survive it by her firm belief that it was our just punishment for our illicit union together. That was my chance to end the affair between us, but God help me, I didn't. Instead, I convinced her our punishment was fulfilled. No snake-oil salesman was more convincing than I in duping that dear woman. I couldn't give her up, not even in the face of tragedy."

Willy stares at Simon, stares so hard Simon asks again if he is all right. He doesn't answer, merely stands, places his coffee mug on the silver serving tray. He walks to the window and looks out, moving the drape slightly. He straightens and folds his hands behind his back.

"I think I see a mockingbird. This late in the day. Yes, there the little fellow is."

Simon is rather confounded by Willy's reaction to his stories, but says, "Oh, that's grand, William. Their songs often brighten my sad days." He clears his throat. "Young man... I-I don't know what came over me to share such dreadful tales of my past with you. None but a very few have ever heard of these happenings, and yet, I wanted to share them with you. God knows I'm unsure as to why."

Willy turns and gazes evenly at Simon.

"I do... I know why... *Father.*"

Simon gasps. "Pardon me, my dear boy... but I am truly not a priest. Far from it!"

Willy puts his head back and laughs. A rich, relieved laugh. Simon, baffled, watches the young man quickly cover the distance between them. Willy kneels and clasps both of Simon's hands in his. "You know, the Holy Book says the Lord rains on both the just and the unjust. I've never felt more strongly that He has rained his glory upon both of us this momentous day, dear sir."

"Well, I, um, that's certainly true... that is, I suppose so."

"Simon... Dad... I'm Willy, your stolen boy."

CHAPTER
Fifty Two

In the Air

Aboard a TWA
1966

ercy and I are both slim, so when we pulled the airplane seatbelts across our laps and nearly to the other side of our bodies, we had to giggle about it. Honestly, I think we'd snicker at a Walter Cronkite news broadcast right now—maybe even a chemistry pop quiz. Our excitement has spilled over into non-stop chatter ever since we left St. Louis for Los Angeles.

I thought Mercy would be in France again this summer. That is, until she came roaring into our driveway on her motorcycle and ran into the house through the backdoor shouting at the foot of the stairs, "We're going to San Francisco, Annie! For a month! We leave June 29, only two weeks from now. Pack your bags, girl."

I dashed down the stairs and stopped mid-way. Causing shockwaves is one of Mercy's favorite things in life. She assumed a runway modeling pose like I had taught her and pivoted gracefully in a circle. She patted her new hairstyle. "Isn't it groovy?"

"Is that one of those, uh, I don't know, I forget the name."

"Afro. Yes, it is! Latest thing, especially on the West Coast and the university campuses."

"What, uh, I mean… how do you fix it? It's so round."

"Easy. You use a pick and lift the hair from the roots out."

"No more straightening?"

"Nope. It's perfect for me, Annie, admit it."

"I have to get used to it, Mercy. You've always been so finicky about your hair. What are you going to do with your cabinets and drawers full of hair products and all those millions of hair ribbons, barrettes, and such?"

She waves a dismissive hand in the air. "Already threw them out. And, it wasn't millions, just thousands. Now, listen, can you postpone whatever you've got planned for this summer? I already have. Wait, you have no choice… you're coming with me, Annie! Aunt Viola has invited us, and we just have to, have to, have to go!"

I looked at Mercy's lit-up face thinking two things; 1) Mercy hasn't wanted to do anything with me in such a long time, and 2) I need to cancel all my local modeling assignments for July. I wasn't going to miss the chance to have new adventures with Mercy the summer before we start college for anything in the world.

Now, here we are flying on Trans World Airlines to Los Angeles. Chinaman Bill and Aunt Viola are picking us up. We're supposed to go somewhere famous to eat tonight, sightsee tomorrow, and then drive up the coastline to San Francisco. The stewardess gathers our soft drink glasses.

We smile at her until she moves on.

"Imagine it, seven years. I haven't seen Chinaman Bill or Aunt Viola since they ran away in the night. You've seen them how many times since they left St. Louis?"

"Twice, but it was always on the fly when we were catching flights to go somewhere else. Mama went out there several times, but I was always in school. Oh, how I wish Barbra Streisand wasn't doing her play in London and was on tour somewhere in California."

"That came out of nowhere. How do you know she's in London?"

"I read, silly."

"You always were a fan of hers. I like her, too, but you know I prefer male singers, especially rock and roll guys."

"Like the Rolling Stones?"

"After the Beatles, they're the best. Did you hear their *Paint It Black?* I love that one."

"Ugh. Hideous. Hurts my ears."

"You just hate rock and roll."

"Not everything. I like the Beatles okay, and that Tom Jones guy is cute. I adore Aretha Franklin."

"She's a blues singer."

"Not entirely. Her songs play on the same radio stations. Now Ella Fitzgerald... can't beat that voice."

"I can't argue that, but why don't you like rock and roll?"

"It's just so... guitar twangy and drum heavy. Almost caveman tribal, you know? Most of those guys need a shave and a haircut, if you ask me."

"Says the little soon-to-be college rebel with the new afro hairdo."

"Not the same thing."

I shake my head in good-natured disagreement, and we

both jump back into the novels we brought on the plane. In a few minutes, Mercy says, "Annie?"

"Yes?"

"Don't call him *Chinaman Bill* anymore, okay? It sounds kind of, you know, impolite."

I study the back of the seat in front of me. It never occurred to me not to call him that. "Okay. What should I call him?"

"How about *Bill?*"

CHAPTER
Fifty Three

Heritage

Magnolia Manor, San Antonio, Texas
1921

*I*f she weren't so annoying, he would find it easier to put his foot down. If he argued with her, she brought up every supposed transgression from the creation of the Garden of Eden. Joseph sits moodily in the bedroom chair as Julie circles him, eyes blazing. Her temper tantrums have grown worse. Married twenty-one months with a thirteen-month-old son, the young family lives in a built-on addition to Magnolia Manor *until they get more settled,* his parents say. The truth is, he's twenty-two and still has no say in his own life.

If not for little Davy, Joseph is sure he'd have gone stark raving mad by now. If it's not his mother or Jack telling him how they will gladly support his family *here* while he returns to Harvard to finish his schooling to become an esquire or a doctor, it's Julie harping on one or a thousand things. At least his parents take his brothers to France every spring and stay until fall. He, Julie, and Davy have the place to themselves for a few months while they're gone, and that cuts down on half the prattle in his life.

Right now, everyone's gone, and it is still pure hell. Joseph is a quiet man who loves solitude. He has a temper, but he keeps it controlled. The few times he hasn't, it was awful. If he's ever going to be a lawman wearing a gun, he has to be in control of his emotions, or so Jack has always told him.

All he ever wanted was to be a Texas Ranger like his step-father, but it was always out of the question with a mother like his. Her preoccupation with everyone, namely him, *bettering oneself* is sometimes insufferable. In fact, it's what egged him on to court Julie the summer after his freshman year at Harvard. She was, after all, one of the Durants from Georgia, a known southern family *of good breeding*. Frankly, he found that kind of stuffy nonsense far worse than cow manure, but it mattered to his mother.

Julie was the prettiest young woman he'd ever seen, and he was amazed that she was so open and warm to all his attentions. He found her fun in a light way, but he would have preferred to put off any wedding plans for an unspecified length of time. He wanted the chance to live some adventures, to ride the wind a while. To be honest, he had planned to quit college after his sophomore year, join the Rangers, and everyone else be damned. He had grown tired of all their expectations that didn't line up with his own dreams.

As the months passed after his marriage to Julie, he realized with sickening dread that she had set a trap for him, one he had fallen into and that now bound him to her for life. That summer of 1919, they dated profusely, attending every social event on the San Antonio calendar. His normal, but slight, physical advances were met with coquettish *no's,* which he completely expected from a girl of her caliber. When he shared with her one hot June evening that he planned to complete one more year at the university before traveling for a few years, probably join the Rangers and not finish his formal education, things took a different turn. Those *no's* from Julie turned quickly, that same night even, into teasing *maybe's*.

A few nights later, while her parents were in Amarillo for the weekend, Julie invited Joseph to eat dinner at the family home. After dinner, she dismissed the household help. No sooner had they left the house when she began mournfully crying into a perfumed handkerchief over his leaving in a few months for "cold, old Massachusetts" and what was a "poor little thing" like her to do with no man around to protect her, not even to escort her to any functions for those years while he had rambling fever? Didn't he care a single bit about her?

If only she hadn't been so beautiful.

When her tears turned into near hysterics, Joseph felt he had to comfort her. He wrapped his arms around her and patted her back. She snuggled close, still sniffling, and then warmed toward him in a way he found irresistible. It didn't take long for him, a red-blooded male, to throw caution to the wind with such a lovely and willing partner.

A week before his departure back to the university in August, she came to him wailing pitifully, telling him she was with child and now she would be sent away and mortified forevermore—a disgrace to her family name and an outcast in this cruel world.

What else could he do but marry her? It was the only gentlemanly thing to do.

"Joseph, are you even listening to me?" Julie screeches. She stops in front of the chair. "I declare, you're like being married to a stone wall sometimes. Did you hear what I said?

My daddy knew the Livingstons in New Orleans. As soon as you told me you were adopted by Jack and had the name Livingston originally, I told my parents. Daddy did some digging and—"

"What are you talking about, Julie?"

"I'm talking about your heritage."

"What about my heritage?"

"It isn't right, Joseph. You should have told me. Mama and Daddy are flat out dismayed. Mama's had to take to her bed she's so upset. Oh, my poor little boy. Davy, what have I done?"

"I have no idea what you're spewing about. What are your Mama and Daddy dismayed about this time?"

Julie sighs and flounces down on the bed. "I just don't know what I'm going to do now. I can't be married to a Colored man. I just can't! After all, it's against the law." She puts her hands on her cheeks. Oh, my Lord, I might go to prison for marrying you!"

"What in hell are you saying, woman?" Joseph bounds from the chair and stands by the bed with his feet apart, his arms at his side.

"I'm saying that you, your mama, and now our little Davy are all Colored people! Why, it's a wonder he didn't come out dark-skinned. Oh, my Lord in the Heavens, what would I have done then? It's too dreadful even to think of it!"

Joseph reaches down and lifts Julie from the bed by her bent elbows in one swift movement. He holds her in the air for a moment, strongly considering throwing her to the floor. The veneer of calm he practices so carefully is close to shattering. The look in his eyes is terrifying to her.

"My daddy will kill you if you hurt me! Put me down, you... you... son of a dark woman!"

Joseph, growling like a dog ready to attack, flings her forcefully onto the bed. She lets out a cry, rolls to sit up while keeping an eye on the man she feels she no longer knows or trusts.

"You-you savage! Don't take your wild blood out on me. It-it's not my fault your mother had a Colored grandmother. Why, I think she was even a slave, your great-grandmother, wasn't she?"

Joseph shakes with fury, fighting an intense urge to attack. Staring at her, he no longer sees the lovely girl with the golden mane. He sees a shallow, spiteful creature uglier than the bottom of the most neglected horse stall.

"Well, are you going to deny your heritage? Daddy found out your blood father, Mr. Livingston, who was White, of course, kept your mama like a prostitute."

"Stop talking, Julie." Joseph's tone is rich with covert threat.

"But, you—"

His glare as his face lowers close to hers silences her. She skitters to the other side of the bed like a spooked rabbit. Speaking slowly and distinctly, he says, "Don't you ever call my mother that name again. Do you understand? In fact, don't ever say her given name again."

"But, she—"

"Do you understand?" he says, his words coated in ice.

She stares at him, then rolls her eyes. "All right. Calm yourself, Joseph."

"Calm myself? I feel like tearing your arms out by the roots and throwing them to the wild boars. I suggest you do not speak, not one word." Joseph points a finger at her. "Not one word."

Julie's bottom lip sticks out at least an inch. She trembles and nods her head.

"My mother is a gracious, kind woman. She saved my little sister and me from calamity and prejudice, subjects you are too weak and foolish to even grasp.

"You have a sister?"

"I told you to be quiet."

"Joseph, please—"

"Hush! Are you even capable of understanding anything deeper than that powder you cake on your face? Life isn't all parties and pretty clothes and easy living. Out in the world, most women aren't like you. They—"

"And how am I, Joseph?"

"You really want to know? You're a vain, pretty doll with nothing but sawdust inside."

Julie gasps.

"Try to think deeper than a puppet for a minute, Julie. Before and during the centuries of slavery, people had interracial relationships, sometimes voluntary, but usually forced. Do you hear what I said? Forced conjugal relations! You think you have the right to judge those women? To judge my mother? Are the resulting children from these unions less human, less righteous than you?"

Julie has never seen her husband angry until now. His chest heaves, his fists are closed, his eyes blood red. She moves one leg off the bed in a move she hopes seems benign. Her thoughts are on escape. Joseph begins to pace.

"I seem to recall how easily you surrendered to me before we were married. Yes, like a prostitute! Did anyone have a knife to your throat, dear Julie?"

Julie's hands fly to her throat. "My God in Heaven, you're cruel! What if I did lose control a few times and let you—"

"Ha! Let me? You practically *forced* me! For two months, I

never heard a peep of an objection. How available you made yourself to me! How was it that you managed to find me alone so many places, or to be alone with me with no guardians around? No, this was your plan from the moment you met the oldest son of one of the wealthiest families in San Antonio. It's as obvious as your nose. In fact, I'll lay odds your parents were in on your scheme."

"Why, I never... we-we did no such thing!"

"You know what? I think the whole town needs to hear about you, about how you enticed me to have relations with you by approaching me like a common Jezebel. Of course, most of our friends have already done the calculations on how long we were married before we had a child."

He laughs a low, mocking laugh. His disgust knows no bounds now that the lock of his emotions and temper has been picked and thrown to the ground. He sits down in the chair. "You know what, Julie? I've had enough of your pretentious drivel. I think we should split up."

"You've had enough? What about me? A girl from an established southern family finding out her husband is of Colored blood?"

"Colored blood? That's how you see it? Not that you can understand numbers beyond ten, but my mother having a Colored grandmother makes me one-eighth Colored. It makes Davy one-sixteenth. Even to your little brain, you should see that makes me no more Colored than you. Whatever amount it is, I'm proud to bear it and proud of my ancestors. All of them! God bless their souls!"

"How-how can you say that? You're proud of having Negro blood?"

"Damn right I am. You know what else? I'll wager you have the blood of lunatics running through your pale southern veins. In fact, given your limitations, and since *y'all* like marrying your own cousins where you come from, you're probably as inbred as hell. Bred too close, you are. A bunch of morons."

Julie jumps off the bed. "Take that back, Joseph!"

"Oh, I see. The truth hurts."

She stomps into her private dressing room and slams the door. Joseph is at a loss as to where to go from here with this woman. He never loved her, and now, he feels the tentacles of hatred for her and her family viciously clawing his insides.

He had learned of his so-called *heritage* when he was seventeen. He had been forbidden to mention it for years, but one day, there they were, Jack and his mother, sitting with him and explaining his former life and name with all the love in their hearts. His mother shed tears over her forfeited baby girl, but she had, with God's help, she explained, accepted it at last. She wanted her first son to know the truth. The way his mother and Jack presented it, he felt proud of his one-quarter Colored mother, his Colored great-grandmother—God rest her soul—his White father, and his White step-father. They didn't tell him where Monique was, but his mother promised him that one day, when the time was right, she would.

The only one he wanted to exact revenge on was his half-brother, Bradford Livingston of New Orleans. Joseph promised himself he would find that man one day, and it would be a "family reunion" like no other.

Julie emerges from her dressing room in riding clothes. Her nose is stuck up to the heavens, her face powder streaked, her hat on lopsided. She strides quickly to the door. "I have to calm my nerves, so I'm taking Coal for a ride. When I return, Davy and I shall be moving back in with my parents. Coal is coming, too."

"All fine, but you're not taking Davy anywhere."

"I'm his mother, and Davy goes with me. I won't abide a Colored man, and I'll make sure Davy never knows he's one. After all, he shows no signs. I've thought this out, and in a few months, he and I, and my horse, of course, are moving back to Georgia to live with my aunt and uncle."

A hot heat flushes through Joseph, stinging his face.

"You won't win this battle, Julie. My family is too established here for your silly southern nonsense to matter one speck. Now, you either stop acting the pitiful fool and make up your mind about our family, or leave. Whatever you decide, you won't take my son with you."

"I will not be married to a Negro, and that's what you are. I don't care how you want to use arithmetic or any of that. You had a Colored great-grandmother, and that's not acceptable from where I come from. No one will blame me, not even a little."

"Do you realize how often Judge Matthews goes bird hunting with Jack? How often all of the judges and attorneys come to our get-togethers, or eat here after a big deer hunt? You're more touched in the head than I thought if you believe you'll take our little boy away from this family."

"We'll see about that, you bull-headed... uh, darkie!"

She leaves in a huff of overly done, childish anger. Davy cries from the nursery, and Joseph goes to him. He is holding the boy in the air making him smile when Maria, Davy's *niñera*, enters the room.

"I'll see to him, *senor*," she says.

He hands Davy to Maria and hears Coal's rapid hoofbeats galloping on the path from the corrals to the house and then onto the dirt road.

She's riding him too hard again.

It strikes him that everything his wife ever does is too much or too little. He looks out the window and sees her whipping Coal's rump with her riding crop. A cloud of dirt follows them as they disappear over the rise.

CHAPTER
Fifty Four

Two Fathers

Tujague's Restaurant, New Orleans
1921

J he Travers Stakes race is being pleasantly discussed this late afternoon at a table at Tujague's, a New Orleans restaurant across the street from the French Market. The men, one a red-cheeked, jolly Frenchman, and the other two tall men of color—all dressed lavishly in the gentlemanly urban style of the day—converse quietly over roasted duck breast, butter-poached asparagus, crispy pork belly squares with fig jam, broiled oysters, and champagne.

The favorite gossip among anyone affiliated or interested slightly or heavily in horseracing is the Travers Stakes a month ago at Saratoga. The outcome of the race incites wild discussion and numerous speculations, causing hot tempers to flare when there are the slightest differences in opinions. The consensus, though sometimes hard won, is that Arnold Rothstein—that New York gambler and assumed dirty dealer—is a crook.

Such harsh judgment of the man is based on his alleged involvement in the Black Sox scandal in the 1919 World Series, and now, the 1921 Travers Stake race. It is said he bet one-hundred-fifty thousand dollars on his own colt, *Sporting Blood,* for that race. Before the day ended, he acquired the winning purse, as well as his wagering earnings, leaving thousands of people with unanswered questions.

Jacque spears a piece of duck and pauses with it on the end of his fork. "The question is, why didn't Harry Payne Whitney's filly, *Prudery,* win the race when she was always the favored horse to do so, so much so the race was almost declared a walkover? What is all that prattle after the race of her being off her feed? Anyone knows those details for a horse of *Prudery*'s caliber are scrutinized more than the blue Hope Diamond, wherever that gem may be in these times. How did Arnold Rothstein, that scoundrel, know she was off her feed?" He contemplates what he just said, pops the morsel into his mouth, follows it with a drink of champagne.

"This entire charade makes no sense," Willy says. "Uncle Jacque, every horse except for Rothstein's *Sporting Blood* had withdrawn from the race, so why did Sam Hildreth enter Harry Sinclair's *Grey Lag* the very morning of the Travers, only to scratch the horse shortly before the race? Everyone knows *Sporting Blood* could never legally beat a horse like *Prudery.*"

Jacque shakes his head. *"Mon dieu,* all if it… crooked as a tree branch, my son."

"Not that I attended the races often, but I was most glad when they allowed it to come back to our state," Simon says, forking a broiled oyster. "William, you say you desired to become a horse jockey at one time?"

"Yes, sir, I surely did. It was my only dream until I was

fortunate enough to get some righteous sense beat into me."

"I beg your pardon?" Simon says.

Willy wets his lips with his nearly untouched glass of champagne. "Perhaps I can explain it by saying that I believe anywhere there are high stakes to be won or lost, such as in horseracing, you will find good and bad characters. As a foolish boy with no experience other than natural horsemanship, far from home, no known sponsors, and Colored, too... well, it made me fair game for the ruffians on the outskirts of the profession."

"Ruffians?"

"Yes sir." Willy sighs, carefully arranges his fork and knife across the top of the plate. He wipes his mouth and places the napkin at an angle over his plate signifying to the wait staff he is finished eating. "You see, it's like the carnivals, uh, Father. The guys out there barking for the people to come inside and spend their money are usually the tough guys. They, and the ones putting up rides and tents and taking them down later, are hired for their loud mouths or their muscle, not their character. Former convicts... men running from the law, woman beaters, that sort of thing.

"I'm not saying the characters hanging onto the flaps of the horse training and racing businesses necessarily fit that bill, but there are some who would just as soon bust you in the mouth or knock your teeth out as teach you anything. They get a kick out of abusing a kid or an older man because they simply can. There's no one to stop them."

Jacque looks at Willy with a sad face. "You never told Dovie and me all those stories, Willy. I know you bear some terrible memories, and it hurts my soul now to think of it."

"Don't let it, Uncle Jacque. It cleansed me of the anguish I carried inside myself those years, and look, it made me tough enough to go to war." His wide grin is infectious. Both older men take their time relishing their pride in the young man they both consider to be their son. Willy begins to squirm under the starry-eyed scrutiny of his two fathers. He clears his throat. "So, let me confirm that I understand both of you gentlemen correctly. You want me to contact the trainer I worked for, Mr. Benjamin Allyn Jones, and have him help you buy your own racehorse, one that you will both own equally but that Jacque will act as the front man for because his skin is lighter?"

Both men nod and smile.

"I'll see what I can do, but I can't promise…"

Willy stops talking and glances at an older gentleman and young woman who walk past their table. The gentleman stops, turns, and touches Jacque on the shoulder.

"Pardon me, but are you Jacque Boyer of Baton Rouge?"

Jacque sits up straight. "*Oui,* is it Monsieur Laurent of my joyful racetrack days?"

"It 'tis!"

Jacque stands. The men grasp one another's forearms, nodding and grinning.

"Allow me to introduce my son, William, and his father, Simon." Jacque says, nodding at Willy and Simon.

"Excuse me, Jacque. For a moment, I thought I heard you say this is your son, and this is his father?"

"I did at that! But you must join us for dessert and coffee so we can explain. It's a wonderful story!"

The man looks at his watch. "We are meeting Alice for dinner, so we must decline your most generous offer to partake of dessert. However, we are early, so perhaps a cup of tea? You have sufficiently whetted my appetite to hear your tale, gentlemen. Yes, we shall join you!"

Monsieur Laurent leans in conspiratorially. "Dear Jacque, also allow me to introduce to you my new track-training jockey." He nods toward the young woman and seems to relish greatly the surprise on the three faces of the men sitting at the table. He chuckles. "Yes, she is a beautiful female, and the best little jockey in the country. She lives with us as *our niece*. It is our most delicious secret that she is a girl except at the track. Isn't it rich?" He nods his head while looking mysteriously right and left as though he is divulging a great secret, and by the looks of it, he is.

"Alice... you remember my wife, don't you, Jacque? Yes, she found this little jewel working at the salon, so terribly underused she was, tending to fat, wealthy women who prattle and preen when, all the time, she was hiding a monumental talent for containing and, dare I say it, *speaking*, with even the pricklest, wildest of stallions!"

With his arm, he gently curves the young woman forward to introduce her. Willy is speechless looking into her blue eyes.

"My protégé cleans up nicely from her breeches and plain shirts, yes? No one would ever suspect the little slip of a 'lad' working my horses at the track is this lovely young lady. Of course, some rather stringent binding of her person by my wife is necessary, you understand, to turn this eighteen-year-old ingenue into a jockey boy. Gentlemen, allow me to introduce to you... Ruby-Monique."

CHAPTER
Fifty Five

A Wild Hair

San Francisco
1966

"But we have to see either the *Purple Onion* or the *Hungry i*, Aunt Viola," Mercy pleads, "It's history."

"Bill doesn't want to take you girls to North Beach. It's full of sleazy strip clubs like that Condor Club. Just shockingly low-class. Definitely not a place for ladies. I might see if he'll take us for a coffee at Enrico's Sidewalk Cafe after dinner one evening. We could arrive by cab right there in the front. We don't walk around those nightclubs in North Beach."

"What's Enrico's?"

"An outdoor bar and café with live jazz. Now, understand, it's in the heart of North Beach, so you wouldn't get to walk around and do tourist things."

"But the *Hungry i* is where Barbra Streisand and Woody Allen got their start, isn't it? Bill Cosby, too. Are you sure we can't go?"

"You have to be twenty-one, Mercy, so, no."

Mercy scoots back on the large crimson sofa woven with gold threads. It's placed to face glass doors opening to a view of San Francisco Bay. In the distance is Alcatraz Island with its federal prison facility buildings. It exhibits no hint of its infamous past from where we sit, only a white-washed splay of buildings with a tower and a rugged surrounding skirt of an island.

"I'm going to go read some pamphlets," Mercy says.

"Oh, good, honey. I'm repotting succulents in the kitchen," Aunt Viola says.

I take a crocheted throw off the back of the sofa and snuggle in it to review our experiences since we got here. Our second night, we went to Bill's restaurant and lounge, *The Electric Chop Stick*. It was nothing like his restaurant in St. Louis. It was packed with people, lots of blue and red lighting, and Aunt Viola, still striking, took the mike in the lounge and sang a bluesy repertoire of songs that made the crowd wild with clapping and elicited calls for an encore.

Mercy and I sat just outside the lounge, Bill's orders, because of alcohol being served in the bar area, but we didn't mind. We sat in a large half-moon booth and nibbled shrimp and crab appetizers brought hot to us from the kitchen.

"Why didn't they have any kids, you think?" I asked Mercy during the intermission.

"Actually, they did."

"You didn't tell me that."

"Because he died soon after he was born. They were so heartbroken, they didn't want to try again. But, guess what? Viola told me last night they're adopting twin girls from China. Orphans. They're somehow related to Bill's family in China, but I don't know any details."

"And it skipped your mind to tell me?"

"I was too busy reading something and forgot about it."

"Yeah, a manifesto on how to disrupt every civil and community law in the nation."

Mercy's eyes gleam. "Maybe."

And that was the end of that conversation that evening.

I rehash it in my mind and look around at Bill and Aunt Viola's beautiful city apartment. It's an old-world wonder on the third floor of a Victorian-era building with a concha-shell stairway leading up to the third floor. It's furnished in silk and hand-woven fabric furniture. True to the time period of the building, there's thick oak casing around the windows, eight-inch baseboards, and old, carved doors with marble door knobs. Tapestries and art hang on the walls, Persian rugs are scattered on the old wooden floors, hand-crafted wood and glass tables dot the rooms.

Their dishes are hand-made pottery pieces from Sausalito across the bridge, the water and wine glasses made from a Tiberon artist famous for one-of-a-kind sets. Swirled candles and hand-blown glass decorate shelves and tables. Macramé plant holders hanging from the ceiling add greenery to the décor. It's stunning, and it has caused Mercy and me to stay awake discussing decorating into the wee hours of the morning. It's the only subject besides civil disruption I can get her to talk about for more than five minutes.

Over the past two weeks, we've found that life in San Francisco is different than anything we've ever experienced. The fog rolls in daily off the bay, and its damp cold chills you through and through. The sun burns away the fog, and it's like springtime, crisp and fresh. Windows are usually open for outside air, and the constant smell of patchouli, sage, and sandalwood incense burning throughout the apartment building and in the little shops blankets everything with exotic scents.

Every morning, Aunt Viola, Mercy, and I go for a walk up and down the strange, steep sidewalks along the streets of San Francisco, our nostrils luxuriating in the odors of sourdough bread baking and garlic sautéing. The effort shows Mercy and me we need to do more strenuous exercise when we get home.

My hope is that Mercy unwinds a little—not so bent on saving the world. Me? I just take it all in and tell myself I'll write about it one day. Some of it startles us pretty bad, though, like some of the hippies with half-naked girls hanging on their arms wearing gauzy, see-through blouses. A lot of the girls wear sleeveless shirts with unshaved underarms. Mercy said she might throw up the first time we saw it. I'm not far behind.

Hair. The hippies all have long hair. Hair under their arms. On their legs. Hair everywhere. Most wear ensembles of bell bottoms and color-print or silkscreen shirts, or assorted mixed clothes like I've never seen before. Barefooted or old-world-looking sandals are their footwear, and sometimes they stop and laugh at my matched high-heel pumps and purse. The very first day, I gave up wearing white gloves downtown as we do in St. Louis. Mercy ditched her more conservative clothes and has taken to wearing jeans and t-shirts with photos of Black singers or civil-rights leaders printed on the fronts. Honestly, with those clothes and her hairdo, she fits right in. I feel a little bit like the odd man out, but it's okay.

We see young Hare Krishna cult members on the corners wearing saffron-colored robes. White paint on their noses means something to them, and the women usually have a red dot in the middle of their foreheads. The men shave their heads—some keep a long ponytail with the rest of their head shaved. Bill told us they're part of some Eastern religious movement gaining momentum this year in California.

At night, walking around even the nicest tourist spots, we run across plenty of people who seem out of their minds. They talk to themselves or spin like tops on the sidewalks. They call out to tourists in lunatic fashion and sometimes dance around madly, slinging their heads, bells from their pockets or sewn on their clothes jingle in chaotic rhythm. Bill keeps a tight watch on our little band of women as we walk from one establishment or landmark to another.

At times, we step over passed-out drunks, addicts, and bums that panhandle every day and night for their next fix or drink. No one seems to mind that they're strewn about like trash instead of humans on some of the public streets. Mercy and I have seen bums and derelicts before, but nothing like what we've witnessed here, especially near the parks or that infamous North Beach section of town. Bill says it's from the drugs infiltrating the city, and that it's a crying shame they don't do more to stop it.

"If they don't get this situation under control, someday it will be a problem that cannot be solved," he says.

That element of this city is a *downer*, as they say here, but it's all part of life in San Fran. We call it San Fran since Aunt Viola tells us to, and to never, ever call it *Frisco*. Naturally, we acquiesce. A few days ago, Aunt Viola took us to see the fresco murals depicting life in 1930s San Francisco in the Coit Tower lobby. The tower, in the Telegraph Hill area, was a gift to the city in 1933. I was in heaven, of course, enjoying the vintage art, but Mercy seemed bored. We took a cab down the crookedest road in the world, Lombard Street, which has eight hairpin curves in a one-block street. We finished the day by having Crab Louis at the Fisherman's Grotto at Fisherman's Wharf since that's where it was invented.

At breakfast at the end of our third week, the four of us sat at the table with, as usual, the windows and the glass doors open to chill us half to death. Bill and Aunt Viola don't seem to think it's cold, but Mercy and I have to wrap blankets around our shoulders in the mornings. Fresh fruit, rye-bread toast and bagels with cream cheese, juice, and coffee with fresh cream and raw honey are the usual breakfast fare. Mercy slathers a half of a bagel with cream cheese, takes a bite, and puts it down on her plate. She sighs loudly.

"Why wasn't I here last year when they were having sit-ins and picketing those posh downtown hotels? What I wouldn't give for a rowdy demonstration to throw myself into. Yelling. Police intervention. Handcuffing ourselves to street lights. Maybe some bloody heads. What fun!"

Three sets of eyes turn to stare at her.

Aunt Viola says, "Sometimes, our voices are louder when they whisper."

Mercy rolls her eyes. "What is that, Chinese wisdom? Sounds like a fortune cookie, and I don't happen to agree."

That was rude, and everyone at the table knows it except Mercy. She attacks her bagel with gusto and pours more cream in her coffee.

"Didn't your Grandfather say the pen is mightier than the sword?" Bill asks.

"Say, how did you know about that? But, to answer you, yes, he did. I agree that change starts from within, but sometimes violence is called for."

"Violence is never the answer, Mercy," he says.

Mercy rises, pushes her chair underneath the table. Her lips are pressed together. Her look of defiance changes her face to that of a stranger.

"If you'll excuse me, I have reading to do," she says, leaving the room in quick steps.

All of us look down, barely picking at our food. "Bill... you don't suppose Mercy has inherited her grandmother's *wild hair*, do you? I truly hope not. Mama's *wild hair* was her downfall," Aunt Viola says.

Wild hair? Her downfall? It scares me to think of our Mercy having a downfall in the years to come. I wish I knew more about that grandmother, but how can I when she seems to be a recluse and a family secret?

CHAPTER
Fifty Six

Fate

Magnolia Manor, San Antonio
1921

Scattered groups of family and friends thin out, sympathy burning on their faces when they look at Joseph. Hugs. Heavy sighs. He can read their minds as they glance at him or walk sadly through the rooms.

Most of the women are dressed in black dresses with demure scarves and broaches at the neck, the men in somber clothing, hats off. All caring people showing respect for the dead and the living. The kitchen is loaded with hams, ribs, roasts, casseroles, barbequed chickens and turkeys, pies, cakes, every kind of fresh fruit, paper sacks of shelled pecans, and homemade breads, some still rising under thin dish towels. Everything that can be served, heated, or baked has been brought to feed Joseph after his great loss.

He'll give all the perishables away to the hired help when everyone leaves; the rest his parents and brothers can have when they get home from France, which they are attempting to do as quickly as possible.

Poor, poor thing. And he with a baby to raise on his own. What a tragedy! His wife was such a pretty little thing, too. But where did the Durants go immediately after the funeral at First Baptist Church? Shouldn't they be here with Joseph and Davy, especially with the rest of his family so far away?

Those are the snippets of conversation Joseph overhears as he moves like a plaster figurine with blank eyes and sealed lips through the people standing in the great room and kitchen. He gathers most folks believe he should live permanently at Magnolia Manor and let Davy's paternal grandparents—his parents—help raise him, especially since the Durants expressed at the funeral they were moving back to Georgia right away.

What people are saying may be true until Davy is a little older, but Joseph already knows his mind is set on living his own life away from Magnolia Manor. Now that Julie is dead, he can go wherever he wants.

He's numb—has been for the past week since Miguel found Coal after he galloped back to the corral wide-eyed and snorting, fully saddled, his reins tangling in his hooves. Miguel ran to find Joseph who, after Julie left on Coal in the middle of their argument, was set to drive to town in Jack's automobile to eat dinner. Steak and whiskey with other reasonable men at the private club in town had seemed a most pleasant diversion after the heated argument and the derogatory things Julie had said about his mother and their heritage.

He was literally stepping into the car when he heard Miguel shouting at him. The two of them drove up the dirt road, it wasn't far, to the rise where he last saw Julie beating her horse with a crop. At that point, the men went on foot to search for her. Miguel said Coal's legs were covered in sand burrs, so they knew to head for the sandy wash past the line of live oaks and wild pecan trees.

Their calls to Julie were answered by the normal buzz of cicadas heard on a hot Texas afternoon. They found tracks once the Johnson grass cleared, and Joseph, his heart in his throat, knew without a doubt Julie had forced Coal down into the wash, most likely at breakneck speed. He had warned her of the cave-in nature of that gorge and that riding a horse in or around it had to be approached with slow assiduousness.

She knew better!

The hoofprints in the bottom of the wash were easily followed and confirmed that Julie had been loping as if there were no tomorrow. It was Joseph who spotted her first, her slim body lying in a crumpled position on one side, one of her legs partly up the slant of the wash wall. Running faster, he spied the blood in her mane of golden hair, the rock where she had hit her head, and a pool of blood beneath the side of her face. Mostly soaked into the sand, the blood left a raised-margin spot of darkened sand.

Miguel called out behind him, "No, *senor!* Allow only me to see her. Go back, *senor!*" but Joseph continued as a sleep-walker toward the mother of his child.

Foolishness was definitely Julie's middle name, and now the consequences of it lay tragically before him. The bend of her neck suggested her neck was broken. He bent and lay his hand on her throat to check for a pulse. He squatted and duck-walked around her, touching her on the cheek with his palm, stroking the piece of hair that lay across her shoulder. He looked up into the sad face of his hired man and shook his head.

For Julie, no more tomorrows.

For Joseph, a biding of time.

CHAPTER
Fifty Seven

Rock Stars

San Francisco
1966

I'm on my stomach on the bed writing a letter to Donnie. He's the one I miss the most, and he's getting ready to move to Houston for his first job after graduating from college last spring. Why Texas, I had asked him, and he said he liked it, that's all. Mercy is sitting on the floor next to me reading a book. Aunt Viola pushes the French doors to the guest room open slightly.

"Girls, dinner is served in about half an hour. That husband of mine is making all his most special dishes for you tonight."

We fly home in two days, and I'm actually ready to resume life as I've always known it. I roll over on my back and sigh. "I can't believe we're going to that concert tomorrow night, Mercy. Bill is the absolute greatest. I never dreamed I would get to see the Rolling Stones in person."

Mercy doesn't say anything. I dig in my stationary bag and

pull out a yellow No. Two pencil. I stick it a few inches into her hair, eraser end first. Mercy bobs her head a little. I push it further into her afro so that it slides across the top of her ear. She reaches up and feels it.

"God, Annie, what are you doing?" She takes the pencil out and throws it on the bed. For a moment, I think she's mad, but her frown turns into a smile. "You're a brat. I ought to throw you out the window."

"Just as well. It's always open and ready."

She sighs and puts her book on the nightstand, face down. Stretches. "How do I get roped into these things? I have to suffer through a rock and roll concert at where? Oh, yeah... a cow palace? Whoever heard of such a name?"

"Not a cow palace, *The* Cow Palace, and its famous, silly."

"Oh, lucky me."

"You'll love it. They're going to sing the songs from their latest album, *Aftermath*... oh, so many groovy ones! *The Last Time, Under My Thumb, Time Is on My Side, Get Off of My Cloud,* and my favorite... *Paint it Black*. Is it really happening tomorrow night?"

Mercy groans. "Maybe I should just have a heart attack and die right now."

"Oh, stop. You're bound to like some of the opening acts. They say that new Jefferson Airplane group is pretty good."

Mercy rolls her eyes and falls onto the bed. "I will admit to you I've heard of the Cow Palace before now. The Supremes were there last February. Now, I could get excited about seeing something like that."

"You and me both. I love Diana Ross. Her hairdos are the coolest!"

Mercy turns and looks at me for a long moment.

"What?"

"Sometimes I forget what a great friend you are."

Wow, maybe our summer trip together was exactly what we needed.

"Yeah, but he looks a little like a pretty girl with pouty lips," Mercy says staring at the glossy black and white photo of Mick Jagger I bought in the lobby.

"He's skinny, but sexy, too. I hear he loves the ladies, and they sure love him."

"I have to go to the bathroom again. Those Cokes are going right through me."

"Me, too. I think it's because we're excited."

"Correction. You're excited. I just need to go to the bathroom. Save my seat while I scratch my way to the ladies room through ten million miles of screaming, empty-headed females."

"Hurry back. I really have to go."

She gives me a baffled look because we both know it'll be at least twenty minutes, probably longer, to and from the restroom plus the waiting in line to even get a chance at a stall. It's okay because there are forty acts lined up before the Rolling Stones, and about half have performed so far. We've heard bands named the Trade Winds, McCoys, and bunches of others. So far, I've liked the Jefferson Airplane group the best.

It's finally my turn to step over toes and say excuse me and try not to get maimed or killed as I make my way to the bathroom. If we both leave our seats at the same time, they get stolen, or so a girl told us when we first sat down. Judging by the fervor building in the room, I feel anything is possible. It's loud and crazy, and the second-best concert I've ever been to, or it will be once I get to see the main act.

I see the line extending out the door of the restroom and into the lobby hallway. I wonder if it's any better if I walk further down, and decide against it. I take my place in line. We move forward like maimed snails, and I'm getting kind of miserable. No more sodas while we wait, I decide.

A group of guys walks by, obviously a band by the way they're dressed in matching Nehru jackets and engaging in a special camaraderie. They're joking and being goofy, which causes me to smile as they pass. One of the guys stops and looks right at me. He smiles. I turn around to see who he's smiling at. I turn back around and there he is, about a foot in front of me.

"Hey, luv. How did you get so gorgeous? Is it magic?" he says.

An English accent. I don't know what to say, so I smile, probably stupidly. He's tall, has blue eyes, full brown hair to his collar, and I find him very attractive. I'm not experienced with a lot of dating or interaction with the opposite sex, so I feel my face heating up.

"You're a model, aren't you?"

"How did you know that?"

"Everything about you, luv. Say, we're on after the Sopwith Camel. Are you sticking around after the show? I'd love to buy you a cup of Joe or something."

"Uh, no, we'll have a car waiting for us when it's over."

He snaps his fingers. "Oh, bother! Well, then, can I convince you to give me your telephone number? I'm Rory, by the way. Our group is..." he gestures at the guys now halted and watching us. "... The Rory Stills Blues Band. We're all from L.A., at least right now. Guess you can tell where I'm originally from, right? What's your name, beautiful?"

"Annie, uh, Ann, actually." Suddenly, a name like *Annie* sounds so backwoods.

"You live around here?"

"St. Louis."

"St. Louis? Yeah, we played there this summer. Bummer! That's on the other side of the world. No matter. You give me your phone number, and we'll make it happen. Righteous?"

He's standing there looking at me with those blue eyes and smelling great and my face is hot and... I simply blurt out my phone number. He looks me in the eyes too long after that, and I feel myself melting like candle wax.

"That number..." he taps his head with his index finger "... burned in my brain, Ann, you can count on it. Brilliant! Gotta run, luv." He leans in and brush kisses me on the cheek. In a moment, he's back with his group walking away. He looks back and waves, blows me a kiss.

What just happened? I touch my cheek where Rory touched it with his lips.

CHAPTER
Fifty Eight

Bewitching

Tujague's Restaurant, New Orleans
1921

illie is fascinated with Ruby-Monique the second he dives into her eyes. Finding out she is a woman of great horse skill sharpens his interest, as does hearing of her ability to pull off a farce like the one she and Monsieur Laurent are construing at the track—passing her off as a boy, no less. No simpleton is capable of pulling off something so rich with potential discovery. Sitting there pretending he is listening to his "two fathers," he decides that, in addition to her physical attributes, Ruby-Monique must be brilliant, as well. That means a great deal to him.

The whole time Simon and Uncle Jacque relay the highlights of Willy's life story, and he is squirming with discomfiture, her demeanor exudes a controlled amusement of life. He can't stop stealing glances at her, exercising all his will power not to stare at her continually. When she speaks—and she isn't afraid to—she has an air about her that intrigues him.

Auntie Dove, whom he considers his true mother in this world, is soft, pliant, and generates gentility from her every pore, as do most women of station in the deep south. This woman sitting at the table this afternoon is from Texas, a rugged, quite wild place, he presumes, and she bears a self-confidence and strength that seems equal to the reputation of that state of the union and of which Willie has never before sensed in a woman.

Considering her palest of olive skin tone, her thick brown curls, and those astonishing blue eyes, he guesses her heritage is possibly Italian and Spanish. The Spaniards he has known, many of them, are fair-skinned with blue eyes. The Italians, dark eyes, dark hair, and slightly tan to light brown skin.

As the men are hooting and remarking at the conclusion of the story in which Willy finds Simon at Florentine Estate, he decides to venture forth, for he has to know, and asks Ruby-Monique if she is Italian with a touch of Spanish or perhaps Irish blood. He'll never forget the flash of fiery mischief that flickers in her eyes for the briefest of moments. She levels her eyes at his, and truthfully, their beauty makes him weak.

"Sir, I do not know all the different mixes of blood I carry in my veins, for I was given up as a babe. Yet, I can truthfully tell you that my great-grandmother was a Negro slave."

The men sit dumbfounded with raised brows, bulging eyes.

She raises her cup of tea delicately, holds it out a few moments as if in a solitary toast to life and perhaps to herself as well, then takes a sip. She peruses each man at the table and smiles. "Therefore, gentlemen, I venture to call myself a woman of the ages, nothing more… nothing less. Do you agree?"

Oh, the shuffling and coughing that takes place in the next few minutes at that table in the restaurant. Quickly checking their pockets of prejudice—for all of mankind has those pockets in varying degrees—each man determines he gives not a jot about her hereditary lines. Bewitchingly beautiful, mysterious, talented in the horse world, and courageous enough to speak her mind, the woman seems to these gentlemen to be the germane jewel fallen from a mighty crown, waiting only to be lifted up and put back in her rightful place.

Willy knows by instinct that she has, at her tender age, mastered the art of handling —dare he say, manipulating? — the male species. Without a doubt, she matches the last of his wild side in multitudinous ways. He aches to know this girl, to share his deepest ideas and dreams with her. Hope gives way to dread as he mentally summarizes the state of affairs before him. By society's standards, she is considered a woman of Color, yet no one would ever know this by simply beholding her. The world will see her as White. What then, is he to do?

Every hormone and cell in his body prays the young woman will agree to step out with him, obviously a man of Color, under the proper circumstances. Dare he even try? She admitted to being a third-generation Colored person, but she looks otherwise. How will they ever overcome such odds… such formidable laws of the land if she cannot prove her racial status?

Such thoughts for a man who just met a woman! It doesn't matter. Willy is determined to make her a part of his life.

CHAPTER
Fifty Nine

Avenging Angel

New Orleans
1922

Gnarled roots grip the ground in hardened, moss-covered knuckles. One hundred and fifty years old, the trees and their roots greedily claim much of the space in the front yard on either side of the neglected pathway leading to what Joseph presumes will be the home he's searching for. He leans against one of the massive oak trunks letting the rain fall on his face unhindered. Behind him, his hands touch soft ivy leaves on vines crawling up the rough trunk as if trying to escape the prodigious knots of wood below. Humidity and adrenaline press on his chest like a fist. It's hot, he's sweating under his shirt, and the summer rain offers no relief.

Inside the iron fence with its rusted *fleur-de-lis* emblems once proudly adorning the spikes, he found it difficult to make progress. A rainy night and the abundance of ancient oaks with their arthritic, desperate grasp for sustenance above the ground has hampered him. For at least a quarter of an hour, he has tripped and stepped over, between, and on top of the above-ground lumps slick with wet moss and mire. His ankles are bruised, but he presses on to what he must do.

Beyond the gigantic watchman trees, Joseph finds it easier to navigate. An atmosphere of despair surrounds him as he pushes aside banana leaves and fragmented bushes with more dead than alive branches grasping at his shirt and hair. At last, a house appears as if the ground belched it forth, pushing its balconied, two-storied front porch front and center of the jumble of foliage around and in front of it. In the darkness, it looms as a frowning white ghost... questioning why he is trespassing. Only the palest of lights show somewhere in the interior of the house, the reflection dying before reaching the glass of the front doors.

He turns on his flashlight momentarily, careful not to shine it directly at a window or at the door, but instead tracing the slight pitch of the roof, the squareness of the eaves, the two-storied, square pillars in the front. From his travels in Europe, he determines the architecture is Italianate with its over-hanging bracketed eaves, stylized wood trim on the windows, and elaborate carvings. From the straight-up, protuberant porch, the house extends equally on both sides in rectangular boxes with windows, tall on the first floor, and shorter on the second floor, grouped in threes with carved wood serving as brows.

It is merely a gentleman's summer home, a family's second home for when they wish to holiday in New Orleans, certainly not the lavish mansion Joseph expected to find. Only five shallow steps rise to the narrow porch and double-door entry.

Where shall he position himself to look into that house

and find the object of his search? He puts the flashlight back in the pouch hanging over his shoulder by a thin strap. He fumbles inside for the flask, finds it, takes a long drink. Putting it away, his hand grasps the knife inside, feels its shape, releases it.

He sneaks along the front edge of the house, exploring first the left wing. The foliage is thick and unkept, making his steps slow. A flash of lightning fully reveals him as he rounds the corner from the left side to the backside of the house. He dips down with his arms shielding his head and face. He is every bit the crafty fox sneaking into the henhouse to violently murder the sleeping inhabitants.

He stands, takes another long drink from the flask, rolls his eyes to assess his surroundings. Loud claps of thunder shake the atmosphere with force. More lightning. The rain coming in torrents. Through the dense greenery, he spies a small screened porch clinging to the back of the house, a dull yellow light shining inside. From his inquiries in town, he knows the owner of this house lives alone.

He retrieves the knife and continues to inch toward the screen door on the side of the enclosure. Only the white paint of the house and the faint light ahead keep him from becoming disoriented. Saturated tree limbs overhead offer no respite from the wetness pouring down on the house and its overgrown grounds. His purpose drives him on—his single purpose, and that is to kill the man who lives in this house.

Approaching the porch, he sees a man reclining in an adjustable chair-couch with a low-lit kerosene lamp beside him on a small table. Though the summer weather has produced formidable humidity and heat, the man has a blanket tucked in around his legs up to his waist.

The mud and moss at Joseph's feet are impossibly slick. He is forced to hold onto the house with both hands, the knife clenched between his teeth. Lightning illuminates the entire sky in all directions as Joseph hangs there knowing that if the man by chance looks sideways, he will see him. The next boom of thunder shakes the house, and Joseph, whose grasp has been slipping, loses his footing. He pitches backward into a reckless spray of angry palmettos. Nearly stabbed, and certainly cut, from the saw-like teeth along the stout stems, he curses. The muffled sound is lost in the storm surrounding him.

Taking the knife from his bruised mouth, he curses the plants, the rain, the blood now dripping off his back, arms, and hands into the rivulets of water running from the raised ground around the house to whatever body of water or ditch is nearby. Rolling over, he attempts to stand but can't get a firm foothold. He gropes on all fours until his hand feels a hard shape. He pats it. It's stable. He grabs hold, attempts to steady his climb back onto his feet. The sky once again illuminates the night with strange amber light. Joseph, his face pointed upward, stares into the ferocious expression of a tall angel statue dressed for war in plaster armor. In his right hand, an unsheathed sword.

That face!

Joseph shouts in alarm, the sound carried away by the tempest. The angel stares furiously down at him. He can't look away. His hands clasp the plaster until his legs give way entirely. On his belly, he begins to weep.

Is he, like the angel Michael, an avenging angel sent to destroy evilness and balance the scales of life itself? If so, who gave him such an appointment? A resounding roll of thunder sounds to his ears as a chastisement.

The anguish of the last year overtakes him. His face rests on the angel's hard foot. Memories and regrets deluge his mind... the savage beating his mother endured that fateful night so long ago. A baby sister gone forever. Being tricked into marriage by a conniving woman and her family. Guilt over that same woman dying with the shards of their worst argument still in her heart. His irresponsible behavior as a father since Julie died. His dead dreams. And, oh, his drinking. It seems he has preferred to stay intoxicated most of the past year. Now, here he is in the dregs, rain violently beating down on him, a knife in his hand ready to end a human life.

A self-appointed avenging angel.

Joseph loses the concept of how long he stays on the flooded piece of yard letting the frenzied storm drain him of his anguish. The storm and his grief abate with the storm moving northwest, leaving him with a weary desire to see for only an instant the man inside the porch—the man who is his and Monique's half-brother.

He presses his face to the screen. Bradford Allen Livingston appears to be sleeping. Joseph carefully makes his way across the front of the porch to the other side where the man's chair is but a few feet from the screening. Once there, he peers inside. What he sees jolts him to his bones.

A wretched sight!

His hands fly to his mouth to keep from crying out. Where the man's nose should be is a cratered, sunken hole. His eyes appear as white holes. He has not a shred of flesh on his frame, and the way he suddenly jerks, then feels for the glass on the table, it is obvious he is blind. Joseph has heard of an insidious disease such as this, a destroyer of a person's body piece by piece. He knows without a doubt, he is seeing a victim of *syphilis*, an incurable malady that reduces a human into a deformed skeleton, stealing his body, mind, and finally, his life.

He feels a gush of sympathy for the poor soul before him who will surely die a horrifying death. A strong desire to go home and hold his young son in his arms permeates his being. He makes his way out of the neglected yard the same way he came through it, but it is a different man leaving than the one who entered.

CHAPTER
Sixty

Lunch at Catfish Alley

St. Louis, Missouri
1966

ercy wheels into the parking lot outside the Liberal Arts building in her new Suzuki X6 Hustler, turns off the motor, and flips the kickstand down. I have to chuckle when I see her these days. She was so prim and proper as a girl and early teen. Now, she goes most everywhere in sweatshirts, slogan T-shirts, bellbottoms, ankle boots, and, of course, sporting her afro hairdo that gets longer all the time.

"Hop on, White Mama!" she calls.

I don't like riding on motorcycles for many reasons. A big one is that it messes up my long hair, which I'm fastidious about. I also wear dresses to classes, mostly minis, and that isn't conducive to straddling a cycle. More importantly, in high school, a friend of ours riding on the back of a motorcycle with her boyfriend was in a terrible accident. It left her limping and full of metal plates in her body for the rest of her life.

Mercy blows off that story with a "Phfft, she should have been careful who she rides with. Me? I'm an ace."

I've conceded to ride behind her for short distances, such as eating at close-by restaurants and only if we take it slow riding through neighborhoods or on uncrowded city streets. If she tries to take me on a freeway or starts darting in and out of traffic, I shut it down. I have a desire to keep myself in one piece, and that's final. She thinks I'm being ridiculous, but she honors my misgivings.

Mercy has definitely been crazier than me for a few years, sometimes taking risks in violent demonstrations that could really get her hurt. All of us are against her participating in the movement in a careless way, but she won't listen. I still haven't met her grandmother who lives in New Orleans, but I haven't forgotten what Aunt Viola said about her having *a wild hair*. Mercy most likely did inherit it from her. Her mode of transportation, her Suzuki, symbolizes her personality exactly.

"Where are we eating?" I ask her.

"I need some soul food, Mama. All my studying lately is wearing me down."

"No chitterlings."

She laughs. "I hate them, too. I want some good fried chicken or catfish. Maybe some smoked ribs."

"Okay, as long as they have cornbread and beans. That's Momma's specialty you know, from her hillbilly days. Think they'll have fried okra?"

"I know just the place. Get on."

I straddle the seat behind her and try, not very successfully, to do so without showing my underwear. "You're going to get me arrested one of these days for indecent exposure."

"Then I'll come bust you out of the slammer."

"Comforting," I reply as we roar noisily toward the street.

Seated in Catfish Alley at little tables with blue and white checkered vinyl tablecloths, we chatter about our classes, professors, homework, research papers, and finally, what we really want to talk about comes up.

"So... what do you hear from Rory?"

"Oh my gosh, Mercy, I think I'm in love with that guy."

"But you met in person only once."

"Yes, but it was meaningful. I heard him perform, don't forget, and he's a top-ten voice for sure. We write so many letters, I feel like we've known each other forever. I play his albums every day. Thing is, his managers are about to disband his current band and put him with another group with three lead male singers. Sounds kind of odd, but, if it happens the way everyone is projecting, he says they'll be world famous. It's something different, and it's being handled by some real money people in the business. See? That's how great his voice is."

Mercy traces the rim of her glass with a finger. "Just be careful. He's a musician, after all, and they have girls beating down their doors and offering their... you know, their *merchandise,* to them at every concert and maybe every time they leave the house. Teenyboppers are nuts."

"I know, and I hate it, but Rory isn't like that. He's coming here for a concert June fifteenth. He won't tell me if it will be the Rory Stills Blues Band or the new one. He says I have to wait and be surprised. I'll be sitting in the V.I.P. section out front, and I have a backroom pass he already sent me."

"That's actually kind of impressive. You don't want to end up with a musician, though, Annie. Not long-term."

"Why not?"

"It has no meaning. It's his gig, not yours, so you wind up being window dressing. At some point, he'll move on. They never stay with the same woman for long. You need to concentrate on your career when you get out of college. Didn't you say you're transferring after you finish your core courses, after you get your Associates?"

"I think so. I really do love art history, and I should go where the best college is for that. Not a lot of options for my kind of specialty, but I'm really interested in museum studies, too. I'm kicking around the idea of minoring in archeology and history, and I'll need a Masters if I go into museum work. It's a lot, so I may have to continue it later."

"Why?"

"Because if Rory asks me to go on tour with him, I'll be postponing college for a while."

"Now you're just talking stupid."

After all the backing I've given Mercy for what she believed in from the first day I met her, her quick, curt statement makes me mad. I take a long drink of lemonade before I answer. "That's your opinion, Mercy, not mine."

"Girl, you have to be kidding. We've planned on getting our four-year degrees and beyond since we were in elementary school. What about our moving off together to California or Boston after college?"

"Things change, Mercy, you know that. You should, anyway, considering how involved you've been in civil rights these past few years. Too busy to even… well, look, you can't always follow your childhood dreams. Especially if they don't apply anymore. I mean, look at you. You're supposed to become a university professor and a world-renowned writer. All I see you doing are sit-ins, radical protests, and writing scalding hot papers against the establishment. Except for me asking you to tone it down for your own safety, you haven't heard me criticizing your goals, have you?"

Mercy's eyes narrow. "Because it's all for *the cause,* Annie. You know that."

"Yeah, I do. You've been obsessed with *the cause* for almost six years now. I think you ought to do something else sometimes, like be closer to your family and friends. There's more to life than fighting one big war."

We look at each other over our half-finished plates. It's a stand-off, and neither of us wants to bring it to a head. I glance at my watch. "Hey, guess what? I have a psych class pretty soon. I think we should head back to campus. When's your next class?"

"I'm through for the day. After I drop you off, I'm heading over to the Pascal Hotel for a pro... uh, to meet with friends."

"Right. Meet with friends. Well, that's fine, Mercy."

We pay and leave, both of us mute on purpose.

When did we grow in two different directions? Are we really destined to go our separate ways in life?

Before she drives off, Mercy gives me one of her million-dollar smiles. "Hey, little Mama, keep the faith. You know I loves ya."

"Be careful out there, brat. I'll call you tomorrow."

I watch her until she's a tiny spec, rolling down the street.

CHAPTER
Sixty One

It Simply Must Be Boston

Baton Rouge, Louisiana
1922

Willy repeats each line of the vows as the minister says it.

"I, William St. Clair, take you, Ruby-Monique Adele, to be my wife, to have and to hold from this day forward, for better or for worse, for richer, for poorer, in sickness and in health, to love and to cherish, till death us do part, according to God's holy law, in the presence of God I make this vow."

The bride-to-be repeats her vows. She is dressed in a flowing white moiré and uncut velvet full-length gown trimmed with pearls and Limerick lace. Her crown above her veil is a garland of white roses, orange blossoms, and myrtle—symbols of purity. A chatelaine of fragrant orange blossoms hangs from her waist.

The minister pronounces them man and wife, and Willy presses his beloved's hands between his and looks deeply into her blue eyes. He is, quite frankly, the happiest man alive, even if he did see his new wife look briefly to the side when he was reciting his vows to her.

The wedding and reception are at the home of Jacque and Dovelle Boyer of Baton Rouge. In attendance are all of Willy's brothers, their wives and children, Simon St. Clair, and Isabelle Smith, *Smith* being Isabelle's chosen new surname. Also attending is Dovelle's cousin from New Orleans, Mrs. Caroline Franklin—her husband, Dr. Robert Franklin, was unable to attend with his gruelingly busy schedule—and an entourage of friends and distant family members who have come to see a happy couple unite in holy matrimony… people who admire the Boyers for both their wealth, yes, that is so, as well as their charitable acts of taking in fatherless boys.

A first glimpse of the bride in her finery, for those not in the closest inner circle, produces a collective gasp when they believe they are about to witness an interracial marriage, one prohibited by Louisiana law. Enough planted persons who are aware of the true facts are seated throughout the audience to soothe the worried brows of those certain people. The interceptors are waiting and watching for the panicked looks, the gasps, so they can lean in and enlighten the poor souls with carefully planned words.

The bride is of Colored descent.

Her great-grandmother was Colored, don't you know?

Mulatto, she is, as she is only seven-eighths White. Still a Colored, yes?

Isn't it amazing that she is Colored and yet so blue-eyed?

Of those recruited to be the purveyors of this great truth, Isabelle and Mrs. Franklin are the most enthusiastic. "I'm just tickled pink, Dovie, to help. Can you believe our little lost Willy boy has grown into such a fine man? So tall and handsome, he is! Did you say he finished his university studies in business and finance? I hear his other father, Mister St. Clair, is of high standing in my very own city of New Orleans. My, my, such a miracle it all is, and look at his wife! I've never seen such a beautiful thing in all my living days," Mrs. Franklin gushed in her deep southern accent, hugging Isabelle and Auntie Dove several times.

A few weeks earlier, as the wedding plans were fully underway, Auntie Dove and Uncle Jacque called for a private session on the veranda with the engaged couple to offer ways to maneuver some of the complexities of their forthcoming marriage ceremony and subsequent lives together. Willy mentioned some of the intolerant behavior they had already encountered in their secret courting ventures of the past year.

"Oh, how I understand, *mes chers*. Jacque and I have battled these perceptions and enigmas for so long," Auntie Dove said. "You know that I am also of Colored descent, yet no one questioned me when I married a French man because I appeared non-Colored. We offered no insights, and we were asked none. It was when we began taking in our boys of all different races to cherish as our own children that onslaughts of prejudices came from people whom we thought were broad thinkers... some who were very close friends of ours. Unfortunately, as it turned out, many had the capacity of a peanut to understand that love knows no color or race. It simply is *love*."

Uncle Jacque, who had been listening to his wife and puffing on a cherry-wood pipe with a carved face, now held the pipe in his hand, leaned forward, and said, "I am very fortunate that I come from a long line of shipping merchants and magnates with more money than they know how to spend." He chuckled, his belly jiggling, cheeks red. "When *gens stupides* try to make trouble, I have my ways. *Mon dieu,* I make them pay!"

"Dear, perhaps we should, um… as I was saying, children, I have thought of a way to ward off unwanted suspicions or untrue gossip. It is, unfortunately, necessary. We shall not have anyone discounting this Godly union or anything pertaining to it. Yes, it is an evil world that judges its own inhabitants by the lightness or darkness of one's skin. But, children…" she said, taking hold of one of Willy's hand and one of Ruby-Monique's, "… it is the law of the land that we must at least *appear* to respect. Do we truly, in our hearts, uphold such a disgraceful law, perceiving it as noble and holy? Not for a moment! But it is for the sake of appearances and for your own future that we must be wise and forethoughtful."

Willy had been delighted that his "mother and father" were so prudent and full of love for him and his bride to be. Ruby-Monique, who had never thought of race and bias until she found out she had a Negro great-grandmother and had consequently run away to the South, sat silently during the family talk. Sometimes, her far-away looks and silence worried Willy, but his infatuation was stronger than any doubts that intermittently flashed across his mind.

"My sweets," Auntie Dovie said, "may I be so bold as to suggest you consider moving to Boston? Now, I realize that Ruby-Monique is from Texas, and you are a Louisiana resident your whole life, Willy, but Boston is perfect for the two of you to make your home."

"Why Boston?" Willy said.

"Livelihood, for one. We are happy to announce that Mr. Bouchard, our long-time and trusted superintendent of all our Atlantic shore interests, is about to retire." She looked at Jacque. He nodded. "Willy, you can fill Mr. Bouchard's position and go as far with it as you wish, son. Isn't that right, Jacque?"

Uncle Jacque affirmed with a tilt of his head.

"Oh, the people you will meet!" Auntie Dove said.

"What do you mean?" Willy asked.

Auntie Dove clapped her hands together. "Did you know that most of New England has never forbidden interracial marriages? Not that you will be an interracial couple, but you appear to be to outsiders. Boston itself has an overabundance of educated elites of Color, Willy. Both you and this lovely young woman will enjoy a social and academic stimulation like you've never experienced here. Dance, theatre, art, prose and poetry... it's all there and, many times, Colored people are at the helm.

"I had no idea," Willy said, glancing at Ruby-Monique. Her face bore no expression.

"Oh, it simply must be Boston!" Auntie Dove sat back in her chair on the veranda and sighed. "And, if you decide to move there, I shall accompany Jacque on his every trip to see you."

Willy did a lot of thinking after that conversation. Considering the business opportunities it afforded him, and the chance to escape the deep biases of the South, he decided it befitted him to take Ruby-Monique and move to Boston. He was somewhat concerned, however, that his intended voiced neither favor nor protest of his decision.

CHAPTER
Sixty Two

A Lonely House

Denton, Texas
1925

"**D**addy, why is the barn door coming off?"

Joseph looks at the weather-beaten structure whose life seems to have been squeezed out little by little. He takes Davy's hand and moves him out of the way before taking hold of the door and pushing it all the way back on its hinges. It protests in soft metal groans.

"Stay back for a minute, Davy"

He peeks inside at two rows of empty horse stalls opposite one another and separated by a wide alleyway littered with hay and dirt clods. Cobwebs hang in the corners. Several dirt-dauber nests in long hollow coils resembling a woman's curled hair hang from the rafters. A door at the far end of the alleyway is closed. Corrals are visible through the small windows on each side of the door.

"Daddy?"

"Well, son, what I see is a very nice barn that used to have lots of horses and got a little run-down." Joseph takes the boy's hand and steps inside. "Don't touch anything without asking me first. Maybe there'll be some old saddles to look at in the tack room."

They are startled by a rattly cough behind them. Joseph turns to face the second thinnest man he's ever seen in his life. The man's bony shoulders are points sticking up from the yoke of his faded western shirt. His Levi's are puckered at the top where his belt has cinched them to the fullest to keep them on his frame. He is stooped, yet he was once tall. The man has a shock of straight gray hair pushed to the side on top of his head, and he badly needs a shave. Three or four days of gray whiskers cover his lower face—a cigarette dangles from the side of his thin, wrinkled lips. His skin is sun-browned and full of creases. What Joseph notices most is the shotgun braced against the old man's leg.

Joseph and the boy step out of the barn.

The man's eyes narrow. "Can I help you?"

Joseph maneuvers Davy behind his legs, dons a sheepish smile. "I'm sorry, sir. I knocked at the door of your house, but no one answered. I was letting my son satisfy his curiosity about this barn. He loves horses and—"

"You lost?"

"Well, I'm thinking I might be. I'm looking for a Mr. Ernest Adele. I thought I had the right place. Do you know where I might find him?"

"Who's asking?"

Joseph puts out his hand. "I'm Joseph, and this is my son, Davy. We're down here from San Antonio."

The man looks at Joseph's hand, switches the shotgun to his left arm, shakes hands. The skin on his hand is rough, but his grasp is firmer than Joseph expects.

"I don't know what happened. My dad, Jack, drew me a map for finding the Adele ranch, but I must have taken a wrong fork in the road somewhere." Joseph smiles, and the man cocks his head as if he hasn't heard right.

"You said *your dad*... would that be Jack the Texas Ranger?"

"Yes sir, it sure is."

"Well, why in the hell didn't you say so in the first place, son? I'm Ernest Adele, and I'm mighty glad to make your acquaintance."

Now the man is grinning from ear to ear and reaching again for Joseph's hand.

"His son! How is the old rascal? I haven't seen him in... what is it... six or so years? He just quit coming, except for that time right before..." The old man hesitates, then says, "Still get his letters twice a year, but I haven't had much heart to write him back. Say, y'all come on in the house, and I'll make some coffee that'll put hair on your chest just in case you need some. Think I can rustle up a glass of cold well water for your boy, too."

They follow Ernest into the house—a nice home with a good-sized covered front porch but, like the barn, in need of attention. Joseph notices as they walk through to the kitchen the house is neat and orderly but looks unlived in. Heavy dust on every surface, window cobwebs hanging from the heads of the frames over the glass panes like intricate lace. The most noticeable characteristic of the house is the feeling of loneliness that pervades every corner.

The kitchen is another story. The old stove is covered in years of over-boiled coffee and grounds and a small, cluttered table sits in front of the windows. Thin metal ashtrays overflowing with cigarette butts and ashes and two or three days' worth of coffee mugs with splashes of stale coffee inside litter the surface. Ernest puts an aluminum pot of coffee on to boil and tells them to have a seat. He gestures toward the table and chairs.

"Oh, let me get that mess off there. I don't think about it much, but now I have some company, I see it's downright unsightly."

He clears away the cups and empties the ashtrays in a galvanized bucket in the middle of the kitchen. It's as if he notices for the first time the receptacle is out of place and moves it to just out of sight beside the small refrigerator. Joseph need not be told there's no Mrs. Adele living there—the place screams of bachelor living. The old man reads his expression and says, "The missus passed some years back, so I guess I'm just an old codger all alone and living like one." He attempts to grin at his own comment, but Joseph sees anything but humor in his face.

Settled in at the table, they exchange small talk about the rains all summer and the tornadoes that went through Fort Worth and Denton on their way to Oklahoma, whether or not the wild pecan trees will produce a better crop this coming year, and how the upcoming quail season ought to be a good one for bird hunters. Ernest inquires of Jack and Selene's health and asks Joseph which one of Jack's sons he is.

The time has come to tell Ernest why he is there.

CHAPTER
Sixty Three

Mama is a Little Crazy

St. Louis, Missouri
New Year's Eve 1966

*I*t's New Year's Eve, and I'm a bit nauseated from too much eggnog on top of Cheetos and potato chips. I'm leaning back on my bed pillows watching Mercy pace back and forth in my bedroom. We didn't see one another all through the holidays, or much at all the past few months. Christmas Eve, I called her. We decided we owed ourselves a fun night together, so rocking in the new year with eggnog, junk food, soda pop, and waiting to watch the ball drop in Times Square sounded perfect.

Since we have another hour to go before midnight, I have the sound turned down on my television. Mercy sits down in my plush rocker with her elbows on the armrests.

"She's driving Dad and me nuts."

"I told you Momma said she's probably going through menopause. I'll bet she can't help it."

"How can my mother be old enough to go through the

change? She's not even forty-three yet."

"You want me to look it up in the encyclopedia?"

"No, I'll do it when I get some time. Maybe she's just bored with Jerome off to school again with his basketball scholarship and me in college and busy all the time. Maybe she's acting out for attention, you know?"

"Mrs. Washington is too mature for that."

"You don't live with her. She's changed."

"What do you mean?"

"She's always hot, for one thing. We're about to freeze to death this winter with her continually turning off the heat, cracking a window in every room, shrieking if we try to build a fire, 'It's too hot in here! Don't light a fire!' It's ridiculous. She gets up in the night now and walks around fixing or cleaning or trying to research those new genealogy charts she's working on."

"Genealogy charts? You mean like so and so begat so and so, and he begat so and so and all that stuff in the Bible?"

"Uh-huh. Can you believe it? Who cares about a bunch of dead people?"

"Oh, I don't know. It might be fun to know who's who. Look at us kids in my family. We know nothing about our dad's side, or him, for that matter."

"Well, yeah, in that case." Mercy expels an exasperated sigh and throws herself stomach first across the foot of the bed. "I think she's just doing it to occupy her brain since she can't remember if she's coming or going anymore. Who knows? Actually, who cares?"

"Mercy, you seem so... I don't know... harsh. Is something wrong?"

"Maybe."

"What does that mean?"

"Nothing."

"Yes, it does. Come on, tell me."

"It means I kind of like a guy, but I have too much to do to date and be stupid. College and writing for the underground press and making myself available everywhere to raise some hell where it's needed means I have no time for frivolities."

I sit straight up. "A guy? Who? Where? When? Tell me, girl!"

She flips onto her back, crosses her arms over her stomach. "Stop it. It's no big deal. I can't allow myself distractions, Annie."

"Now that's where you're wrong. You *must* allow yourself some distractions or you're going to burst. You're way too intense, and I mean it. You act like the weight of the world and the entire civil rights movement is on your shoulders. So, who is he?"

"Third-year biology major. Goes to U of Mo. Wants to be a marine biologist or some other scientific job of that ilk. I met him at a bookstore about a month ago. We just kind of... oh, I don't know."

"Instantly fell for each other?"

"That's too arcane. We simply started talking and found out we have some similar interests."

"Is he cute?"

She sits up and bites her lip to keep from losing her serious *no big deal* face. "Gorgeous."

I hug a pillow and roll off the bed giggling.

"Don't get all ridiculous on me, Annie. It's really nothing. I told you, I have no time for relationships."

I sit back on the bed cross-legged and make a pretense of removing the happy look on my face by swiping my hand across it. "Okay, in honor of this most scientific guy, we shall dip into our twelfth-grade science class and say this situation is as serious as the Coriolis force causing whirlpools of liquid iron to generate electric currents. On my honor, I shall not giggle or laugh or smile."

In a few seconds, we both crack up.

CHAPTER
Sixty Four

A River Losing Itself

Denton, Texas
1925

"This here was her room, Joseph. I left it just the same way it was. She was always a neat little thing, so I didn't have any picking up to do." Ernest's voice trembles on the last few words. He steps behind Joseph. "Hey, little fella, want to go see my hens? I got two left so's I can have an egg once in a while."

The old man and young boy clasp hands and walk down the hallway. Joseph keeps the deep disappointment of not getting to meet his only sister in check by scrutinizing the room she called her own a mere six years ago. It's almost austere. A bed, a dresser with a mirror over it, curtains over the window a dull blue color matching the smooth bedspread, a straight-backed chair. On the shelves built into the wall are trophies, awards, and ribbons for various horse fairs and shoeing competitions. A framed document for serving as assistant-trainer of a famous thoroughbred horse from Dallas is on the wall, as well as two large blue ribbons.

All the years of wondering where she was, and, all the time, Monique was three hundred miles to the north of him, growing up not knowing her real mother or any of her brothers. Ernest had tried to explain the temperament of the girl to him, that she was a restless soul who showed no outward feelings but surely had them inside somewhere. She had won his heart early on, and, from the looks of it, had irrevocably broken it. Anyone can see the old man is seriously ill in body and soul.

Joseph walks into her room and sits in the chair staring at each item. Why would she walk away so coldly? He had read the note she left, and it bruised him sorely for Ernest, a widower and a father who had already buried two babes and a wife. Her note was indifferent. Calloused. Nothing.

Not even seventeen, she had taken it upon herself to flow out into the big world like a river losing itself at sea. She had never written Ernest one word afterward, and she left no trail that the law was able to trace.

Ernest told him how Jack had come to tell him the truth of marrying Ruby's mother, told him the events that inspired him to help a young woman with two children escape New Orleans, and how Ruby had obviously overheard them discussing it that day in the barn. Somehow, what she heard propelled her out the door.

Why would the truth of her life make her flee? Why didn't it at least compel her to come to San Antonio and find her mother and brother? She knew Jack's whole name and surely could find the address from the letters Jack wrote to them twice a year. Hadn't he and his mother grieved fiercely for years over that lost girl?

The questions in his mind find no answers.

He recalls the time right before Jack took them on their first excursion to the South of France. Jack had packed a leather duffle bag and taken their new car. He told the boys he was going car sporting and may look in on his old Texas Ranger friend up in north Texas. Obviously, Jack was coming here to tell Ernest the whole truth about Ruby's family.

If Joseph had only known the truth back then, perhaps he could have prevented his sister from running away. And again, perhaps not. She sounded nothing like him or their mother, and from Ernest's stories of her, she may have had one foot out the door long before Jack came calling that fateful day.

CHAPTER
Sixty Five

Where's Annie?

St. Louis, Missouri
1967

*I*f Mercy could get her hands around Annie's neck right now, she might wring it. Or, she might hug it and never let go. She sits sideways on her motorcycle under the shade of an expansive maple tree in Forest Park. In her hand is a pastel purple envelope. Sadness and guilt are eating her up alive.

A wobbly-voiced Zeenie called her earlier to come over as soon as possible, and she had gone immediately... scheduled protest at a restaurant be hanged, to use one of Annie's Uncle Dew's sayings.

It was Annie's uncle and Zeenie who opened the door for her before she rang the doorbell. "Come in, honey," Zeenie said, sniffing and wiping her nose. She hugged her a long time, then motioned for her to follow her to the living room.

"Where's Annie?" she asked on the way.

No one answered. Zeenie merely shook her head as she

walked in front of her. As soon as Mercy sat down, Uncle Dew handed her a piece of paper with Annie's handwriting on it. "Read it, sweetheart," he said.

Dear Momma, I love you. Please don't worry about me. I know you won't understand my flying off to England without telling you, but I didn't want you trying to stop me. I am nineteen, after all, and I love Rory with all my heart. His new group, Three-Part Harmony, is already making headlines all over the world. Judging by their record sales and the size of their concerts, I believe they'll be as famous one day as the Beatles and the Stones. You know I'm a responsible person and always have been, but I want to do this. Think of the educational value if nothing else! I'll resume my studies one of these days, and you know I ended the year at the university with a 3.9 average. Pretty groovy, right? I promise to call often. Please give Mercy the sealed note I left for her, and tell my knothead brothers to stay righteous. That means to do what's right, you know, even if they think I've done something I shouldn't. I just want this chance to be part of my future husband's life and career. Really, who can blame me? Love always, Annie.

Mercy looked up from the note with a flabbergasted expression. "I can't believe she would do something like this."

All three of them sat in disbelieving silence.

"I-I never thought…" Zeenie said.

"Who would have?" Uncle Dew said.

"She's nothing like this," Mercy said.

"How could she?" Uncle Dew said.

"Here's your note, sweetie," Zeenie said, handing Mercy a sealed envelope. On the front was Mercy's name in Annie's handwriting. On the back, a few lines of shorthand. Mercy studied the scribbles for a moment.

"What does that gobbledygook say?" Uncle Dew asked.

"It says to please look in on her momma as often as I can. That's all."

The silence in the room was terrible.

No Annie? It was unthinkable.

"Why is it that people are most cherished when they aren't around anymore?" Uncle Dew said.

"Stop it, Dew, she's not dead," Zeenie said.

He fidgeted himself right out of the chair and gave Mercy an intense look, "Um, hon, if you don't mind… could you read what's inside your note before you leave and let us, uh, kind of know what it says?"

"Of course."

He handed her a letter opener he retrieved from a small desk in the corner of the room. It was the first time she had been around Annie's uncle that he wasn't making some kind of joke or doing something to make everyone laugh. She sliced the envelope open cleanly and pulled out the note. Naturally, the stationary paper matched the color of the envelope. Annie loved matching things.

Mercy, I know you won't approve of what I'm doing, but you're the one who always told me a person has to follow her convictions no matter what. Yes, you taught me that, and so much more. You gave me the wings to fly, and now I'm ready to use them. My conviction right now is to be by Rory's side. I will write you from England, and I'll try to call in a few weeks. I didn't want everyone (or anyone, for that matter) telling me not to go, so I left clandestinely.

In the meantime, there's something important I've been meaning to say to you and haven't found the words. I worry about you, Mercy, and I've been worried about you for quite some time. I thought maybe our own Mr. King might be the right one to sum up my concerns and feelings about the important work you do. Never stop your passionate pursuits, but please do them as Mr. King suggests… non-violently. Do it that way for yourself and for all of us, especially me. I can't ever lose you—you are the sister I never had. Here it is:

"And so I plead with you this afternoon as we go ahead: remain committed to nonviolence… we must come to see that the end we seek is a society at peace with itself, a society that can live with its conscience. And that will be a day not of the White man, not of the Black man. That will be the day of man as man."

(You probably already know this, but this excerpt is from that speech Mr. King gave at the conclusion of the Selma to Montgomery march in Montgomery, Alabama, March 25, 1965.)

Remember what your Grandpa Grafton always says, that the pen is mightier than the sword. I believe he and Mr. King are in agreement about using non-violence to win this battle.

Love you,
Annie

Mercy put the letter back in the envelope and into the leather purse strapped crisscross over her shoulder. Looking at the hopeful faces of Annie's family, she said, "She said she wanted me to be careful and that she'd been worried about me. Said she'd write and call soon. When she does, I'll definitely let you know."

Their expressions registered disappointment, but she couldn't help it. The note hit her right between the eyes, and she didn't want to talk about it. She stood, hugged Zeenie and Uncle Dew, mumbled a few promises and consolations and left before she completely broke down.

Under the maple tree, she flips the kickstand down and goes to sit on the grass. She leans against the tree trunk and rereads the letter. Annie gone? Was this the end of their girlhood, their teen years… the end of their lives together as best friends? But they are only nineteen. It isn't supposed to end this way, or this early. Yes, she had given Annie a set of wings, but not to fly away with some guy across the ocean! With a musician none of them even know personally?

What about their getting an apartment together after college? What about... everything else? Why had she ignored Annie so much the past years, put everything in front of their friendship? How many hundreds of times Annie had asked her to do things, to go with her here and there, to be part of various activities, but she was always too busy, too wrapped up in her own pursuits. Now, it was too late.

Hot tears drop onto the front of her silk-screened T-shirt.

CHAPTER
Sixty Six

It Wasn't Enough

Boston, Massachusetts
1931

illy had given her everything his wealth and love could get for her, and it wasn't enough. Their home in Boston was the envy of all their associates. Her clothes and shoes were designed by the likes of Elsa Schiaparelli, Jean Patou, Salvatore Ferragamo, Jeanne Lanvin, and Coco Chanel. He took her on lavish European trips. They were patrons of all the arts. He bought her jewelry to match her beauty. Cars. And, though she was never as happy about it as he, he gave her three beautiful children and the nannies, cooks, and housekeepers to make life easy for her before and afterward.

Nothing he did, nor one thing he acquired for her sake, added the sparkle of warmth he continually searched for in those azure eyes. She stole the light from his own eyes the day his hired detective, a Mr. Mike O'Malley, came to his office to share his findings regarding the lovely Mrs. William St. Clair.

His report claimed she had been seeing a certain doctor in a certain nearby city, and that the lady was, in fact, according to his sources, four months pregnant. Willy had leaped from his desk and had his hands around the throat of the hapless detective in such an unguarded second of time the poor man nearly died of heart failure.

"You, sir, are a liar and a scoundrel!" Willy shouted as they tumbled to the floor.

Grunts and wheezy pleas for his life were O'Malley's responses.

Willy stopped choking the man just short of garnering a murder charge. O'Malley scuttled off the floor and hurried across the room with an offended glare at Willy.

"I shall have you jailed if you so much as lay another finger on me!" he rasped. "I believe my findings shall make fine reading in the newspapers, now won't they? Naturally, what I have with me are copies. The originals are in my desk drawer with instructions."

Willy stumbled back to this chair on the other side of his desk. He knew O'Malley was telling the truth. He'd experienced Ruby-Monique's icy indifference, felt her slight shudder if he so much as tried to hug her lately. She had refused his bed for more than half a year for one or a hundred excuses.

"I beg your forgiveness, sir. Please... sit down, Mr. O'Malley."

Willy leaned forward on the desk on his elbows, his head in his hands. He raised his face—and oh, what a weary, sad face it was—to look at the detective. "Who is the father?"

"You know it gives me no pleasure, lad, to bring news of this kind to a young husband, especially one as charitable and tolerant to our fair city as you are. However, I suggest you get hold of that temper of yours for any future business between us." He reaches into a satchel and takes out a photograph. "'Tis this man," he says, placing the photo in front of Willy.

Willy gasps. "Could you be mistaken?"

"Afraid not, sir."

There before Willy was the picture of his best friend, André Bissett, the man who was a weekly guest for dinner at his home, someone who accompanied him and Ruby-Monique to the theater, to charity events, and who happened to be Willy's closest confidant. André was a good-natured, gray-eyed Frenchman Willy had met at the track one rainy day. Willy had convinced André to move to Boston so they could continue their friendship and do business together. He had set André up in a dry dock and shipping business, and the man had flourished and become wealthy.

Now, it was gut-wretchedly understandable why André had refused any of Willy's suggestions regarding the eligible young ladies of Boston he might court, or at least have on his arm as escorts when they attended events all over the city.

Right under his nose, André and his wife... it was absurd. Traitorous.

The next day at the St. Clair home, at least twenty people plus all the house staff packed and sorted the belongings of the family. The house was up for sale, and Ruby-Monique had two choices put before her the very night of the disclosures: Stay in Boston and be André's paramour without benefit of any further connection or sustenance from Willy, his family, or his businesses. Their children would, of course, go with Willy, and she would have no more contact with them. Naturally, divorce proceedings would commence immediately thereafter.

Her other choice was to leave Boston and remain legally married to him. Willy had been dabbling in financial opportunities in St. Louis for several years, and, thanks to his myriad connections, he knew he could start fresh there. He would buy a small home for Ruby-Monique in New Orleans and bring the children to see her periodically, discreetly, keeping a low profile so as not to provoke the *stigma of the South* of his and Ruby-Monique's *perceived* interracial marriage. For all practical purposes, she, appearing as a White woman, could live in New Orleans as a White woman, raise her fourth child as one, claiming to be a widow.

Mortified at the news of William's discovery of their affair, and of learning that the object of his desire was with child, André immediately sailed for Europe, leaving the running of his company to his board of directors.

Ruby-Monique chose the second of Willy's options, and within less than a week, the St. Clair family takes their leave of Boston, Massachusetts, leaving tongues to wag at will.

CHAPTER
Sixty Seven

Tell My Girl

Denton, Texas
1931

he room is sickeningly warm to Joseph. The curtains are drawn against the dark night outside. The only light is a low-flamed kerosene light flickering across the room. Ernest's air is racked with congestion and wheezing as it moves slowly in and out of his sunken chest. Death hangs in the air.

He gurgles, chokes, coughs. Joseph is immediately at his side lifting the man's shriveled shoulders a few inches off the bed and handing him another rag to use for spitting out the bloody phlegm. The old man moans in between the coughs. The lung sickness is taking its time. Joseph curses it under his breath. He has grown to care deeply for this man the past six years, and it hurts to see him suffer so terribly.

A light knock on the door, and eleven-year-old Davy sticks his head in. "Any change, Daddy?" he whispers. Joseph shakes his head and smiles wearily at his son. Davy goes to the bedside and peers down at Ernest. "I wish I could help him," he says. The man opens his eyes.

"Davy?"

"Yes sir?"

"You did real good at that junior rodeo, son."

"Aw, I could have done better."

"You will, boy, you will. Take your time and live every second like it's a year when you're riding those broncs. Slow that time down in your head. Watch where you put your spurs." He coughs and again, Joseph assists him. He lies back on the pillow. "Don't you be climbing on the back of no bulls yet, you hear? Wait till you're at least fifteen. When you do, remember this... take each time by itself. Ain't no two bulls alike. When the bull goes forward in a buck, lean forward over your arm and stay square with your rope. When he lifts his front end up, keep your butt square and your weight down in the seat of your pants. Stay in the middle of his back. You shift around even a few inches, and you'll be eating a dirt sandwich. Got that?"

"I sure do. I won't ever forget, Ernest."

"You're my good boy, Davy"

The long flow of words seems to steal a little more life from Ernest, but a small smile plays on his face. His eyes are closed. "Joseph?"

"Yes, sir. I'm right here."

He reaches an arm into the air. "Can't see too well, boy."

Joseph puts his hand over the man's lean fingers and brings his arm down to rest on the layer of blankets covering him.

"Don't break your promise to me, Joseph. If my little Ruby comes back, she gets half this ranch. You helped me make it worth something again, so she might like it now. See,

she can build her a beautiful house over by the springs
bordering the Crawford land. It'll work out real fine for both
of you. She can have all the pretty curtains and doilies and
such her mama Arlene made for this house. You and Davy
don't need them, do you?"

"No sir. That'll be just fine."

"I finished filing the papers in town about the deed and
all, didn't I?"

"You sure did, sir. Everything is tended to. Don't worry."

A smile plays around the man's wrinkled mouth. His eyes
remain closed. "I sure am grateful to you two fellas for making
my last years mean more than a plug nickel. I thank you
kindly."

"No need to thank us, Ernest. Davy and me were looking
for a new start, I reckon, when we came here and found you.
It's been our great pleasure to know you."

"And my old partner Jack is still living, ain't he?"

"Sure is. Ailing a bit, but alive."

"You tell him I'll see him up the trail, okay?"

"You betcha."

"Joseph?"

"Yes?"

"Tell my girl... tell her I never stopped loving her, not
for one minute or hour. Tell her I don't hold nothing against
her. She's my baby girl, yes sir, always has been. Always will
be."

Tears stream from the sides of the old man's closed eyes.
He opens them abruptly, stares wide-eyed at the ceiling.
"Ruby?" he whispers. His head raises from the pillow, falls
back as he breathes his last.

CHAPTER
Sixty Eight

The Ledge

San Francisco
1968

Sol Swartz, owner of the deli downstairs, steps outside his shop in a full white apron smeared with remnants of the day's cooking, including kishkeh and other kosher delicacies. Even in my emotional agony, I am reminded of abstract expressionism as I stare at what looks like sliced green olives in those food smears and ultimately see *Rhythm, Joy of Life* by French artist Robert Delaunay in them.

Art? I'm thinking of art at a time like this?

"*Oy vey,* Ann-uh-luh, get down from off that ledge. Get back in the window. You wanna bust your *keister* with those damn platform shoes? What's the matter with you kids today?" He rocks back and forth on his heels. "So, you look pale, Ann-uh-luh. Go to the ocean and get some sun, for God's sake. Hey, you want I should send up some chicken soup?" He waves his hand. "Don't even tell me. I'll get some chicken fat from the larder. No trouble at all. Work is what I do."

He starts toward the door, stops, backsteps onto the sidewalk. Looks up at me. "Get inside already. You got no worries. You're a *sheyn froy*. Wait till you get bunions. Then you can climb out a window." He watches me for a minute. "Did you smell my *carciofi alla Giudia* frying this morning? Geez, what you gonna do with a Jew who had an Italian *bubbe* like me, huh? Fry the artichokes and make the matzo soup, that's what." He puts his head back and laughs, but I see through all his chatter. He's worrying about me.

"Sol, please, this is bigger than food. It-it's the…"

Sol stares at me through narrowed eyes. Rubs his chin. "So, Chana's making latkes. I'll send some up with the soup. Get down off there and go wash your hands. Sheesh, what you hanging around for? Food's coming. You think I do all this work for nothing?" He shakes his head. "Hippie generation… *mshuge*, all of them."

He mutters all the way back into his shop. Sol always mutters.

A guy with bare muscled arms and a black leather vest covered in chains comes out of the head shop next to the deli. He mounts a tricked-out Harley parked along the street. Noticing a few stragglers staring up at me, he looks too.

"Hey, babe, uh, cute-face. Yeah, you, blondie. You looking for some climbing experience? Come on down here. I'll give you something to climb you won't ever forget." He cups his hand over his groin and laughs lustily. He starts the motor, revs it, and zooms down Beach Street, his long air blowing zigzag around his head. Under different circumstances, I'd have kicked him in the face.

A few feet to my right, the bedroom window of this apartment slides open. Star holds a dull beige phone receiver partly out the window, followed by her head. Her bright yellow and blue tie-die shirt and dyed black hair are too much to absorb on this last day of my life.

"Phone call, Annie."

"What?"

"I said, you have a phone call."

"Are you kidding me?"

"Someone named Marcy or something like that. Want me to take a message?"

Doesn't anyone have respect for the last moments of a person's life?

I bend in half with my bottom headed back into the open window behind me. It lands in the bathroom sink. I pull my legs in and swing them around to the floor. I stomp across the narrow hall and jerk the phone from Star's hand. She snorts and gives me a dirty look as she exits the room. I slam the door behind her. A thumbtack pops off the back of the door. The raging blue, purple, and red Jimi Hendrix poster swings downward at an angle held now by a single tack.

"Hello."

"Hi, babe. How's my favorite White Mama?"

I don't say anything.

"Listen, I can't talk long. I'm on my way to a protest. Don't worry. It's a tame little get-together. I don't do dangerous ones anymore because, wow, you know, I have this friend who used Dr. King's own words against me. I'm definitely reformed, kiddo. I use my pen and not my neck anymore to make my points." She laughs.

I almost want to laugh, too, but it seems absurd at this particular time. After all, my life is over, isn't it?

"We're in finals this week, but I had to hear your voice. I don't know. I've had a bluesy kind of feeling about you the last few days. Kind of fatalistic. I haven't heard from you for a month, then you send me that cryptic little note with your phone number telling me you're back in San Fran, no updates at all, and... I don't know. You and golden boy doing okay? When did you get back from London?"

Her voice is splintering the hard wad of cold steel inside my guts, turning it into razor-sharp pieces. How can I express the tragedy of the sum total of my life and dreams dissolving in abject failure?

I can't. I need a megaphone, an earthquake, a tidal wave to do it right. Mere words through a telephone? It's impossible.

"I-I..."

"Annie?"

I drop to the bed hunched over like a hundred-year-old man. My throat burns with suppressed sobs. I rock back and forth, tears flowing silently but torrentially, hugging the phone like it's my only salvation.

"What's happened? Where's Rory? Is he there? Who was that girl who answered the phone?"

No answer.

"Annie?"

Silence.

"Okay, give the phone back to that other girl... what's her name, Startle?"

Nothing.

"Shirly Ann Blackburn! Get that idiot girl back on the phone!" Mercy roars. It slaps me out of my spell. I jump off the bed and throw the phone on the bed.

"Star," I try to call through the open door, but a hoarse rasp is all that comes out. I stagger into the tiny kitchen-living room, my stomach convulsing with pent-up sobs. Star is flopped out on the sultan pillow by the wall smoking a cigarette and reading Linda Goodman's *Sun Signs*. She frowns at me and turns over, purposely presenting her backside. I walk around her and stand there holding my stomach.

"What is it?"

"Can you, uh... please?" I gesture for her to follow me.

"Oh, wow, you're a piece of work, lady." She throws her book down, follows me noisily into the bedroom. "Okay, what do you want?"

I point to the phone.

"I got a call? Funny, I didn't hear it ring."

She picks it up. "Yeah? Uh, yeah, this is Star." Her face contorts as she listens. "Uh-huh. She broke up with her boyfriend. Found out the jerk was married all along. Had a family in England, a kid even. One of the band guys finally outed the sumbitch. Uh-huh, yeah, a real bummer, but what do you expect? The guy's a famous musician. Probably has babes in every town. What? I don't know. I think so. Got herself out on the ledge a while ago, but it's only one story down. Pretty hard to do yourself in from a second story."

Star chuckles, takes a drag of her cigarette.

"The ledge, you know... that thing they have outside a window?" She stubs her cigarette out in the incense burner beside the bed. "Well, how would I know? Why don't you ask her yourself? Me, I just think she wants some attention. You know how air-headed blonds are, right? Always doing something to grab the spotlight. Hey, you mind holding a sec?"

Star rummages through the drawer in the night stand, finds a joint, lights it while cradling the phone on her neck. She takes a deep draw and flashes me a wicked grin. She holds it out to me. I shake my head as she slowly exhales.

"Hey, look, I did her a big fat favor letting her crash on my couch until she gets on her feet. Only did it as a favor to

Sol. No, he's the dude who owns the deli downstairs. He was worried about her. She and lover boy used to eat at his deli when they were in town. Uh-huh. That's right. Been here about ten days now."

Star leans one knee on the bed.

"Hey, princess, don't act like I'm her shrink or something. I'm just the shmuckie gal who pays the rent around here. Huh? What was I supposed to... what's that? No. Yeah, well, the same to you, sister!"

Star throws the phone on the bed and bangs out of the room. I grab the phone and hold it to my chest.

"Annie? Hello? I know you're listening. Look, I'm coming out there. Don't even try to argue with me. Whatever's happened, we can work it out. This is Big Sis now, so don't give me any lip. What is this... Sunday? My finals are over this coming Wednesday, and I'll be there Thursday. Give me that address again. Listen, you do anything stupid like step out on a ledge, and I swear I'll pull your legs and arms right out of your body. You'll be whimpering on the ground like a limbless rat scooting around in a circle."

"That's BS, Mercy."

"Ah, she finds her tongue at last! What's 'BS' about it?"

"You hate naked dolls with missing arms and legs."

"What? Oh, my God!"

She breaks into laughter, and, amazingly, so do I. One more time, Mercy is my magic.

CHAPTER
Sixty Nine

The Trouble with Genealogy

St. Louis, Missouri
1968

ercy and I are contemplating renting our first apartment together as soon as I get a job. She's sort of engaged to her biologist, but it doesn't really feel solid yet since he has so many more years of education to complete. I don't feel like going back to school for a while, and everyone has supported my decision. I know I'll return when I get better. Right now, I'm bruised inside. Rory broke my heart, and it still hurts.

I'm leafing through the want ads outside on the patio when I hear the phone ringing in the house. Momma's at the coffee shop giving pep talks to her managers today, so I go answer the phone on the kitchen wall.

"Hey," Mercy says.

"Hey."

"Feel like hearing some wacko news?"

"Sure."

"Mama's planning what she calls a Genealogy Party, and she says you, your mom, your uncle, and the boys all have to come. Says she won't take no for an answer. She's acting strange. Giddy. Singing through the house and giggling sometimes when she looks at us. We're all going along with it, but she's making it a huge deal. She's renting a banquet room at the Magnolia Hotel on Eighth Street, having it catered, the whole bit. That's the hotel where Cary Grant used to stay, you know. Fancy stuff. Two weeks from now, five in the evening."

"Does that make any sense to you?"

"No."

"Is she still hot all the time and getting up in the night and all that?"

"Not anymore. She went to the doctor, and he gave her something. I guess she really was going through menopause."

"But she got hung up on to the genealogy thing?"

"Oh, more than ever. She's been everywhere talking to people, visiting courthouses, making gravestone rubbings, taking pictures. Goes to meetings, too. We think she's obsessed with it."

"That's the trouble with genealogy. I mean, I hear it can be as addictive as gambling."

"I don't doubt it. Keeps her busy and happy, though, so Dad and Grandpa are okay with it."

"And she wants all of us to look at her family tree she's put together? Wow, she must be proud of it. I hope we don't have to look at two or three hours of slides."

Mercy snorts. "No lie. So... I can tell her you're coming?"

"I'm in."

"Can you be in charge of rounding up your family for me so I can tell her it's done?"

"Sure."

"Let me know in a couple of days so she knows how much food to order."

"She remembers Joey is in Viet Nam, right? Cross him off the list, naturally. Jackie is super involved with his business in Colorado. I hope he can get away."

"Yeah, I know. But he has plenty of advance notice. He can fly in, stay the night, and go back the next day. Does he need a little help funds-wise for a plane ticket?"

"Good grief, no. He's doing great with the restaurant in Steamboat Springs. Learned everything about running one from working with Thomas, you know. It's a matter of prying him loose, but I'll work on it."

"You have to admit, it might be fun for all of us to get together again. Tell Jackie to bring his fiancé if he wants. I'm sure Donnie will want to bring his wife. Tell him to bring the baby so we can all see her. Glad he moved back here from Houston. Mama said the more the merrier. Sounds almost like a reunion, doesn't it?"

"Yeah it does. It's pretty far out, Mercy. Do you think my family is going to love hearing about your mom's genealogy charts, though?"

Mercy laughs. "God no, but let's humor her this one time. The food will be outstanding, and, like I said, it's been a long time since we were all together like this. She said to explain it will be "a blast" for one and all. She's been trying to use some younger lingo lately. Mostly, she gets it all wrong, and it cracks me up."

"Okay, I'll start calling right away. A Genealogy Party it is."

CHAPTER
Seventy

Reunion

Magnolia Hotel, St. Louis, Missouri
1968

*M*y family acted like they'd been waiting for an invitation such as this for years. Everyone agreed to come the first time I mentioned it. Of course, Joey won't be there, and none of us ever stops worrying about him off fighting in a war. Uncle Dew is bringing someone special—a girlfriend—he said. Donnie didn't even hesitate. I think he's a little stir crazy these days with a baby in the house, and, at the very least, wants to see Jerome again. Jackie's flying in but not with his girlfriend. Momma and I complete our group on the guest list.

Tonight is the big night, and Mercy and I are here early to help Mrs. Washington oversee last-minute preparations. Walking into the banquet room, we see her in a dazzling blue moiré dress with a spray of flowers pinned to the bodice. She's walking the length of the long table inspecting the place settings and the flower-strewn runner in the center. A whole line of amber-glass globes with flickering candles inside are placed among the flowers, creating a cozy, elegant atmosphere.

The surprising thing is how the tables are positioned in a long-U lengthwise in the room with the settings on one side of the table only. The chairs face a podium with a lectern next to a door. An easel frame holds a blackboard next to the podium.

"Wow, your mom is taking this genealogy presentation seriously."

"I have no words," Mercy says.

Mrs. Washington looks up and walks straight to us. She encircles us in her arms in a threesome hug and almost forgets to let go.

"Mama, you can turn us loose now."

She doesn't.

"Girls, girls, girls. This has been a long journey, and it has produced fruit that will last our lifetimes and far beyond." She sighs with an air of contentedness. There we stand for the longest time. At last, she lets go but continues smiling at us like we just invented the cure to all worldwide famine.

"Um, I really love the pale-pink recessed lighting in here, Mrs. Washington."

"Darling girl, my little Annie, isn't it time you called me by my given name? Please, call me Hope, won't you?"

"I, uh…"

"Mama, what's gotten into you? Have you been sipping champagne?"

Mrs. Washington laughs heartily with her hand covering her mouth. "Of course not, I'm just happy. By the way, have I told you how much I love your new hairdo, Mercy? I understand the afro hair style meant so much to you, but this one makes you look like Diana Ross."

"I hate to break it to you, but Diana Ross has about a

hundred different hairdos, Mama."

"She's right, though, Mercy. This teased look with the flip looks boss on you."

"Um, anyway, you sure have lots of plates set up, Mama. Annie's family equals seven guests plus a baby, and there are only nine of us with your two brothers and their wives coming, right? So, who else is invited to this... this somebody-begat-somebody-else party?

"Somebody-begat-somebody-else party? Oh, I see now. As in the Bible." She giggles, her eyes shining. Mercy and I exchange side glances. Whatever she has planned, she's ecstatic about it. "Well, dear, I have a few surprises up my sleeve."

I start to ask about the lectern and chalkboard when Mrs. Washington says, "Girls, would you mind telling the manager I have a few more requests?"

In the hotel lobby after summoning the manager, we run into one of Mrs. Washington's surprises—Bill and Aunt Viola with two young girls dressed alike. After greetings and hugs, Mercy asks, "Why didn't Mama tell me you were coming? You two haven't been back here since, uh..."

"1959," Bill says.

"My sister is being very secretive about this party, girls. I don't know what's really going on, but we wanted the chance to introduce the whole family to our daughters."

Bill whispers something to them, and they smile at us. One has a missing front tooth. They have long, black ponytails, matching green and gold party dresses, and crystal barrettes in their hair.

"This is Lì húa, which means *beautiful pear blossom*, and Lì meim, which means *beautiful plum blossom*. They're six years old and working hard to learn English," Bill says.

We don't have a chance to comment because Jerome and Donnie with his family arrive at the same time. The two men go through a whole series of crazy handclasps like I've never seen before. Donnie told me recently that Joey had written him about the Black soldiers in Viet Nam coming up with new kinds of handshakes, so I guess he's trying them out on Jerome. While they're laughing and cutting up, I greet Donnie's wife and smile at the baby inside the carrying bassinette.

By the time we're back in the banquet room, more guests have arrived, including Mrs. Washington's two brothers and their wives. I've met them all over the years, so we're not strangers. In our absence, trays of appetizers, pitchers of water, and buckets of chilled champagne have been added to the tables.

Another thirty minutes, and everyone that Mercy and I know of has arrived, but there are still empty seats with no place settings. During the four-course meal, Mercy and I decide Mrs. Washington has miscounted the attendees. The waiters clear all the plates other than the ones with partially finished desserts. More coffee and water are poured. The baby is passed around for about the tenth time. The buzz of conversation dies down as one by one, we notice Mrs. Washington standing behind the lectern.

When she has everyone's attention, she says, "I am so honored and excited to have all of you here tonight. I don't think any of us are strangers, are we?" She pauses as everyone looks around smiling and shaking their heads. "No, we are truly not strangers. I have titled this evening, *Beautiful Ashes,* because that is what we are, beautiful ashes. The meaning of it shall become clear as the evening progresses. Right now, I want to introduce a friend of mine, Mr. Francisco Salazar.

Mr. Salazar is a professional narrator, and he is going to tell us some stories in his wonderful, rich voice. Afterward, we shall have a few surprises.

A man rises from a chair at the very end of the table.

"Did you see him come in here?" I ask Mercy.

"Yeah, a few minutes ago. He said something to Mama and sat down. I'm kind of impressed Mama hired a narrator."

I nod and sit back to listen.

"Good evening, ladies and gentlemen. I'm delighted to have this opportunity to relay several incredible stories pertaining to this amazing family. As Hope has requested, I shall begin with a story of a child being kidnapped by a voodoo priestess along the marshes and swamps of Lake Pontchartrain and Lake Maurepas. Ah! I already see the surprise and excitement building! Shall we commence?"

CHAPTER
Seventy One
Beautiful Ashes

Magnolia Hotel, St. Louis, Missouri
1968

I'm spellbound as the story unfolds of a young boy taken by a crazy priestess, rescued by one of the woman's own daughters, and given to a wealthy family. A boy, who when he was fifteen, ran away from home to be a horse jockey, went to war, and, afterward met and married a ravishing young woman who was posing as a boy to ride and train race horses. At the end of the story, he tells that boy's mother's name. Mercy gasps.

"Flo? So my middle name of Florentine is from *her?*" she whispers to me.

Mr. Salazar says, "Let's meet Willy, shall we? William Grafton St. Clair... Willy... will you please stand?" Mercy's Grandpa Grafton stands. A collective gasp is heard around the room. I turn to stare at Mercy. "Did you know all of this?"

"Only about his war experiences. I-I'm essentially

shocked."

"Do you think he minds everyone knowing his past?"

Mercy blows out a big breath. "Well, he's grinning at Mama, so I guess it's okay."

Grandpa Grafton smiles kindly at everyone, slightly bows, then sits down. I want to go hug him and ask him millions of questions, but Mr. Salazar starts speaking again.

"The brave young girl who rescued Mr. St. Clair that terrifying night, risking her life and carrying him over that infamous Suicide Bridge… Miss Isabelle Smith… will you join us, please?"

The door opens and an older woman with a cane steps into the room. Her eyes sparkle as everyone claps for her. She greets the room with gracious head nods. Mrs. Washington leads her to a chair at the end of the table.

"And now…" Mr. Salazar waits for the conversation to ebb "… we have another remarkable story of a young woman of twenty years of age with a babe in arms and a young son. Those three were victims of the closed and perilous society of New Orleans in the early twentieth century—a society seething with ancient prejudices, old and new money, race-mixing, and young hot blood."

Without breaking my stare, I nudge Mercy with an elbow. She nudges me back. Even my hair is alive with anticipation.

Mr. Salazar, his rich tones rolling over the words, tells the story of how the young woman was driven from a little house in New Orleans, a house she owned, and how she was thrown out by the cruel son of the woman's caregiver after the older gentleman's untimely death.

"Ah-ha, a kept woman," Mercy whispers in my ear.

"The woman, in a state of utter desperation, threw herself on the mercy of a kind man who was staying at the St. Charles

Hotel. He not only saved her that very night, he also fell in love with her and married her. He raised the boy as his own, but alas, the poor mother of two, somewhat deranged at the time, gave up her six-month-old daughter in fear of that cruel man, a man who promised to sell the baby to a merchant who dealt in child bartering and slavery in international waters. Later, that decision to give up her little girl broke her heart a thousand times. Yet, she refused to rip out the hearts of the couple raising her daughter."

Mr. Salazar stops talking, and the gap in conversation is soon filled with chatter as the guests absorb and discuss all they have heard.

"Would you like to meet some of the characters, the real characters, of these stories?" Mr. Salazar asks in a lilting voice.

The flurry in the room is palpable as everyone titters with excitement. The door beside the podium opens, and a slender, well-dressed woman walks in. Her silver hair is in a fashionable upsweep, her neck graceful, her face—while bearing the wisdom of the ages—still exotically beautiful.

"She-she looks so much like my grandmother," Mercy whispers.

Mr. Salazar extends his hands to the woman. She smiles and takes them as she steps onto the stage.

"May I present Selene, the mother of the young boy and baby girl in our last story?"

Everyone stands, and as if by signal, starts clapping. It's infectious. We keep clapping, and I'm feeling tearful for some reason. I lean toward Mercy. "Who is she, though? Are you related to her?"

Mercy shrugs. "I have no idea."

Selene steps to the side of the lectern.

"I would next like to introduce you to the baby girl, the

daughter of Selene, who, though raised by a different family, has recently been reunited through the efforts of Hope Washington with her own long-lost mother and brother."

The door opens and a woman who looks very much like a younger version of Selene enters through the door.

"Grandmother?" Mercy says.

The woman comes onto the stage and stands by Selene. Her lovely but serious face is stamped with both sadness and endurance.

"Oh, but there's more to this story for those of you who do not know. This woman is Selene's daughter, yes, but she, Ruby-Monique, is also the wife of William Grafton St. Clair." He extends an open hand toward Grandpa Grafton. "Of course, that makes them the parents of Hope Dovelle Washington, and her brothers—Simon Boyer St. Clair and Jacque Boyer St. Clair. Ruby-Monique is also the mother of Viola Chen."

Momma, Donnie, Jackie, Uncle Dew, and I all stare at each other in bafflement. I knew that Grandpa Grafton's estranged wife lived in New Orleans, but I had no idea she was given away as a baby, posed as a boy to train race horses, and now... she is standing up on the stage. I shall at last meet Mercy's illusive maternal grandmother, the one with the *genetic wild hair?*

"Who would like to meet the brother of Ruby-Monique, the son of Selene?"

Polite clapping ensues from a group of people mostly silenced by amazement. Mercy looks at me with pure confusion on her features.

"Whoever this is, he'll be my great uncle, Annie," she whispers, keeping her eyes on the door. "All these years, I thought my grandmother was an only child."

The door opens to reveal an attractive man with a thick gray moustache and a straight-as-an-arrow back. He's wearing cowboy boots, a gray cowboy hat, and a fancy jacket.

"My God, it's Joseph from Texas!" Momma says, and all of us in our family, except Uncle Dew, stare at her like she's crazy. Uncle Dew stands and bends forward over the table scrutinizing the newcomer.

"One last person to introduce, and Hope hopes… forgive the double words… but she hopes that, let me see, is it Zeenie?" Mrs. Washington nods from her chair. "She hopes Zeenie will forgive her and understand. Without further delay, may I present David Jackson "D.J." Blackburn, son of Joseph and Julie Blackburn, grandson of Selene and Jackson "Jack" Blackburn."

A handsome man who looks a lot like my brother Donnie enters the room. He is dressed in similar fancy western clothes as Joseph but with a huge belt buckle with, as best I can make out, a bucking bull with a man on his back. Momma emits a startled cry as the man goes to stand beside Ruby-Monique and Selene. Either it's the lighting playing tricks, or both men beside Selene have tears in their eyes.

How can these men be Mercy's relatives but have our last name? The room feels too hot. I glance at Momma. She has both hands over her mouth. I feel dizzy.

"It-it's our dad. What the heck…?" Donnie stutters, looking at Jackie and me.

Mrs. Washington steps to the microphone. "I know this is quite a shock, but please bear with me while I draw a quick lineage chart for you."

She draws a large square at the top of the board with a piece of chalk and writes *Selene* inside it. She draws two lines coming from that box and draws a box at the end of each line.

She writes *Joseph* in one, and *Ruby-Monique* in the other. She draws one line and box from *Joseph;* four lines coming from *Ruby-Monique.* In the one box from *Joseph,* she writes *David.*

In the four boxes coming from *Ruby-Monique,* she writes *Simon, Jacque, Hope,* and *Viola.* From the *David* line, she draws lines to four boxes and doesn't write in them. From the name *Hope,* she draws two lines with two boxes at the ends. Inside those boxes, she writes *Jerome* and *Mercy.* From the lines coming from the David box, she writes *Donnie, Joey, Jackie,* and *Annie.*

There is no sound in the room.

Mrs. Washington continues in a gentle voice. "Dear ones, from trial, sadness, and the ravages of time come the ashes of our lives. Because we never give up... because we are always there for one other... because there is love, we become the *beautiful ashes.* Beauty from the ashes of loss.

"Life is a journey of mystery, is it not? When I began my adventure into genealogy, I had no thought of unearthing such incredible stories, such links between our lives. What a joy it was to do so! I think you will see from this chart that David's children and my children are second cousins. What relative do they share? They share this elegant lady whom I met only recently, my own maternal grandmother... Selene. She is the connecting link, the great-grandmother of my children and the great-grandmother of Zeenie and David's children as well."

Mrs. Washington draws a line between the boxes that say *David* and the ones that have her, her sister's, and her brothers' names. Then, she draws a line between my brothers and me and Mercy and Jerome. She takes the chalk and points to the first line. "Let me explain it again. First cousins, such as David and I, have children, and they..." she points to the line connecting her children with us... "are second cousins to one another."

This time, it soaks in. Mercy gets it, too. Maybe the whole room does because a low murmur rises above our heads at the table. I don't know what to do. I'm deliriously happy in ways I've never felt before, and yet, I'm angry, too. There are my real dad and my grandfather, a great aunt and a great-grandmother stepping off a little podium in a St. Louis hotel. They are strangers, and yet they are part of us.

What does it mean? Where have they been all these years? Why are we only now finding out about them? Why didn't our dad try to find us? If our grandfather Joseph wasn't dead, why didn't we ever go see him? Momma has a lot of questions to answer, and I think I'm pretty mad about it. How could something so preposterous and providential as this happen in real life?

I glance again at Momma, and she's staring at David, my father, like he's a ghost. Joseph, my grandfather, walks over and puts his arms around Momma, and I can see that she's crying against his chest. Uncle Dew is hopping around like he has crickets in his shoes. I've never seen him so giddy.

Jerome and Donnie are shaking hands and laughing, then they kind of half-way hug and grin some more. Jackie is in line to do the same. I feel as if I'm hiding in the velvet curtains of a theater watching a play unfold on the stage. It feels like fantasy. I look from person to person as they shake their heads, shake hands, laugh, hug. Aunt Viola comes from behind and wraps her arms around me.

"I'm really your cousin, Annie. No wonder I've always been so crazy about you. Can you believe it?"

I return her hug, manage a weak smile, and glance at Mercy. She's in the same bewildered state as I. Dumbfounded, she stares at everyone, kind of turns in a half circle, then turns

the other way. "Annie…" she says, pivoting as she speaks, "…
I don't know, uh, well, everybody tried to keep us apart since
we were ten years old. Nobody could. We didn't care what
anyone thought. Now we find out we're actually blood?"

I don't say anything because I can't. Not yet.

Mercy drops into her seat and pulls me by the arm into
mine. "Man oh man, uh, cousin… one thing about it. You
were right about people being like those shorthand brief
forms. You look at them and see a few angles, a few strokes,
but that tiny portion you see on the outside is the tip of the
iceberg, almost nothing to do with what's on the inside. Who
they really are, what they are, has to be unveiled like a piece of
art. I mean… just look at us. Real-life cousins, for heaven's
sake!"

Mercy puts her head in her lap, shakes it back and forth,
sits back up. "Wow," she says. "Just wow."

I shake my head in mutual shock. It's going to take time
to absorb all that we've heard tonight and all that is true going
forward. From the shining faces all around the room,
especially the one on our dad's face—and Momma's—as he
walks toward her, perhaps the possibilities in this life are
endless. Maybe it's like searching for Atlantis or the Lost City
of Gold. You can believe or disbelieve all you want, turn the
world and the oceans inside out, but it doesn't count unless
you actually find whatever you're looking for.

Is that to say all dreams come true? I think Momma's may
have. Mercy and I fought the world and its predispositions in
order to be best friends, so our dream of people accepting us
as we are came true, too.

Yet, long before anyone knew our bloodlines crossed to
make us relatives… long before the world accepted that two
little girls of different races wanted nothing more than to be

best friends... Mercy and I were family. Hearts are what make people family—not bloodlines or belief systems or skin color—and nothing on this earth is stronger than that.

About Brief Forms

Having lunch in the fancy *Trois Fontaines* Restaurant, Mercy wants to take Annie's mind off her problems by engaging her in what she has learned about an unusual notetaking process called *shorthand*. It works! The more Mercy explains how a series of strokes, curves, and dots represents the phonetic spelling of any spoken word, the more intrigued Annie becomes. For example, "ph" in the word *telephone* is written as an "f." All silent letters are left out. Annie is ready to sign up to learn this crazy system of writing immediately! In her excitement, she makes a comparison of people to the shorthand code, aweing Mercy in the process.

When did shortened methods of notetaking come about, and was it always based on the sound of the word and not the spelling? Actually, it is recorded that a man named Xenophon used a type of shorthand system to write the memoir of Socrates in ancient Greece. In the Roman Empire, Marcus Tullius Tiro invented the first Latin shorthand system called the *notae Tironianae*. Through the centuries, speed writing has been used based on phonetics, symbols, and shortened versions of normal spelling.

The system Mercy and Annie will be learning in 1963 is known as Gregg Shorthand, named after the man who invented it, Irish-born John Robert Gregg. Gregg, a shorthand prodigy born in 1867, taught himself at the young age of ten a current version of shorthand. He studied several other versions before inventing his own at the age of eighteen. The

Gregg chart *of Brief Forms*, a chart of common abbreviations, is what intrigues Annie and Mercy the most. I mean… a short upward stroke stands for "the"? Too easy and fun for the girls to resist.

Here's an example of a brief form chart:

Drill 1.—The fifty most common words

The, and, of, to, I, a, in, that, you, for, it, was, is, will, as, have, not, with, be, your, at, we, on, he, by, but, my, this, his, which, dear, from, are, all, me, so, one, if, they, had, has, very, were, been, would, she, or, there, her, an.

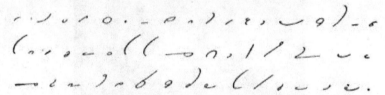

Drill 2.—The next fifty most common words

When, time, go, some, any, can, what, send, out, them, him, more, about, no, please, week, night, their, other, up, our, good, say, could, who, may, letter, make, write, thing, think, should, truly, now, its, two, take, thank, do, after, than, sir, last, house, just, over, then, work, day, here.

Note: The words "some," "night," "last," "just," and "over" are written according to advanced principles. "Truly" and "been" usually occur in phrases and are then abbreviated to "T" and "B".

About The Author

Jodi Lea Stewart

Jodi Lea Stewart's writing reflects her life starting in Texas and Oklahoma, moving to an Arizona cattle ranch next door to the Navajo Nation, and resuming later in her native Texas. As a youngster, she climbed petroglyph-etched boulders, bounced two feet in the air in the back end of pickups wrestling through washed-out terracotta roads, and rode horseback on the winds of her imagination through the arroyos and mountains of the Arizona high country.

She left the University of Arizona to move to San Francisco, where she learned about peace, love, and exactly what she *didn't* want to do with her life. Since then, Jodi graduated *summa cum laude* with a BS in Business Management, raised three children, worked as an electro-mechanical drafter, penned humor columns for a college periodical, wrote regional western articles and served as managing editor of a Fortune 500 company newsletter.

With an Okie mom and a Texas dad, an eclectic mix of Native Americans, Southern Belles and Gentlemen, not to mention Cow Punchers, as her life companions, Jodi walks comfortably through the hallways of anything Southwestern or Southern. She currently lives in Arizona with her husband, a crazy Standard poodle, a rescue cat, and numerous gigantic, bossy houseplants.

Jodi is a member of the Southwest Writers and New Mexico-Arizona Book Co-op. *TRIUMPH, A Novel of the Human Spirit* is Jodi's sixth novel.

For more information about the author, visit her website at **https://jodileastewart.com/**, or visit these other sites:

Facebook Profile:
https://www.facebook.com/jodi.lea.stewart
Facebook Page:
https://www.facebook.com/AuthorJodiLeaStewart/
About Me:
https://about.me/jodileastewart
Amazon:
https://www.amazon.com/Jodi-Lea-Stewart/e/B0085YFWZ6
LinkedIn:
https://www.linkedin.com/in/jodileastewart/

Progressive Rising Phoenix Press is an independent publisher. We offer wholesale discounts and multiple binding options with no minimum purchases for schools, libraries, book clubs, and retail vendors. We also offer rewards for libraries, schools, independent book stores, and book clubs. Please visit our website to see our updated catalogue of titles and our wholesale discount page at:

www.ProgressiveRisingPhoenix.com

CPSIA information can be obtained
at www.ICGtesting.com
Printed in the USA
LVHW112136160920
666201LV00001B/151

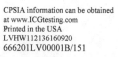

9 781950 560295